D0962147

How to SPEAK BOY

Also by Tiana Smith

MATCH ME IF YOU CAN

How to Speak Boy

TIANA SMITH

Swoon READS

SWOON READS   NEW YORK

A Swoon Reads Book

An imprint of Feiwel and Friends and Macmillan Publishing Group LLC

120 Broadway, New York, NY 10271

How to Speak Boy. Copyright © 2020 by Tiana Smith. All rights reserved.
Printed in the United States of America.

Our books may be purchased in bulk for promotional, educational, or business
use. Please contact your local bookseller or the Macmillan Corporate and
Premium Sales Department at (800) 221-7945 ext. 5442 or by email at
MacmillanSpecialMarkets@macmillan.com.

Library of Congress Control Number: 2019940969
ISBN 978-1-250-24221-1 (hardcover) / ISBN 978-1-250-24222-8 (ebook)

Book design by Sophie Erb

First edition, 2020

1 3 5 7 9 10 8 6 4 2

swoonreads.com

FOR MY PARENTS,
SORRY IN ADVANCE FOR ALL THE KISSING SCENES.

Chapter One

Pantyhose were invented by the devil. This is a well-known fact. They squeeze the life from your ovaries while simultaneously giving you a wedgie big enough to make any middle school bully proud. And to make things worse, they are *never* a perfect color match, no matter what the package says. But right now, they were the perfect distraction.

I picked up two different options and turned to my best friend, holding them close to my face to compare.

"Do you think my skin tone is closer to Peaches and Cream or French Vanilla?" I asked.

"Don't they know it's not good to call skin by food names?" Naomi asked, leaning in close to get a better view. "The girl in this one looks like Emma Watson. Think she modeled for Hanes back in the day?"

I shrugged.

She grabbed the one from my left hand. "This one."

"M'kay. Help me find all the ones in size small."

Naomi scrunched her nose and stepped toward the rack. "There's no kind of organization here. Why do you need so many?"

"Because they get more runs than a marathon, and I need enough for the whole speech and debate season. Coach's rules. If I ruin a pair each tournament, that's sixteen pairs."

"You know, if you got some nicer quality ones, they probably wouldn't snag as much." Naomi looked behind a pile of tights to see if more Peaches and Cream nylons happened to be hidden there. Her black curls fell into her face, and she brushed her hair out of the way.

"Like I have forty bucks to spend on a single pair of pantyhose," I said. "I'm seventeen and I don't have a job."

Naomi didn't reply. She just held out another package for me to add to the pile we'd started collecting on the floor. This was why we were friends. She didn't judge me for my geeky love of speech and debate, and I didn't act awkward around her because she was taller than Taylor Swift and 99 percent of the boys' basketball team.

"Thanks again for driving me to the speech and debate barbecue," I said, gathering the pile up in my arms. We'd only found eight, but that would have to last until I could get more. "And thanks for stopping here on the way."

If I'd taken the bus, it would have eaten up half my day. And stopping for nylons would have added at least an hour to the trip. It wasn't like Boise, Idaho, was known for its impressive public transportation system. I definitely didn't need all that time alone with my thoughts right now. Then again, the whole point of this trip was to distract me from what was going to happen at the barbecue, so maybe I should have taken the bus after all.

Naomi slung an arm over my shoulders as we walked to the checkout.

"Life wouldn't be worth living if I was actually on time for a game," she said, and a pang of guilt zipped through me.

"Tell your volleyball coach it's my fault," I said.

Naomi grinned. "I always do," she sang. I tried to slug her in the arm, but she danced out of the way.

We made it to the front of the store and I let the nylons tumble to the counter. The worker raised his eyebrows, but I didn't feel like explaining why a high school senior needed so many pantyhose on a Friday night. Let him imagine what he would.

"September's almost over," Naomi said to me as the worker scanned my items. "Volleyball season ends soon anyway. If my coach hasn't cared before, she won't now."

"What must that be like?" I mused aloud. "To have a coach who doesn't have a death grip on every detail of your life?" Mine was a tyrannical robot in human skin. She controlled how I did my hair for tournaments (French twist—classy but alluring), how tight my skirt suit was allowed to be (just enough to remind judges I'm a woman and should be taken seriously), and even the MAC Ruby Woo shade of lipstick I reapplied between each round (okay, full disclosure, I really loved that lipstick).

"Forget your coach. And her opinions," Naomi said, helping the worker put all my nylons in a bag. "Like, take tonight, for example. You nervous?"

I grimaced. I'd been doing so well at not thinking about it.

Naomi saw my expression and put a hand on my shoulder. "See, Quinn? That's what I mean. It makes zero difference what your coach thinks. You're still A-plus team captain material, no matter who she announces at your speech and debate welcome barbecue thing."

I paid the cashier and we walked through the automatic doors and into the crisp fall air.

"If she doesn't pick you, it's her loss. You know you're the best on the team." Naomi clicked the button on her key fob, and her Jeep chirped.

"That's not true," I said, climbing in the passenger seat and placing the bag at my feet. Naomi turned the keys and I messed around with the temperature controls until I wasn't dying. This time of year always ping-ponged between hot and cold, and the leather interior of Naomi's car magnified it by infinity. "She could pick Grayson."

Grayson Hawks. My mouth twisted in distaste. He was the poster child for Tall, Dark, and Handsome, and he wore trendy hipster glasses that were all kinds of pretentious. He had everything in life handed to him, no matter if he deserved it or not. Spoiler, usually he didn't. We'd been competitors in practically everything since he'd moved here, and he came out on top more times than I cared to admit. Sometimes I won, but he was always just *there*, making my life harder than it needed to be. In speech and debate, in school, in gym class—it didn't matter what it was, he made it a competition.

Everyone loved a good-looking geek, especially someone as charismatic as Grayson. He had this perfect light brown skin and wavy black hair that looked so smooth and shiny. Everyone thought he walked on water, even though it was all a show. It really wasn't fair. He was almost guaranteed the team captain spot.

He'd probably do anything to get it too. Just like when he ran for class president junior year, when he'd dated Zara, his only real competition, only to dump her right before the election speech so she'd bomb it. He never denied the rumors either. My friend Carter asked him about it once and Grayson had only laughed. Who does that?

Naomi snorted as she backed out of the parking spot.

"If your coach picks him, it's because he's the governor's son and she's playing favorites. As much as I think you're wrong about him, you're still the one who's been on the varsity team all four years."

Yeah, and once he'd made varsity, he'd proceeded to taunt and torment me at every competition. It was like he defaulted to some kind of "annoying" preset whenever I walked into the room. What made things worse—he routinely beat me at competitions. Like the universe had it out for me.

But I tried to believe Naomi. Tried to stop my racing heart from banging out of my chest. I wasn't sure if it was because I was anxious about tonight or simply because thinking about Grayson made my blood boil. I hummed along to the radio for a measure or two, but my throat turned dry and I swallowed instead.

More than anything, I really wanted to beat Grayson at *something*. Maybe he got better grades and he had all the teachers in his pocket, but I wanted to take something from him that he wanted for himself. So that just once, he could know how it felt to come in second.

I changed the radio station again and again until Naomi swiped my hand away from the controls. We'd first bonded over our love of boy bands, and now music was a common theme of our friendship. But her Jeep was older than we were, and didn't have any way to connect our phones to the speakers. We had to endure whatever happened to be on the air at the moment.

As we drove closer to my coach's house, my pulse picked up speed. Before I was ready, we pulled up front and I was out of reasons to delay.

"You sure Carter can give you a ride home?" Naomi asked, putting the Jeep in park. Carter was my closest friend on the team. Off the team as well, except for Naomi. We grew up together, so he'd seen me through all my worst stages, including the years of braces and the time I'd accidentally gotten a brush stuck in my hair and had to shave the left side of my head—he stuck by my side the whole time. That was true friendship right there.

Carter had no filter whatsoever, and I liked that he was so open with his thoughts. So many people in high school were fake, but with Carter, I knew where he stood. I was always so introverted and I counted on him to bring me out of my shell. When we were together, he didn't act quite so out there, and I didn't hide from all social interactions. I clung to that with a strange kind of desperation. It wasn't like I had a whole lot of friends to begin with.

I would have asked him for a ride here, but shopping for pantyhose might have actually killed him.

"I'm sure," I said, unlocking my seat belt. I took the nylons out of the plastic shopping bag and began placing them in my shoulder bag, taking my time. Naomi saw through me, of course.

"Go on, get. Your coach has already made her decision by now, so you might as well get it over with."

I sighed and stepped out of the car. Naomi was gone by the time I'd made it up the sidewalk and walked around back, the way we always entered. Coach was grilling on the patio and she nodded in approval as I took off my shoes and left them in the pile already gathering outside. We'd had enough events at Coach's house to know wearing shoes inside meant murder. Voices drifted from the open door and I made my way inside the kitchen, smiling at Carter when I saw him leaning against the counter, talking to someone. My smile froze when I saw that it was Grayson.

I wasn't sure I could make polite small talk right now, at least, not with the one guy who could take away my chance at being team captain.

"Quinn!" Carter called, motioning me over before I could pretend I had someone else claiming my attention. I moved slowly. Grayson was wearing a blazer. Like an actual suit coat with jeans. The suck-up.

"Hey, Quinn," Grayson said, turning to me. "You ready to lose tonight?" His question, and the way he said it, with eyebrows raised and cheeky grin in place, set my teeth on edge. I wondered what his mom would think of his political mind games.

"Oh, I'm sorry, are you talking to yourself again?" I asked.

That's when Carter cut in, probably sensing the verbal spat coming this way. Grayson always knew how to get under my skin.

"Did you get whatever girly things you needed at the store?" Carter asked.

My cheeks flamed and I very carefully did *not* look at Grayson so I wouldn't see his reaction. I knew he'd look smug. I fiddled with the strap of my bag and tried not to overreact.

"I told you I had to buy pantyhose for the speech meets, not period stuff," I said.

Carter's eyes opened wide. "Oh, no, that's not what I meant. I was just saying—" He stumbled over his words and brought his hand to the back of his neck. "Never mind, sorry." The tips of his ears turned pink and his lips formed a tight line, like he was trying not to say anything else. He ran a hand through his disheveled hair and shrugged an apology.

I wanted the floor to eat me alive, but Grayson smiled like he found the whole thing amusing, as he would. He grabbed a chip from a bag on the counter and popped it into his mouth with a crunch. Glancing around, I tried to find someone else I could talk to. Or maybe the nearest exit.

No viable escape routes opened up, so I said, "So, uh, Carter, can you give me a ride home after this?"

"Did your mom bring home any leftovers from the diner last night?" he asked.

I nodded.

"Then yes."

Carter was the definition of a mooch. Or maybe it was just the teenage boy in him that made him inhale any food within a ten-foot radius. Even now, he'd taken a handful of the chips from the counter and was busy shoving them into his face like we weren't all about to eat dinner in a few minutes.

"You know how her mom works at that diner on Ninth?" Carter asked Grayson.

I didn't know why he bothered prolonging this conversation, but that was just Carter. Always thinking the best of people and being friendly to everyone, like a shaggy puppy dog. I wanted to be more outgoing like that. Just not with Grayson.

"At the end of the night, they let her take food home if they made too much," Carter said.

"Nice," Grayson responded. I couldn't tell whether he was being sarcastic or not, so I bristled in silence. Sure, my mom worked at a diner. But it wasn't like Grayson was any better just because his mom was the governor. My mom was also an amazing photographer, and one day that'd be her primary business. I'd been helping her set up a website and portfolio, and since she let me take over her Instagram account, she'd had more bookings than ever.

I loved doing it too. Seeing results like that? It was intoxicating. Maybe it was geeky, but my plan for college was to go into marketing. I couldn't get enough of it, and even after I helped get my mom's business up and running, I'd still use those skills in influencing the world around me. I wasn't entirely sure what industry I wanted to go into the most, but everybody could use a good marketer. In the meantime, I'd be able to help out my mom. Okay, yes, most teens might not be that excited about working with their parents, but then again, I never claimed to be normal.

"Oh!" Carter slapped his forehead with his palm. "I forgot I said I'd give Mike a ride home already. But I can tell him to get someone else."

Carter didn't drive a two-seater convertible. It had five spots. But the back of his car was a literal pigsty, with more fast food bags and questionable gym clothes than anyone should ever be forced to touch, let alone sit on. I'd probably contract some kind of deadly disease.

"That's okay. I'll find someone who—" I started.

"I can help you out," Grayson said.

I froze. What fresh torture was this? Grayson lived on the other side of the city. I knew, because Idaho was one of a handful of states that didn't have a governor's mansion, so his mom got paid a stipend to live in their home.

"Oh, I don't want to bother you," I said overly sweetly, hoping he'd let it drop. "I know how much it physically hurts you to think of anyone else before yourself."

"Maybe I joined the Boy Scouts," he said, smiling. His teeth were so white, I wondered if he used bleaching strips. "Or maybe I just want to try some of your mom's leftovers."

I sucked in a breath while plotting how to get out of this. There was no way Grayson was taking one step through my front door.

Coach came inside the kitchen, looking at us from the doorframe.

"Hamburgers and hot dogs are ready," she called, and a surge of twenty teenage bodies headed toward the door. I picked up a paper plate and grabbed on to Carter's arm, holding him back from the crowd so Grayson could move ahead. Carter glanced back at me incredulously.

"We're going to be at the end of the line," he said, and I picked up some more chips and put them on his plate.

"You'll survive. That's your payback for forcing me to talk with Grayson. And for not giving me a ride."

Carter sighed and looked wistfully at the grill on the backyard patio. "You can still come with us, but we're going to leave a little early. I can make Mike sit in the back."

I patted his arm. "Thanks, but I'll figure something out. I don't hate Mike enough to do that to him."

We moved forward a foot in the line, and for a bit, neither of us spoke. Then Carter broke the silence.

"You know, if you're team captain, you'll have to talk with Grayson a lot more," he said, picking up a chip from his plate.

Oh, I knew that, unfortunately. I was trying not to think about it.

"If I win, then there won't be a problem," I responded, stealing a chip for myself. "He can't talk back to the team captain."

Carter's look was skeptical, and I didn't say anything else, knowing there was no reality in which Grayson would ever not talk back to me. I chewed on my lower lip while we waited. Grayson was one of those naturally gifted people. I wouldn't fault Coach Bates for picking him. Sure, I'd been on varsity longer. But would that be enough? Maybe Grayson had already sabotaged me in some way and I just didn't know it.

"What if he wins?" Carter said.

It was the one question I hadn't allowed myself to actually ask out loud. The noise around me muted to a buzz, and I focused on taking one step after another. My paper plate was shaking a little, so I gripped it harder. Traitorous plate.

"I mean, what if he wins *and* you have to ride in his car all the way to your apartment?"

My stomach dropped and I genuinely thought I might be sick, right then and there. I would spend the whole night begging people for rides if I had to. There was no way I was walking into that trap willingly.

Coach was dishing up the meat at the grill as students slipped their shoes back on. Her eyebrows pinched together when Carter snuck a second hamburger patty onto his plate, but she didn't say anything. She had her straight brown hair pulled back in a low ponytail as usual, and her reading glasses were perched on top of her head. She smiled when she saw me, and I couldn't help the flutter of hope that rose in my chest. She wouldn't be smiling if she wasn't planning on making me captain, right?

We took our seats on the grass with everyone else. My teammates were all talking excitedly about something, but I was too busy wondering if Coach smiled at Grayson too.

The whole time we were eating, I couldn't taste my food. Twenty minutes had never felt so long in all my life. By the time Coach stood up on the porch and waved for us all to be quiet, I was pretty sure I was developing an ulcer.

"Welcome to a new season of speech and debate!" she announced, and all I could think was *Blah, blah, blah, get on with it already.*

Coach Bates cleared her throat.

I died a little inside.

"We have a few announcements, like the itinerary, information on our home tournament since we're hosting the state competition this year, and other specifics, but I know you all want to find out who this year's team captain will be."

I didn't breathe.

"There were so many qualified candidates this year. The problem was narrowing it down."

I sneaked a glance over at Grayson, who didn't seem nearly as concerned as I was. I could feel the eyes of my teammates on me like a heavy blanket. Grayson leaned back nonchalantly in the grass, putting his weight on his elbows. I sat up straighter.

"I'm breaking with tradition this year," Coach said. "I couldn't pick only one, so there will be two. Everyone, please congratulate Quinn Edwards and Grayson Hawks, who will be co-team captains this year!"

I heard the clapping around me, but it didn't register. Once again, I hadn't been enough to beat Grayson.

"Think of it this way," Carter said, leaning over, "at least the car ride home won't be so awkward."

But that was where he was so, so wrong.

Chapter Two

So, is it true you and Grayson kissed last week?" Naomi asked as AP Government and Politics was getting out. We'd picked up our bags and were making our way toward the cubbies that held our returned assignments.

"What?" My head jerked back. "That so did not happen." I actually stopped where I was and someone bumped into me from behind. I let them pass before continuing at a whisper. "Who said that?" I was going to kill them.

"Not in so many words," Naomi said. "Carter said Grayson gave you a ride. I guess I was hoping that someone finally managed to shake your resolve."

I resumed walking down the aisle. Yes, I'd gotten a ride from Grayson, because no one else was available. Carter hadn't been kidding when he'd said he had to leave early. I'd barely asked a handful of people by the time I looked around and realized my backup plan had already left.

"I'd rather kiss a blobfish than Grayson Hawks. Besides, schoolwork doesn't allow time for a boyfriend," I said. This was a common refrain of mine, and the more I said it, the more I almost believed it. This way, my single status was something I'd chosen, rather than the sad reality of my life.

Some people were naturally good at school. It was effortless. I was not one of those people. I spent twice as long on my homework as Naomi, but you wouldn't know it by looking at my grades. This was yet another area where Grayson also seemed to excel without trying, which was all kinds of unfair when you competed with him in everything.

This AP Government class was going to be my doom especially. It was the worst of them all. In general, my grades were okay, enough that my guidance counselor suggested I take this AP class to beef up my college applications. I'd picked Government, figuring that if history relied a lot on memorizing events and stuff like that, I would be fine. If I could memorize speeches, I could memorize historical facts.

Problem was, memorizing a speech involved strings of words that made sense one after another, and history involved random dates that had nothing to do with anything else. Besides, speech and debate was all about the presentation. The show. A multiple-choice test didn't care whether you appeared confident or not. It cared whether you knew the answers.

"Did you at least invite him in?" Naomi asked.

I scoffed. "Right. I invited my biggest competition into my home for teatime and cookies. Then my mom showed him her photos and we chatted about world peace. *No, I didn't invite him in!*"

The only good thing about that car ride was that I made it from point A to point B when no one else had been able to drive me. The whole time he'd pushed my buttons and made me flustered to the point that simply stepping out of the car had been a relief.

Naomi nodded like she agreed with everything I'd said, but her eyes told a different story. They were all squinty at the sides and she wouldn't really make eye contact. We made it up to the front of the room and separated to our perspective cubbies. Hers was on the right and mine was on the far left, because our school ID numbers were so far apart.

We never used names for any of our assignments at our high school. School IDs were on everything. Supposedly it was to help the teachers grade fairly, but I was pretty sure they all had my number memorized by now. I bet they laughed about me in the teacher's lounge. *Oh, that poor 15511. Will they ever pull it together?*

I grabbed my assignment from the cubby and shoved it in my backpack without looking at it. Naomi met me at the door.

"How'd you do?" she asked.

"Don't know, don't care," I replied.

Naomi rolled her eyes at me.

"Not looking at your score won't change it. I know you secretly care. This is like when you kept putting off going to the barbecue. Sometimes you simply need to face the facts."

"I *will* look at it," I said. "Just somewhere more private, thank you very much."

Naomi raised an eyebrow, but let it go. "Congrats on the team captain thing, by the way."

"*Co*—team captain," I corrected her. "I have to share the title. With Grayson." I'd been stewing about it all weekend. On the one hand, I'd gotten everything that I'd wanted. But on the other, well, so had Grayson. Was it really so much to ask that I beat him at just one thing? It'd been far too long since that had happened.

Naomi and I walked down the hallway toward our lockers. AP Government was our last class of the day, so we took our time.

Naomi turned to me, and I knew she was up to something. There was that glint in her eye. "So, if you and Grayson are co—team captains, does that mean you'll be spending a lot of time with him?" She waggled her eyebrows suggestively. I pushed her away, but she was not deterred. "Because you two would make the cutest couple."

"Hush, you," I said, looking around to see if anyone else had noticed the breakdown my best friend was having. Thankfully, everyone else was too preoccupied with what they were doing.

"I thought you were supposed to be my friend. Why would you wish that kind of evil on me?"

She raised an eyebrow. "You know he only teases you like that because he's dying for your attention. He likes you."

"Right." I snorted. "Like how he liked Zara Hayer? What happened there again? Oh, yeah, he used her to win the election. We're *competitors*, Naomi. Zara just wasn't smart enough to see it coming."

"Never judge anyone by their exes." Naomi shuddered, and I pounced on the opportunity for a subject change.

"Oh, you mean like when you dated Matt 'Mouth Breather' Brayford?"

"For one week!" Naomi laughed. "In eighth grade!"

"Mmm-hmm," I hummed, playing it up.

The more I got her thinking about herself, the better. Then maybe she'd forget about playing matchmaker between me and my sworn enemy.

I opened up my locker and started organizing the books I'd need to take home.

"You know, I hear Matt's single," I said, hoping to leave the topic of Grayson far behind.

"Speak of the devil," Naomi murmured, and I turned to face her so she could get the full force of my teasing grin.

"Oh, is the mouth breather nearby?" I asked, not bothering to keep my voice low.

That was when I heard him behind me, and it wasn't Matt Brayford.

"Hey, Quinn," Grayson said.

I turned so fast my backpack hit him in the stomach, and he steadied himself by grabbing my shoulder. Why was he standing so close?

"Ummm, hi." I wasn't sure what my face looked like right now. Then again, I wasn't sure I wanted to know. I could already feel the heat creeping up my neck, and I was pretty sure my skin was blotchy. It tended to do that when I got nervous, like when I was waiting for something horrible to happen. Grayson removed his hand and leaned against the row of lockers.

"I forgot to get your number on Friday." He pulled his phone from his pocket, like he had no doubt I'd give him my number simply because he asked.

I looked at Grayson, confused and unable to actually do anything besides stand there. Students moved all around us, but it was like I was caught in my own mini bubble of inactivity. Naomi nudged me from behind and I regained enough sense to utter a single word.

"What?"

"Your phone number?" Grayson asked, his brows pulling together.

Grayson Hawks was asking for my phone number. But why? So he could prank call me in the middle of the night?

"You know," Grayson said. "Because we'll be co–team captains, unfortunately. I guess we should have a way to get ahold of each other."

I stared at his phone, wondering how many ways he could use my phone number against me. Then again, did I have a choice? Whether I liked it or not—hint, I didn't—we'd have to work together this year. Ugh.

"Right," I said, nodding to my internal thoughts as much as I was answering him. "Here, give me your phone and I'll put it in."

My fingers moved robotically, punching the numbers in, one by one. By the time I handed him back his phone, I was pretty sure I could talk civilly.

"Smile," he said, taking a picture of me. I heard the click before I could process what he was doing.

I scowled. "I wasn't ready."

He looked at his phone and pinched his lips to one side. "Whoa, you're right. You're usually much more photogenic than this, Quinn, yikes. What's going on with your hair?"

I quickly swiped his phone from him to see for myself, but the picture I saw was normal. But that didn't matter, because Grayson was already laughing at my response.

"Relax, you take everything too seriously." He took his phone back, presumably programming my picture in with my phone number. A second later, my phone buzzed in my pocket.

"I just texted you so you have my number now." Grayson's eyes crinkled around the corners when he smiled. "I know it might be tempting, but try not to send me anything too scandalous."

I rolled my eyes and he started to walk away, but I couldn't let him get the last word.

"So, you get an awkward picture of me, but I don't get one of you?" I called. Grayson turned, a smirk already on his face. He held his arms out to his sides, as if to say, *Ready when you are.*

I clicked his picture. It was a shame he was so good-looking. What a waste of a pretty face.

"You good?" Grayson asked, and I nodded.

"You have my number. Don't be afraid to use it," he said. Then he turned and walked away again. I brought my phone back to my pocket and spun around to find Naomi watching me, her smugness radiating off her in waves.

"What?" I asked, already knowing what she was going to say, even though she was dead wrong.

"He was flirting with you. I totally saw it."

I scoffed. "I was there too, remember? And he definitely was not flirting." She should know; that was simply part of Grayson's enigmatic personality. Sometimes he was cheeky, sometimes he was smooth, but he always had his own agenda in mind. I knew better than anyone else that he wasn't to be trusted. It was a show, just like his speeches. His mom had taught him all she knew about winning people over, and Grayson was a natural. When he wanted to be, or when he had something to gain, he could be very charming. And sure, maybe sometimes I enjoyed our little spats. When I came out on top. But that was a secret I'd take to my grave.

I hiked my backpack up on my shoulder and closed my locker door. Naomi watched me with one eyebrow raised, but I pretended not to see.

"You're like a pesky little gnat. Or a tall one, rather. Don't you have practice?" I asked, motioning for her to shoo.

She scowled, then sighed. "Catch you later." Her curls bounced as she walked away.

It was only after she'd rounded the corner that I finally allowed myself to look at my returned assignment for AP Government.

I pulled it free from my backpack and stared at the red A at the top, not understanding what I was seeing. Seriously? An A? That had never happened before. Well, not in my hardest class.

Finally, all my hard work actually amounted to something. I grinned and brought the paper close to my chest, clutching it there in a hug. My entire body felt weightless and I leaned back against the lockers before I could do anything reckless, like shout my success to the hallway. But I couldn't stop smiling, no matter how hard I tried. Passing freshman gave me weird looks. Not that I cared. I brought the paper in front of me again, to make sure I hadn't been imagining things. But there it was, a bright red A, slashed across the top like a crimson kiss of approval.

But then I saw something I'd missed earlier, and my grin dropped. The student ID number at the top of the paper was one digit off from mine. Instead of 15511, this one read 15211.

This was not my assignment.

Chapter Three

I had my own practice to get to. But on the way there, I stopped by my AP Government classroom. No one was there to witness my humiliation, including the teacher, thankfully. I didn't need her apologetic look as I explained to her that I'd actually thought I'd earned a good grade in her class for once.

I checked the cubbies surrounding mine, looking to see if perhaps my assignment got shelved to the right or something. They were all empty. Most likely my assignment had gotten switched with 15211's because our numbers were so similar, so I found theirs and looked inside to see if my assignment was there. It wasn't.

But I'd had mixed up assignments happen before over the years, so the odds were pretty good that it'd happened again. Whoever it was must have taken mine home without realizing the teacher's mistake. Poor A student, thinking they'd bombed the homework. Well, I didn't feel too sorry for them.

I ripped a page from my notebook and pulled out a pen to write 15211 a note. If they didn't have my assignment, at least they'd be able to tell me so I could ask our teacher what might have happened.

> Sorry if I gave your AP Government—loving heart some kind of an attack when you saw my grade instead of yours. I'm guessing our assignments got swapped, and even though I'm sure my grade is spectacular in comparison, it'd be great if I could get it back. If you don't have my assignment, please let me know so I can hound Ms. Navarrete about the black hole in her office. But yeah, if you do, please send it back. You know, so I can hang it on my wall of shame or something like that.

More like, I needed to know which questions I'd gotten wrong, so I wouldn't make the same mistake twice, which I was sure to do anyway.

I placed their assignment and my note in their cubby, then walked out the door and to the stairs leading to the second floor. Speech practice was held in the theater classroom, which was ironically one of the farthest rooms from the auditorium where they actually performed. But Coach Bates also taught theater, which was why we met in her room.

At the base of the stairway, my phone dinged with a text from my mom.

> First speech practice as team captain. SO PROUD OF YOU!

She took the cheerleader thing a little far sometimes, but I loved her anyway. I sent back several kissing face emojis and put the phone back in my pocket. I squared my shoulders and walked up the stairs. It was time.

Grayson was already there. Of course. He'd probably come straight here after he'd left my locker because he wanted to make me look bad.

I pulled up the desk next to him and sat down, pretending like I wasn't itching to leave his presence already.

"So," I said, pulling out my notebook, "I guess we need a game plan on how we're going to not strangle each other. How do you think we should divvy up the captain duties?"

He placed his elbow on the edge of his desk, bringing his hand to his chin like he was pondering life's mysteries.

"Not even a little strangulation? What about light hazing?"

I rolled my eyes and he chuckled, leaning back in his chair and placing his hands behind his head.

"Okay, okay," Grayson said. "We should probably do the food planning for our home tournament together, since it's the state meet and that's kind of a big deal. But Coach wants us to work with some of the newer members during practices and we could do that from opposite ends of the room, if you can't stand being next to all my awesomeness. What do you want to do about team activities?"

"Yes," I said dryly. "It's so hard to be next to your . . . awesomeness." I leaned over as if inspecting something unpleasant. "Is that a TARDIS on your shirt?"

He smiled, completely unfazed by my scrutiny, holding out the bottom edge of his shirt to better show off the graphic. "The fact that you called it a TARDIS and not a phone booth means maybe there's hope for you after all."

I sighed. "Back to business, please. I could plan the Thanksgiving party if you want to do the bus cheer on the way to tournaments." The bus cheer was the one thing I did not want to touch with a ninety-nine-and-a-half-foot pole. The team captain had to come up with a different one for each meet and, on the bus ride there, was forced to stand up at the front and get everyone pumped to compete. It was humiliating. And I didn't want anything to do with it.

"Nice try," Grayson said. "But there's no way I'm going to let our fellow classmates miss out on your best performances."

"In that case, I wouldn't want to deprive them of yours either," I said.

Grayson barely gave a hint of a smile before replying, "Fine. We're both doing it. What about the Thanksgiving party?"

"I'm not doing it by myself if you're not doing the cheers alone," I said in warning.

"Guess we're stuck doing that together too," he said, raising an eyebrow.

Great. I tried not to let my dismay show on my face, but Grayson was laughing at me when Coach Bates came over to where we were sitting.

"Hey, you two, I've been gathering the new team members over in that corner of the room." She pointed. "It'd be great if you could give them a run-down of the different speech and debate events so they can pick what they want to compete in."

Coach left to help someone else and Grayson started gathering his things.

"I'll grab the handouts," I said, already heading to the file cabinet. Grayson went to introduce himself to the freshmen and I pulled out enough flyers so everyone could have their own copy. By the time I made it to the group, three of the freshman girls were already staring dreamily at Grayson like he was some kind of Greek god. I dropped the papers on the table with a thump and everyone jumped.

"All right. So, there's different events you can compete in, and you'll need to decide whether you want to do things on the speech side or debate side," I said.

"Aren't they the same thing?" a boy asked, not even bothering to pick up a handout. "Like, you stand up in front of people and talk about something and then it looks good on your college applications?"

I grabbed a paper and placed it in front of him. "No. Speech and debate are two separate things, and they each have at least five different events. You'll see them listed out here." I pointed to the location on the handout. "I'm not going to go through them all since I'm pretty sure you all can read."

Grayson must have thought I wasn't handling things well, because he jumped in. "What Quinn means to say is, read through the options, and then if you have questions about anything, we're here for you. Quinn and I both compete in Original Oratory, which means we write our own speeches, hoping to persuade listeners to adopt our point of view on a particular topic. It's one of the solo events for speech. But there's also pair events that you can do with a partner on both the speech side and debate."

"But Oratory is clearly the best," I said. "Except that then you have to spend more time with Grayson, and I can't recommend that for your health."

"All events are equally great," Grayson said, shooting me a look that was practically begging me to behave already. "So no matter what you pick, you'll have fun. Though, obviously we're biased toward Oratory. Even if the downside means practices with Quinn."

"Does that mean you compete against each other?" one of the girls asked.

I wanted to say, "Only in everything," but I held my tongue and simply nodded.

"Which one of you is better?" she asked.

I coughed uncomfortably.

"Duh," one of the boys answered. "They're both team captains, aren't they? They're probably about the same, right?"

"Sure," Grayson said.

The word was innocent enough. But his tone and the way he said it sounded so . . . so . . . condescending. Like he was patting a grumpy toddler on the head and trying to appease them.

It didn't matter that he was right. Sure, I'd been playing the part of the underdog lately, but it wasn't always like that. This year it was *my* turn. State was going to prove that, when I came home with the first-place trophy.

Actually, it didn't matter what place I got, so long as it was better than Grayson.

"Read over the events," I said, careful to keep my tone even. "I need to leave by five to catch the city bus, so make sure you find me before then if you have any questions." I stood up from the table and turned away, prepared to leave them to it.

"Real team captains stay late, though." Grayson's voice was taunting, the way it was when he was being purposefully obtuse. "I'll be here as long as it takes."

I turned back around and addressed the group. "Practice is usually over by then anyway, so don't worry, you shouldn't have to resort to second best."

"You know, Quinn, I could give you a ride after practices. Consider it my gift to you." Grayson's signature half smile was firmly in place, his dimple pronounced.

"I'd rather have food poisoning for a week," I said politely, smiling the whole time. Grayson leaned back in his chair and crossed his arms.

"You're always so uptight. Relax. It's not like anyone *wants* to ride the bus."

Fun fact: When someone tells you to "relax," the opposite actually happens.

Grayson went back to looking at the handout, but I was bristling. I knew it was all a game to him, but his comments always got under my skin.

"Better the bus than your company," I replied, flipping my hair over my shoulder. Then I turned and walked back to my own desk, fuming the whole time.

I knew working with Grayson would be difficult. But did he have to be so . . . so . . . *Grayson-y?* With that smile that he knew was cute, and his too-witty comments that I never knew how to answer?

I pulled out my notebook and started working on my first speech of the season. There was only one solution to the Grayson problem. I'd have to crush him in the competition. No matter what it took, I'd make sure that happened.

Chapter Four

There was a note waiting for me in my cubby the next day. And it was there before lunch, which meant 15211 either had AP Government sometime in the morning, or whoever it was had realized the mistake too and had gone to return my assignment first thing. There had to be at least four or five classes of AP Government throughout the day, so really, 15211 could be anyone.

I'd checked as I walked to English because it was on the way. Seeing the letter in my cubby, I was glad I'd decided to come early.

I analyzed the handwriting, trying to figure out if it looked feminine or masculine. It didn't really matter, but it was strange not to know. The writing was slanted and bold, sure of itself, but somehow elegant at the same time. It was better than my own, but not as bubbly. I flipped it over, but they hadn't signed their name. I turned it back and began reading.

Dear 15511,

Believe it or not, I hate politics more than I hate cherry-flavored cough medicine, so no, my "AP Government–loving heart" didn't have some kind of an attack, thank you very much.

Sorry you bombed this assignment. If it's any consolation, I'll probably fail the next one since I'm writing to some girl (a guess from your handwriting) instead of paying attention to Ms. Navarrete talk about the role of social media in the latest presidential elections. Have fun with that today. She seems to think everyone's still on Myspace. I think that died like a century ago.

I'm second-guessing whether I'll leave you this note. Maybe I'll just return your paper with a quick "Here you go, enjoy!" Then you wouldn't think I'm a creepy guy. I promise I'm not. Just bored.

15211

By the time I'd finished reading it, I'd made it to English class. I wove through the desks until I made it to the back row, where Naomi, Carter, and I usually sat. I was pretty early and they weren't there yet, so I pulled out my notebook and debated whether to write 15211 back.

I didn't have to. He'd returned my assignment, so really, what more was there to talk about? He'd probably think I was the creepy one if I kept this going.

That was when Naomi dropped her book on the desk next to mine, folding her long legs into the space that was clearly meant for a much shorter person.

"Ooh, a note that isn't from me?" she asked, leaning over to grab the paper on my desk. "Look at you, expanding your circle of friends."

"Ha," I deadpanned. "Don't get your hopes up. I don't even know the guy. He somehow ended up with my assignment in AP Government, so I asked him to return it and it came with this."

"He sounds cute," she replied, looking over the letter.

"How could you possibly know that?" I asked. "Do you have a super-power you never told me about?"

She placed the note back on my desk.

"Well, he's funny. So."

"Comedians are usually funny because they *aren't* attractive," I replied. "They have to develop other talents in order to stand a chance."

"You're going to write him back, right?" Naomi dug through her bag until she found her English book, which she placed on her desk.

"What's the point?" I fingered the edge of my notebook, unsure whether I wanted her to convince me.

"The point?" She leaned forward. "The point is, you need more people in your life besides me and Carter. You're too happy in your antisocial bubble. It's great that you're so techie, and helping your mom in your free time and all that, but you're like a grandma in teenager skin. Besides, a little flirting never hurt anyone. You could use the practice."

"Oh, so not only do I have to write him back, but now I have to flirt with him?"

She tore a piece of paper out of her notebook and handed it to me, as if I didn't have my own right in front of me.

"I could use the entertainment." Naomi didn't say anything else after that. She just raised her eyebrows and motioned for me to continue while she used her phone's front-facing camera to reapply her lipstick.

I sighed as I picked up my pen. I had no idea what to write, despite Naomi's meddling.

Somehow, I'd have to confirm he was right that I was a girl. He'd been nice enough to clue me in, and I wasn't about to share anything more personal. No way was I going to tell him anything that might name me as the person who "bombed the assignment," as he'd so politely put it. I started writing.

> You know "I'm not creepy" is exactly what a creeper would say, right? I'm not holding my breath. Besides, who gets that many answers right on an AP Government assignment? Either you study way too much, or you're too smart for your own good. Either way, I think I've decided not to like you. It's not good for my fragile girl ego to be friends with someone like that.

I smiled as I wrote that. Would he get my sarcasm? I debated starting over. But Naomi was looking over my shoulder and nodding in approval. Besides, if he couldn't get my sense of humor, then it'd be better to know now. Especially if I was going to be forced to exchange notes with a stranger.

I glanced up to check the clock. Only a few more minutes until English started. Naomi was talking to the girl to her right, so I returned my attention to the note.

> Anyway. I just saw Mr. Williams pick his nose, and I had to tell someone. There you go.

It didn't mean I had English class right now, even though I did. I could have seen my teacher in the hall or between classes. And it wasn't like I was delivering this letter before eighth period, so 15211 would have no idea what time I'd written this. I hadn't given too much away. It was strange, how easy it was to talk to a perfect stranger. Like, by not knowing who he was, I could tell him anything. I was like those trolls who felt empowered on the internet. Anonymity made me bold.

I tried to think of anything else to say, but I was all out. My English teacher finished picking his nose, which meant he was probably going to start class soon. I signed my student ID number and put it back in my bag so I could place the note in 15211's cubby when I had AP Government.

Carter walked in, saw us, and smiled so big, I knew he was up to something. The smile stayed there the whole time as he walked to the back.

"I have news," he said, sliding into the chair to my left. His sandy hair stuck out from under his hoodie and he leaned toward me. "I'm switching events."

"For speech and debate?" Naomi asked. She'd stopped talking to the person to her right when Carter joined us. She had this wild theory that Carter had a crush on me, and sometimes, I believed it. He'd randomly say things that made me wonder if he was flirting. Or trying to. Usually, I ignored it, because that would just be awkward. When you grew up with someone as a friend, it was impossible to see them any other way. But mostly, I thought Naomi was full of it. She wasn't super close to him, so she didn't know him like I did.

"What other event would I be talking about?" He shoved his backpack under his desk and looked back toward us.

"But you've always done Impromptu," I said. "You're good at it." I tried to think of why Coach would have him switch, but came up empty. Carter was quick with witty responses and made up facts with such confidence that he could fool an expert in the field. It was like he was handmade for Impromptu.

Honestly, I'd always been a bit jealous, because Impromptu seemed like so much less work than my event. He didn't have to research facts or memorize a ten-minute speech. He didn't rewrite the same line five different ways to get the pacing and cadence perfect. He just showed up.

"Why, thank you," he said, bowing slightly from the waist. So humble. I couldn't help but laugh and Carter joined in. Naomi rolled her eyes and started talking to the other girl again, obviously bored with our speech and debate conversation.

"I wanted something different," he said. "And this way, I'll get to spend more time with you. Win-win." He grinned and reached over to slug me lightly in the arm.

"Wait, you're doing Oratory now?" I sat back and tried not to let my shock show on my face. It was bad enough I had to compete against Grayson, but now Carter, one of my best friends? The guy who always gave me his brownie from the lunch line because he knew I liked them?

"Yeah, so since you're team captain, you have to give me pointers."

Oh, and then there was that. Not only would I have to compete against him, I'd have to *help* him. I'd have to coach him in my own event, reveal all my secrets and tips, and hope it didn't come back to bite me.

I already knew it would. If Carter could channel his natural talent into a memorized speech, then he'd have the perfect one-liners every single time.

This was supposed to be my year. The year I'd win state, and beat Grayson, and actually have things work in my favor for once.

Sure, I'd known I'd need to compete for it, but now even my friends were conspiring against me. Why couldn't Carter have stayed doing Impromptu? Just to "spend more time with me"?

Making things worse, I couldn't even tell Carter how I really felt. Only a week ago, we'd been talking about how hard it was to find time for friends our senior year. This was obviously his solution to the problem. I'd meant it was hard to find time to hang out with Carter and Naomi together when everyone had different schedules, but it wasn't like I could clarify now. How could I be so harsh to express my displeasure when Carter was only trying to do something nice?

I plastered a smile on my face. "That's great news," I said, hoping Mr. Williams would start class soon and end my misery.

Such great news.

Chapter Five

The next day, I got another note.

Dear 15511,

You say you don't want to be my friend. Here are all the reasons why you should be so lucky:

1. I'm a pro at keeping secrets.

2. I'd tell you if you had something stuck in your teeth.

3. I'd never make you sing karaoke.

4. I can beatbox. Okay, not really, but that'd be pretty cool, right?

5. I'm a silent chewer.

6. I know how to pronounce "Worcestershire."

7. I never wear socks with sandals.

8. I always text back.

I'm running out of reasons, and I haven't even gotten to ten, which makes me worried I might not actually be good friend material, so if you wanted to crush my ego, then mission accomplished. With that happy thought, it's probably best if I stop writing now.

15211

I honestly hadn't expected him to write back. This was getting a little ridiculous. How long did he expect me to keep this up? I wasn't planning on responding, but then Naomi found the letter in my backpack and threatened to show everyone on the speech team pictures from when I stuffed my bra during a sleepover if I didn't write back right away. That was more ammo than I wanted my competition to have, so I pulled out a pen and wrote 15211 back. I kept it short.

You know how to pronounce "Worcestershire"? If you tell me you can draw stick figures too, you're hired.

His next note had been a stick figure drawing of two people. One had a regular circle for its head while the other had an elongated oval. He'd captioned it, *Why the long face?* Despite myself, I laughed.

I wrote back.

My best stick figures happen when I play hangman. So here's a word for you to guess. It also happens to be my favorite food.

It'd taken almost a week of back and forth for him to figure out I liked mint Oreos. The following day, a whole pack of them showed up in my cubby.

I'll admit, that went a long way toward making me like the guy. Anyone who bought me chocolate was okay by me.

When he told me it was physically impossible for him to watch a movie without popcorn, I bought him a bag from the vending machine to return the favor.

The white cheddar kind. Because it's hands-down the best. Don't argue. You know I'm right.

Somehow I found myself falling into this new rhythm where I exchanged notes with a stranger almost every day. Sometimes it was one line, sometimes a full page, but it always made me smile. After enough time had passed, Naomi didn't even have to pressure me into it. It became something I looked forward to, rather than a weird social experiment.

Without divulging too much of my personal life, I also asked him advice on speech and debate topics. Our first tournament was coming up quickly and I still hadn't settled on anything.

What issues in the news today do you think are the most important?

Internet privacy. Antidiscrimination laws. The human carbon footprint. Immigration. I could go on and on.

Not only did we sometimes mention the assignments, but I often saw his grades whenever I left a note in his cubby, and his scores in AP Government were a testament to his knowledge of political topics. What was ironic was how much he claimed to hate politics.

Of course, talking about those kinds of things had somehow led to us discussing deeper and more personal topics. In one letter, I learned he didn't always get along with his parents, for one thing.

Dear 15511,

Did you get question three right on the last assignment? I didn't. I think Ms. Navarrete is wrong, but my parents prob-

ably won't let me explain my view. If I miss one answer on an assignment, they ask me what went wrong. More than one and I might as well have failed.

It's like they expect me to be a rocket scientist or president of the United States or something like that. They can't seem to remember I'm just a teenager doing the best I can.

Sorry, that got deep fast. Didn't mean to lay that all on you, random stranger. All that to say, what'd you put for question three?

15211

I deflected his question about our assignments, because the truth was, I'd gotten a lot more than just question number three wrong. Parents, though, that was something I could talk about.

I was lucky. Random spats aside, my mom and I got along. The night before I got that letter, we'd binged *The Good Place* and laughed so hard there was actual waterworks. Later, she'd shown me some of her latest photos from a wedding and we'd both about died when she'd photo-shopped horns onto the bride. Still, we had our moments.

For about a week after that note, I swapped parental horror stories with 15211, leaving my dad out of it since he wasn't in the picture anymore.

My mom didn't like this Goth emo guy I used to date. So anytime he came over, she'd blast the Top 40 hits from her room just so he'd leave. Our walls would actually shake. And no, she doesn't like pop music.

Looking back, it actually was kind of funny. My mom had to have hated it almost as much as he had. Personally, I liked pop, so it was probably all for the best that it hadn't worked out between me and Emo Guy.

*One time my mom locked me out because I missed curfew. I had
to sleep on the porch swing. Luckily, it was the summer.*

His parents seemed a lot stricter than my mom. My mom did things
in good fun, but his parents' expectations were sky high. It was clear he
respected them immensely and put a lot of stock in their opinions, which
was great. But, the more I got to know him, the more I felt bad for him,
and I was getting to know him more every day.

It was strangely exhilarating writing a stranger a note. A physical,
handwritten letter that wasn't something that'd be forgotten on his phone
the minute something better came along. The letters I collected seemed
more solid than anything I'd read in a long time, which was maddening
considering I didn't even know who it was doing the writing. How could
something so full of questions be so concrete at the same time?

He seemed to feel the same way.

*Is it weird that I kind of like not knowing who you are? Some-
times it's not knowing something that makes it all the more
exciting.*

Soon, it wasn't a question of *if* I'd write him back, but a matter of how
quickly I could whip out my pen. Curiosity was nibbling at my stomach, making me anticipate AP Government for the first time ever, simply
because I'd get to put a letter in someone's cubby. Really, it was absurd,
and I knew it.

I didn't even know his name, or anything that could actually identify
him. All I had were pieces of a whole, things that made him who he was,
but when looked at separately, could apply to anyone, really.

On Monday night, Naomi and I tried to figure out who my mystery
pen pal could be while I waited for my mom to come home from the diner.
Music blasted from my computer and we talked loudly over it.

36

"His parents are still together?" Naomi asked as we sprawled out on my bed. Ms. Navarrete's class rosters and 15211's letters were spread out around us like a sea of white foam. A paper cut waiting to happen. Ms. Navarrete had four classes of AP Government throughout the day, and each class had about fifteen guys, give or take. We'd sweet-talked the office aide into printing them out. Well, Naomi had sweet-talked. I'd stood there awkwardly and debated whether this could count as a felony or end up on my permanent record somehow.

"Affirmative," I said. "His parents are still married." I searched through the names in third period.

"There's got to be at least sixty-five guys here." Naomi put down the paper she was holding. "Remind me again why you can't just ask him?"

I had to turn down the music because my mom was going to be home any minute.

"And spoil the fun?" I asked. My voice was light, but inwardly, I was tense, a coiled-up snake. Conflicted. Did I really want to know who this person was? Some things were better off unsaid, after all. I gathered the papers together just as my mom poked her head through my door.

"Nice to see you're so focused on homework," she said. Naomi bounced her head enthusiastically. I sat there frozen, like a meerkat sensing approaching danger. My grades in AP Government hadn't been stellar lately, and my mom had agreed on Naomi coming over as long as we used the time to study.

Well, in my defense, we *had* been studying. But not schoolwork.

"You girls want some dinner?"

Naomi was off the bed and on the way to the kitchen before my mom was even done offering. Like me, she'd probably smelled the apple pie aroma that was wafting through my now-open door.

"I got another photography booking this morning," my mom said, waving her phone at me. "I'm doing newborn shots for a lady across town. She said she found me through Instagram, which you know I can never do without you." She waggled her eyebrows and I smiled. Direct results. It was the best feeling in the world. "You know you're my favorite kid, right?"

I scoffed and said the same line I always did.

"I'm your *only* kid."

"Still my favorite. Now let's eat."

She left and I finished gathering the papers, separating them into two piles. One for 15211's letters, and the other for the lists of potential names in Ms. Navarrete's classes. I debated throwing the lists away. My hand hovered over my trash can, the papers touching the edge.

Then I pulled back, placing the lists of names on my desk instead.

Right now, I wasn't sure I wanted to know who 15211 was. But something told me that might not always be the case.

Chapter Six

I had 15211 to thank for my first speech topic of the season.

I'd talk about the psychological reasons behind why teenagers don't always mesh with their parents and I'd use actual science to back me up. Oratory was all about persuading people to your viewpoint, and I was going to argue that more grown-ups should cut us slack, because hello, it was our hormones' fault we behaved the way we did.

Besides, parents often had completely unrealistic expectations of us. Adults thought we were too old for the mistakes we made, but they never let us have any real responsibility. We weren't old enough for *that*. We were in this in-between world where everything was out to get us.

Sure, maybe the topic wouldn't make the judges love me right away because they'd be grown-ups themselves, but with enough facts, they'd be forced to see I was right. Those were the best topics—they were the ones that won. If you could get judges to agree to something they wouldn't regularly admit, you were in.

It didn't mean I wasn't friends with my mom. But she was still my mom, and of course, we had our moments. Usually, whenever she thought I spent too long on Instagram. It didn't even matter if I said I was doing it for her.

I spent longer writing it than I usually did, but by the time I left speech practice on Tuesday, I was feeling pretty good about myself.

Until I saw the sun setting on the horizon, a gorgeous watercolor painting that mocked my pain.

"Oh no, oh no," I muttered to myself as I pulled out my phone to check the time. The whole time I'd been working, it'd been on silent. Which meant I'd missed the reminder telling me to leave for the bus. I knew the bus schedule almost by heart, but I looked it up anyway and my stomach dropped. The last bus had already come and gone, over an hour ago. I was stuck.

I should have been more aware of my surroundings. Most everyone had left practice already, except for our coach. And Grayson.

I sucked in a shaky breath of cool September air and tried not to panic. The shadows were already lengthening from the trees, but I knew my mom wouldn't be home until late tonight.

Okay, so my mom couldn't help me. What other options did I have?

I could walk. But I was at least five miles away from our apartment, it was getting dark, and it wasn't like I lived on the nice side of town. So that was a recipe for disaster.

I could ask Grayson for a ride. But after the way I'd behaved at practice a couple of weeks ago, that wasn't going to happen. Ever. Even the thought of it made my skin crawl with embarrassment. Sure, I'd talked to him about other things since he'd offered to drive me home from practices, but anything involving a car was strictly off-limits conversation-wise.

My cheeks flushed and I chewed on my lower lip. I couldn't let him see me out here either, standing around like some pathetic loser. What if he finished up whatever he was doing and saw me hanging around, like I was waiting for him? I'd die.

Two large columns stood outside the entrance to the school, surrounded by tall bushes. I went around one of them, scratching my arms in the process as I ducked low and sat on the ground. But from this angle, I was hidden from the view of the front doors.

I could text Naomi or Carter. Or both of them.

Easy. *That* was something I could do. I felt weak with relief and slumped back against the column as I started a group text. Carter hadn't left practice that long ago, but he almost always had work right after, which was why I didn't usually ride with him. Chances weren't good, but I had to ask.

> Can either of you give me a ride home from the school? I missed the bus.

Carter's response was almost immediate.

> Sorry, no can do. I'm working at the climbing gym right now. My shift is over in three hours though if you're still stuck. Let me know.

I sighed and put my phone in my pocket while I waited for Naomi to text back. The fact that she hadn't already though wasn't a good sign. I put my head in my hands while I waited. It was getting colder and my jacket was thin.

I heard the school doors open and I froze. Grayson's voice was unmistakable.

"See you tomorrow," he called back to someone. The doors closed behind him and I counted his footsteps without looking. Looking would mean moving, and that would rustle the bush I was hiding behind.

Of course, that was when my phone dinged with another text.

Grayson's footsteps stopped. "Hello?" he called.

I didn't answer. Sweat dripped down my back as I slowly reached into my pocket to bring out my phone. The display seemed overly bright in the semidarkness and I fumbled with it. But another text came through before I could put my phone on silent.

Grayson came around the pillar and stood right in front of me. At first he seemed hesitant, but when he recognized me, he smiled.

I, on the other hand, wasn't smiling. I just wanted the ground to eat me alive, was that too much to ask?

"Well, well, look what we have here. Hiding, are we?" Grayson asked.

My mouth opened up to form words, but none came out. I closed it and pursed my lips together. Another text came in and I glanced down to read it. All of them were from Naomi.

> I'm stuck babysitting my little brother right now. Or I'd totally come to your rescue.

> P.S. Carter, I think three hours is a bit long for Quinn to wait, but kudos for offering I guess?

The third text was sent just to me, not on the group thread.

> The boy is trying too hard. I told you he likes you.

Naomi couldn't give me a ride either. The panic started setting in then. Because if neither of them could pick me up, that left me with . . . Grayson. Who was standing in front of me, hands in his pockets, a self-satisfied expression written all over his face.

No. I refused. I would not beg him for a ride after everything that had happened a few weeks ago. I'd rather go back inside the school and camp out in the speech room until Carter or my mom got off work in a few hours. Hours with nothing to do, surrounded by empty hallways and reminders of my academic failures. Naomi might think it was too long to wait, but it was better than the alternative. My hands shook and I mimicked Grayson's pose, standing up and putting them in my pockets to cover up my awkwardness.

"I wasn't hiding," I said. "I was waiting."

"For what?"

I didn't have a good answer for that. If I said *a ride*, he'd ask me who was coming. And the answer was no one. I almost laughed. But I wasn't sure I could keep it from turning into a cry, so I stayed silent.

"Well"—Grayson nudged his glasses farther up on his nose and I didn't meet his eyes—"I'm pretty sure there's a bus stop around here."

"Really? I had no idea," I managed to get out. The bush stood between us, and I played with one of the branches, still not meeting his gaze.

"Ah, but the buses don't run this late, do they?"

He had me there. I finally looked at him, and I knew my secret was out. Understanding dawned on his face and I pushed my way out of the bush, walking past him and toward the main doors of the school. I had no words to say. Nothing that could make this moment less humiliating.

"Quinn," he called before I could make it to the doors. I turned around and tried to keep from tears. It was ridiculous, and I had no idea why I felt this way. But my ribs were squeezing together, and I wrapped my arms around my body.

"I do have a car, you know," he said. His voice was lightly teasing, like maybe he could tell how much this moment was killing me, so he didn't go into full jerk mode. Either that or he was afraid I'd go off on him again, which was still a distinct possibility with how high-strung my emotions were right now. My chest hitched and I looked down at the ground. My hair hung in my face and I struggled to put what I was feeling into words.

"It's one of those things on four wheels that can take you places. All you have to say is please." He shrugged his shoulders. "I know, I know. It's hard for you."

"Don't be ridiculous," I said. I wouldn't be able to keep up my indifference much longer. I needed him to leave before I broke down. "I'm perfectly able to hang out here until my mom can get me."

"Oh? Tell me again, when does she get off work?"

I sighed but didn't answer.

He nodded slowly. "The custodian was already locking things up as I left. Ms. Bates went out the back. But, hey, I know you're an overachiever, so if you like creeping around here after dark . . . more power to you I guess?"

His words were a stone in my stomach. I could always wait outside, but it was dark and getting colder by the minute. Grayson rubbed his hands on his arms, as if sensing the same thing.

"It's only one little word," he said, voice surprisingly soft.

I considered my options. Embarrass myself with Grayson, which had already happened and couldn't really get worse, or wait in the dark for hours until either Carter or my mom could come.

I closed my eyes and let out a breath.

"Okay," I said, swallowing hard. "Please."

The word was bitter and seemed to stick in my throat like peanut butter. But I'd said it, and there was no turning back now.

* * *

WE DIDN'T SAY anything as we clicked our seat belts. Like last time, the new car smell surrounded me, and I wondered how much Grayson's parents had paid for it. He pushed the button, the car hummed to life, and we pulled out of the parking lot, all without a word. It would have been awkward, except I was over it now. It was pointless to feel embarrassed, because no matter what I did, it kept happening.

"How'd it go with your group at practice today?" Grayson asked. At the beginning, we'd split the new Oratory members into two groups to go over basics, working from opposite sides of the room. "You need me to pick up your slack?"

"Hardly," I deadpanned. "I think I can handle a few first years." I'd been teaching two freshman and Carter. But it'd been tricky not to show him favoritism when he kept using inside jokes and sidetracking the conversation. I'd had a much easier time focusing when we'd moved on to working on our individual projects. Plus, I didn't want him to get the wrong idea about our friendship, if Naomi was right. Judging from the way she'd written *the boy is trying too hard* she still thought she was right. She thought his actions went above and beyond normal friendship. Maybe it'd be better for everyone involved if he worked with Grayson instead. If Grayson was offering.

"But if you wanted to help Carter transition to Oratory," I said, "I wouldn't say no."

Grayson shot me a loaded look.

"He's your friend, isn't he?"

That was precisely the problem. But it wasn't like I wanted to explain myself to Grayson.

"Maybe he's on my bad side," I said, waving my hand noncommittally.

"Tell him to join the club," Grayson said with a chuckle.

I slugged him on the shoulder and Grayson pretended to be hurt.

"You sure Carter deserves to be on your list? I'm on your bad side simply for being good at what I do."

I snorted.

"You take it personally. But it's not personal, I promise."

Maybe for him it wasn't.

"Keep telling yourself that if it makes you feel better," I said, looking out the window.

"So what'd Carter do to get on your bad side? Is it really that bad? Do I need to beat him up?"

Grayson was smirking, obviously making light of the situation and trying to bring us back into familiar territory where we taunted each other and didn't do nice things like give the other person a ride when all hope was lost, like some knight in shining armor to save the day.

"Like you could ever beat anyone up," I said, rolling my eyes. "You don't have it in you."

"Hey, I can be mean." He glanced over.

"Oh, I didn't say you couldn't be mean. Those are two very different things. You're rude all the time."

Grayson nodded slowly. "I can't help it. I have too much fun arguing with you."

My eyebrows furrowed. "You *like* arguing with me? Are you okay? Are you sick?" I pretended to be concerned and placed the back of my hand to his forehead. Just as quickly, I snatched it away after realizing what I'd done.

Grayson laughed. "Is it so hard to believe that I have fun arguing with you?"

"No, I guess I believe that. You are a pretty awful person."

"See? I never know what you're going to say. I like that."

This whole conversation was surreal. I couldn't tell if he was trying to give me a compliment or if he was insulting me, yet again. Uncomfortable with the unfamiliar territory, I cleared my throat and looked out the window.

The darkness surrounding the car made the conversation feel more intimate and close. Grayson was only sitting a foot away from me, and with his hand resting on the gearshift, his arm was almost touching mine. I shifted away, putting more distance between us.

"You still haven't told me what Carter did to end up on your bad list."

A car passed us in the other lane and the lights reflected off Grayson's glasses.

"He's not really. I just think there's a conflict of interest there with him being my friend. You're the only one on my list."

This made Grayson laugh. We stopped at a light and he looked over at me. "I'm honored," he said, pretending to bow. "That means I'm number one. No surprise there."

I narrowed my eyes at him. "I guess we'll wait and see after this next tournament, now won't we?"

"I don't know, I have a pretty killer topic. I don't think yours can beat it."

He looked over, obviously waiting for me to supply him with my topic. But it wasn't like I was going to cough up the information that easily. I wasn't sure what he'd do with it.

"If you think I'm going to tell you my topic, you're wrong."

"Oh, because speech topics are so worthy of secrecy?" Grayson raised his eyebrows in a dare, and I couldn't back down.

"You know mine is."

He made a "hmmmm" sound as he turned left. "Why don't you let me be the judge of that?"

I drummed my fingers on the car handle. I remained silent and Grayson laughed.

"You know everyone will hear it this weekend, right?"

He had a point. Besides, he'd likely been writing his speech for weeks, and the chance that he'd scrap it all now, mere days before our first competition, was low.

Low, but not impossible.

I sucked in a breath, let it out in a whoosh, and, with it, told Grayson my speech topic. I wasn't even sure why I did it. I didn't need Grayson's praise. Or even his approval. But I wanted it anyway. I wanted him to hear my topic and shake in fear. I wanted him to feel vastly inferior and bow to my superiority.

Instead, he gave a low whistle, followed by a short laugh.

"You sure do make this easy for me sometimes."

I scoffed. "You're just jealous."

"Normally? Hands-down yes." He sent me a smile that strangely stopped my breathing. "But, Quinn, you know the judges are going to eat you alive."

I brushed his backhanded compliment aside and focused on the hidden barb that was always there, like a buy-one-get-one-free coupon for insults. Grayson had this way of telling me his honest opinion, refusing to sugarcoat anything. Half of the time I didn't know what to do with it. Everyone else nodded politely and went along with whatever I said, but not Grayson. He didn't let me get away with anything, and that irked me more than almost anything he could have said. Carter was blunt too, but he didn't actively antagonize me.

"I appreciate your concern," I said dryly. "But I think I can handle it."

"I admire your bravery," Grayson said. "How you don't even try to play their game or tell them what they want to hear. I mean, I think you're wrong, but it's brave nonetheless."

"I think *you're* wrong," I said lightly, waving his comments aside. "But then again, there's nothing new." I looked out the window at the buildings flashing by.

I tried to ignore the conversation, but as was usual with Grayson, I couldn't let it drop.

"So you think I'd win more if I took the opposite stance? If I said we all need to honor our parents or something like that? Mother knows best and we teenagers should shut up and listen?"

"That's exactly what I'm saying."

"But I have facts."

"Since when is winning about facts? It's all about making the judges like you. I'm half tempted to take the opposing argument at this tournament simply so you can see I'm right."

"You wouldn't."

"Wouldn't I?"

I knew he would. That was the problem.

Well, the problem, and the thrill. Because this was also an opportunity in disguise. I could see it on the corners of my vision, dancing around the car in the silence between us. I never could resist a good competition.

My heartbeat picked up as I mulled it over. If Grayson changed his speech topic now, at the last minute, I'd have weeks of research ahead of him. My speech was already written. Plus, it'd give me the opportunity to finally beat him and rub his too-handsome face in it. But there was a definite risk to presenting opposing speeches at a tournament. One of us was likely to win, and the other was bound to tank spectacularly. There wasn't really room for middle ground. But if there was a chance I'd finally beat Grayson . . .

"Do it," I said. I tried to keep my voice as noncommittal as possible, even throwing in a shrug for good measure. If he knew I was pulling strings, he'd never go for it. Grayson was much too smart for his own good.

Grayson stopped at a light and turned to face me. "Seriously?"

I raised my eyebrows. "What, are you scared?" I turned on my winning smile. "Not so tough now, huh? You know I'm right."

"I may agree with you in principal, but that doesn't mean it's a good speech topic," Grayson said, shaking his head. "If I do this, you won't tell Ms. Bates I sabotaged you and you won't throw me under the bus?"

I smiled sweetly. "I would never."

He grinned and held out his hand, which I shook.

"It's a deal."

Chapter Seven

Everyone around me was busy talking to the wall. Literally. This was pretty common at speech and debate tournaments, especially early on in the year when we were all testing new speeches and smoothing out any kinks in our performances. Some students were still reading off notecards and I hoped for their sakes they didn't bring them in with them to the actual rounds with judges. It was one thing to study notecards in the hallway, but at a varsity meet, notecards were the kiss of death.

I was sitting against the wall with my legs sticking straight out in front of me. It's hard to sit ladylike in a pencil skirt, even with years of practice. The more I thought about the competition, the more nervous I got, especially about whatever Grayson had planned.

I tried to distract myself with Goldfish crackers. And music. There were a few things I brought with me to every single speech meet, and Goldfish crackers and headphones were high on the list. Call me superstitious, but the only time I didn't break into the finals round was the time I'd forgotten to bring my music along.

But even Shawn Mendes wasn't helping now. My hands were still shaky each time I brought a Goldfish to my mouth, and despite the volume, I couldn't seem to drown out the sounds going on around me. We had about fifteen minutes until the first round, and because I'd stayed up late going through every possible flaw in my speech, I could barely keep my eyes open. That'd be a great way to impress the judges, falling asleep before I even got to compete. I already wanted to tear my pantyhose off and throw them in a fire, so this was bound to end well. But this tournament needed to go perfectly. I needed this to be Grayson's downfall. So I'd put in the extra time, just in case.

I adjusted my suit coat, relaxed against the wall, and closed my eyes. Nope, that was a mistake. I felt myself falling asleep and I jerked away from the wall. Snacks and music weren't cutting it. I needed something that would really hold my interest.

I pulled out 15211's latest note from my bag and smoothed it out over my legs. We'd exchanged more letters over the past few days, and AP Government had never been so entertaining. He'd never mentioned his real identity, and I hadn't either. We hadn't even discussed the possibility of finding out.

I decided I liked it that way. If I knew who it was, the chances of me being disappointed rose by approximately a bazillion percent. Besides, we'd both gotten a little personal at times, and I didn't want anyone really knowing all those things about me.

Anonymous was safe.

I learned 15211 liked his lists. Half of his notes were in list form. He liked tiptoeing around things that could possibly identify him without actually tipping the scales. Like how he could pronounce *Worcestershire*. It was real information, but nothing I could actually use.

There was more actual information about him in this one letter than all his past ones combined, and I still hadn't written him back. I wasn't sure I could return the favor. It was long and rambly, like the lecture that day had been especially boring. My notes were mostly mindless, but this one of 15211's showed some real thought.

I liked it, and I didn't. Because if these notes actually meant something, well, I wasn't sure what to do then. I'd texted Naomi to ask her opinion, but she'd had a volleyball tournament all day and hadn't responded.

I reread the letter on my lap and found myself smiling.

> I think we should do twenty questions, but our own version of it where instead of guessing one thing, we give twenty facts about ourselves. But until I get your okay on that, I'll just tell you all about myself and hope you do the same. No pressure, though. You can keep your secrets. I know I'm keeping some too.
>
> I like watching sports, even if I suck at playing them. I blame my parents, who never let me play (too many injuries!), so I guess we'll never know what could have happened. I might have been a legend. For now, I watch football on Sundays and pretend I'm coordinated enough to have caught that pass someone else didn't. Does paintball count as a sport? If so, I've got that one down.
>
> I like action movies and video games. And action video games. One day I'd love to be a programmer for them. You know, if the whole "president of the United States" thing doesn't work out. But I doubt my parents would ever let me go into something like programming or coding, so that dream will never happen. Yay.
>
> I've never been in a fight, and would be terrified if I ever were. I'd probably lose. No, not probably. Definitely.
>
> Not that I'm a weakling. I think it's important to note that I am just as strong as most guys. Okay, got that on the record.

I like to cook. Surprised? My parents work long hours, and I got tired of eating frozen pizza, so I taught myself. My younger siblings don't always appreciate it, though, especially when I try something more . . . experimental.

I know nothing about cars except for how to drive them, and even then, I can't drive a stick shift, despite the twenty or so lessons my dad gave me. He said it was something every guy needed to know. So then my mom made me take ballroom dancing classes because she said <u>that</u> was something every guy needed. I can still do the waltz, so it wasn't all for nothing.

I hate camping. Why do people do that to themselves? You have a perfectly good bed, away from mosquitoes and water. Sleep in it.

I will freely admit (but only to you, since you don't know who I am) that I like chick flicks. I'd always complain when girlfriends would drag me to them, but secretly, I'd be glad to have an excuse to see it. I'd much rather see a rom-com over a horror movie any day.

Now, I think all that info deserves at least one fact about you in return, but I'll understand if you run away screaming instead.

All the sound around me had dulled to a buzz as I read 15211's letter. I hadn't even noticed that my playlist had ended. I pulled the earbuds from my ear and put them in my bag. The letter crinkled as I moved, and I smoothed it out again.

I reread the sentence about his past girlfriends taking him to chick flicks. Was he saying he was currently single? The thought made me smile and I rolled my eyes at my own naivety. I didn't even know this guy.

But you already know a lot about him. More than you have some other guys you've dated, my thoughts answered back.

Yeah, well, now I was being ridiculous and arguing with myself, so that was great. I folded the letter and put it away, watching the students around me practice their speeches. Maybe I should be focusing on that. I could use the practice, and my memorization wasn't as solid as I'd like. But my thoughts kept circulating back to the letter.

I hadn't told anyone about my secret pen pal, well, except Naomi, and sometimes we were so in sync I wasn't sure she counted. It'd been going on long enough now that I probably should be more open about it with others. Like Carter. But I never talked with Carter about boy stuff. And what if Naomi was right and Carter did have a thing for me? It'd be cruel to throw this in his face.

It was better this way.

Right now, this was just ours. Mine and 15211's, whoever he was. And it was strangely thrilling to have a secret like this. Each letter was like a clue, hinting at just enough to keep me guessing. Bringing me closer to finding . . . *something* at the end of it. A friend? Something more? The possibilities felt endless. Because while I might not know who he was, I kind of did all the same. The essence of him, at least.

Knowing his name might change that.

I thought of everything he'd told me so far and tried to picture the boy that would match that image in my mind. Even with the letter safely tucked away, I could remember it all, almost word for word.

I didn't know any physical features, except that he was "as strong as most guys," whatever that meant. I knew his parents were still married, which eliminated about half the boys in our grade. He played video games, which eliminated exactly no one.

I readjusted my skirt and took another handful of Goldfish. Whoever he was, I was pretty sure I didn't know him well in real life because I didn't know anyone who cooked and did the waltz. Maybe he kept those facts to himself, though, like how he wouldn't admit to liking chick flicks. After all, he'd said he'd kept some secrets, and my thoughts kept returning to that piece of information like a tongue probing at a missing tooth.

What was he hiding? And should I be worried about it?

Maybe he had a postage stamp collection.

Maybe he fought crime after dark.

Maybe he had the whole periodic table memorized.

Even wondering about those things didn't change the fact that I was way more interested in this guy than I probably should be.

Maybe it was irrational, but perhaps the biggest reason I didn't want to reveal my name was because he was too good to be true. Too good for me, at least. 15211 was obviously smart and talented, and I was . . . just normal ol' me.

Carter slumped to the ground beside me, his suit coat unbuttoned and flapping around him as he slouched.

"Lists are up," he said, showing me his phone and the picture he'd taken of them.

The lists were how we knew which room we'd be competing in. We'd be in different rooms for each round, competing against different people most of the time until finals.

"How many rooms of Oratory?" I asked, taking Carter's phone from his hands. He'd taken pictures of four Oratory rooms, which meant we luckily didn't have a whole lot of competition at this tournament. I found my number listed under room 151A.

"I'm in room 200," Carter said. "Where are you at?" We used numbers to identify ourselves at meets, instead of names, so it wasn't like he knew.

"Not yours." I passed his phone back. "So we're not competing yet."

I wondered if Grayson would be in my first round, delivering his speech that was a direct argument to mine. I almost rubbed my hands together in anticipation, but stopped just short.

"I dodged a bullet," Carter said. "But I'm sad I have to wait even longer to hear your speech. I'm sure it's amazing."

I stood up and started picking up my things. The first round started soon and I needed to be ready.

"Can I ask you a question?" Carter said, standing. I nodded. "Did you tell Grayson your speech topic before this meet?"

I hesitated before answering. Carter knew how secretive I was with my speech topics. If I let him know I'd told Grayson, he'd read into it. But in the end, I couldn't lie to my friend.

"Yes. Why?"

Carter nodded slowly. "Just be careful, okay? Becoming friends with him, I mean." I sucked in a breath and Carter continued before I could say anything. "Remember what he did to Zara. I don't want the same thing to happen to you before the state finals."

I blinked. "Grayson and I aren't friends," I said. "Pretty much the opposite."

Carter gave me a thin-lipped smile, clearly appeasing me. "Sure."

I shrugged his comment off, but tucked the information away for later. Because the fact was, I wouldn't put it past Grayson to do something underhanded to get ahead. Maybe it was his modus operandi for anything involving a competition to seduce the enemy and distract her into sabotaging her chances.

"I just . . . I care about you. So, yeah."

I didn't respond to his comment. There really wasn't anything to say.

"I'll walk you to your room," Carter said. I nodded as I picked up my bag with the letter inside. The letter from the same guy who had inspired my speech for this tournament.

It was time to focus on speech and debate. I had a better chance of beating Grayson at this tournament than I'd probably get all year. So why could I not stop thinking about 15211's letter?

Chapter Eight

*P*ity parties are hard to pull off when you're wearing a power suit and heels, but somehow I managed. Problem was, there were too many people around to witness it. I had to get farther away. Much, much farther. The auditorium doors swung shut behind me, somewhat muffling the sound of clapping. I turned left down the empty hallway, left again, and walked all the way to the end, where a flickering fluorescent light was my only company. Sinking down against the wall, I sat on the linoleum floor and finally let my head drop between my knees.

I sucked in a breath and slowly let it out, counting to ten. Again. Then I released my hair from its French twist, letting it tumble to my shoulders. Now that the speech and debate tournament was officially over—and my poor standing in the still-going awards ceremony was proof of that—I didn't need the headache from all the bobby pins. I gathered them in a pool at my feet, focusing on the tiny ridges instead of the dull burn forming behind my eyes. I. Would. Not. Cry.

So what if I lost to Grayson Hawks? So what if he got first place and I got eighth? *Eighth*. That was literally the worst I could get while still being in the finals. Last place. I was used to placing in the top three, every time. That was expected. So when the middle-aged guy with a microphone had said, "Eighth place, Quinn Edwards," it took me a full ten seconds to realize it was my name he'd called. I'd made a gamble, and I'd lost. Grayson was right, and that fact stung more than actually losing to him.

Another faint wave of clapping made its way from the auditorium to where I sat. They must have announced the winners of another event. Mentally, I calculated how much longer I could stay out here. They hadn't gotten to any of the debate events yet, which meant I had at least another half hour to feel sorry for myself. I pulled my knees to my chest and dropped my head onto my arms.

I'd have to write another speech for the next tournament, and this time, I'd have to think of something the judges actually wanted to hear. If I wanted to beat Grayson, that is.

And, oh, how I wanted to beat Grayson. It shouldn't have been this important to me, but every time he won, I felt my competitive nature get a little bit worse.

The sound of footsteps made me lift my head.

I sighed when I saw who it was. "Did you come to gloat?"

Grayson was the last person I wanted to see right now. Verbally sparring with Grayson took wit, and right now I was running on empty.

"You'd like that, wouldn't you?" Grayson eased himself down so he was sitting beside me, and I tensed at the proximity. I could practically feel his body heat through his suit coat. He was so close, and a traitorous part of me couldn't help but react to the good way he smelled. Now wasn't the time to think about things like that, though, not when I still had to come up with a way to beat him.

"Why would I like that?" I asked.

"Because then I'd be the jerk you could bad-mouth to all your friends."

Despite myself, I grinned. Grayson's voice was deep and smooth—

perfectly controlled, like his polished performances. He'd been amazing, and I couldn't fault him for winning. Carter hadn't broken into finals, so at least I didn't have to live with the knowledge that someone had beaten me who'd been new to the event.

"What makes you think I talk about you?" My voice shook a little as I said it, and I hoped Grayson blamed it on me being emotional over losing, rather than how close he was sitting. He'd never sat this close before, and suddenly, it was the only thing I could focus on.

Grayson raised an eyebrow, like he knew I was lying. I pushed his shoulder and he laughed.

"Maybe I followed you because you looked upset," he said when he'd finished laughing. "And I thought you could use a friend."

Was that what we were now? Before becoming co-team captains, we'd only been competitors. But I found myself looking forward to our little spats, as much as I'd never admit it to anyone, least of all Grayson. He pushed my buttons and distracted me constantly, but I kind of liked it? It didn't make sense to me, so I didn't even try to untangle that hot mess in my mind.

"You can say 'I told you so.' I know you want to." I snuck a glance at him, but he didn't seem smug about his victory. Just casual. One corner of his mouth lifted up at the edge and he sighed.

"Well, now you know my secret to success, so it's only a matter of time before you're outranking me."

"You mean, your secret of giving the judges what they want? So original. I don't think anyone has ever thought of that before you."

"You wound me." He held a hand to his chest in mock horror. "You know, if you want to give me a chance at beating you again, you can always tell me what you plan to speak on next. I'll prepare accordingly."

"You'd like that, wouldn't you?" I asked, echoing his statement from earlier. He caught my reference and smiled.

"Well, you know the judges can't resist me." He smirked. "So do your worst."

"So cocky, aren't we?" I said. "Want to do another gamble?"

Grayson looked cautious, which was flattering considering I'd come in last place at this weekend's tournament. He quickly recovered, plastering on false bravado like a second skin.

"Oh please, you don't stand a chance," he said.

"Yeah? You're so sure you can win no matter what? Let's let the other person pick our speech topics for the next meet. What do you say?"

I was betting on his sympathy here. I'd just lost, so really, it'd be cruel of him to stick me with a boring topic like world peace or the importance of washing your hands. He wasn't that heartless, was he?

We didn't typically have a new speech for each tournament. We usually did two or three for the entire season, but I figured he'd choose a different topic now that I was too. It was hard to capitalize on someone's failure if they stopped giving you the opportunity. Maybe he'd wanted to go back to his original speech he'd planned before our chat in his car, but I wasn't about to let that happen if I could stop it. I needed at least one win to boost my ego.

"The tournament in two weeks?" he asked. I could see he was actually considering my offer, and I tried to hide my grin. "Are you going to that one?"

The next meet was on the same day as our school's fall fling. It was the only meet that wasn't mandatory. But Grayson should know me better to know speech came first. Not that I'd been asked to the dance anyway.

"I'm going to the tournament," I said. "You?" It was pointless to ask. Someone as popular Grayson would be going to the dance, for sure. But Grayson nodded, surprising me.

Another faint round of clapping made it to where we sat under the flickering light. Someone else's dreams were either made or crushed. But the clapping didn't make me feel as bad as it had earlier.

"I already have a topic picked out for you," Grayson said. His grin spread from ear to ear.

I swallowed. So we were doing this, then. It was what I'd hoped for and dreaded at the same time. I squared my shoulders.

"Let's hear it."

"You're going to talk about saving the whales, and you're going to love it."

That wasn't so bad. Obviously, there were better topics out there, but I could make it work.

"Aw, you gave up too easily," I said joyfully. "I'm going to make your topic so much worse!"

"Saving the whales isn't bad enough for you?" he asked. "You're hard-core, Edwards."

I nodded solemnly. "That I am, Hawks. That I am. Let's see now." I rubbed my palms together. "What topic should I give to you?" A flash of inspiration hit and I snapped my fingers. "Women's rights in the work-force!"

"You do realize that the judges will love me," he said. "A guy talking about how women should receive equal treatment?"

I shook my head. "Oh, no, you're getting this all wrong." I laughed. "You have to argue the *opposite* side. You have to say women shouldn't be in the workplace or receive equal pay. *That's* your topic."

He blanched, and I smiled gleefully.

"You're a monster," he said. He shook his head but smiled as if this whole exchange was all a game to him. "Well played."

I bowed from my waist and he laughed.

"Looks like I'll have to brush up on my nautical knowledge," I said. "And you'll have to try not to look like a jerk. I know how hard that will be for you." I raised my eyebrows and Grayson laughed.

"Well, you know what they say." Grayson ran a hand through his hair. "All's fair in love and war."

Was this a war tactic of his? Buddying up to the competition? I remembered Carter's warning clearly in my mind. People said he set Zara up by dumping her before the student body elections went live. They said he'd learned the trick from his mother, who had a "take no prisoners" approach to politics. But was Grayson really capable of something like that? I used to think yes.

I searched his face, suddenly unsure of everything.

Someone cleared their throat at the end of the hall and my head snapped to the left.

Carter was standing there, hands in his pockets as he leaned against the wall in the flickering light.

Grayson stood up, but he wasn't in a hurry about it.

"I'll catch you around," Grayson said. He was grinning at Carter as he nudged my foot with his.

I rubbed my arm, unsure of how to interpret the gesture.

Grayson passed Carter, who came to sit at my side.

"You two seemed pretty cozy." Thankfully, he waited to say anything until Grayson was out of earshot. Carter adjusted his legs so he was sitting crisscrossed and turned his head to face me. "I'm telling you, he's trying to play you. My warning still stands."

I shook my head. "Don't worry. You know I don't have time for boys," I said, realizing something. Carter had given me the perfect opportunity to let him down gently. *If* he was flirting. By turning down Grayson, I could turn down Carter at the same time without him knowing it was about him or feeling offended. It wasn't like I wanted to hurt my friend's feelings.

Carter nodded but didn't say anything, leaving it up to me to fill the awkward silence.

"I really need to focus on school right now. My mom needs my help with her photography business and it's taking me a really long time to figure out how to build a website. Plus, there's speech and debate. You saw how I did today."

Carter shook his head. "Winning isn't everything, you know. Unless you're after that scholarship. Is that it?"

Whoever won first place at the state speech and debate tournament received a financial scholarship to the college of their choice. Sure, it was on my radar, but the competition alone was enough for me. The simplicity of beating Grayson was all I needed. But if I said that, Carter would think I was obsessed with the guy.

So I nodded, hoping he'd let the subject drop once and for all. I was starting to wonder if maybe I was a little obsessed, and not in the way I'd originally thought. *That* thought made me all kinds of squirmy.

"What's so great about going away to college?" he asked. "I've heard you and Naomi fantasize about going to Hawaii, but it's friends that make college great. You don't need the scholarship. You could stay here like me and go to community college. Think of all the fun we'd have." He wiggled his eyebrows and I laughed.

"You know I don't think there's anything wrong with community college," I said. It wasn't even like I was planning on going away, but now wasn't the time to inform Carter of that fact. Maybe it'd be better for him to think I was going away. Of course, as soon as I thought that, I felt awful. Since when did I keep things from Carter? I almost confessed right then and there, but I was starting to see what Naomi meant, and I couldn't bring myself to do it.

The truth of the matter was, I'd likely go to Boise State so I could stay close to my mom. She was the only family I had. Well, except for a deadbeat dad that I never saw who lived somewhere in California. Boise State also had a great business program where I could focus on marketing. I could get a concentrated education on something that fascinated me, without having to move away. Naomi was the one who wanted to go to Hawaii, and let's face it, who could blame her?

"Lots of our classmates are planning on going to a community college, you included. But it doesn't have the program I want."

"What program?" Carter scoffed. "The only thing you're really interested in is speech and debate."

"Not true," I said. "I want to do marketing. Besides, does our community college have a speech and debate team?" Answer: It did not. But Boise State did. Two birds, one stone.

I shook my head. "It's a moot point. It's not like I did well back there."

"I thought you did great."

"You must be a better judge at Improv," I said. "Because what you saw me perform was not great." I laughed at my own expense. "But thanks for trying to cheer me up. You're a good friend."

He smiled. "I try. We should go. They're probably missing us in the auditorium." He scooped up the bobby pins and placed them in my palm. I put them in my suit pocket with a sigh. He stood up, then held his hand out for me as well. Once standing, I squared my shoulders and we started back to the rest of the group. Sure, maybe I'd tanked this meet. But with the bet Grayson and I had made, the next tournament had my name written all over it. Those whales wouldn't know what was coming.

Chapter Nine

Dear 15211,

I never thought I'd say it, but I'm actually glad it's Monday. That means the weekend is finally over. Without giving too much away, I . . . struggled . . . this weekend. It's like I need lessons on how to, shall we say, be more of a people person. Any ideas?

That little request was because most of my judges had left comments saying I didn't appear personable. But how were you supposed to come across as personable in a formal memorized speech?

How to be a people person, a list by 15211:

(And yes, I'm just guessing here, but here's what I think).

1. Smile. A lot.

2. Don't be a downer.

3. Look people in the eye. (But don't be creepy about it.)

4. Don't take yourself too seriously.

5. When in doubt, make a joke.

I made sure to write plenty of jokes into my next speech. My favorite was "when there's a whale there's a way." Yeah, totally lame, but at least I wasn't taking myself too seriously. With a topic like "saving the whales," humor was my only chance. And while it was hard to smile while speaking, I practiced nonstop.

15211 was like a fountain of knowledge. Anytime I had a question, he somehow knew the perfect response. How to win an argument? *Know what can be used against you.* How to appear confident? *Square your shoulders, don't make excuses, and again with the smiling and eye contact.* He was really big on those two things.

He'd ask me for advice too, and I always felt like a superstar when I could help out.

> *How do you apologize to girls? Or if I admit I was a jerk, will that only make things worse?*

I wrote back.

> *You know how you said, when in doubt, make a joke? Whatever you do, don't do that. Since you like lists so much, I'll make this easy for you.*
>
> *1. Fess up and admit you were wrong.*
>
> *2. Don't do it again.*
>
> *That's it.*

All his advice helped me in speech and debate, so without even realizing it, I started trusting him with other things as well. Like my love life.

Another question for you: How do you kindly hint to a guy friend that he'll always be in the friend zone? Especially if I'm not even completely certain he's trying to flirt with me? I don't want to hurt him.

15511

P.S. I realized I never answered you earlier about twenty questions. Yes, I'll play if you still want. Even though I might regret it later.

After class ended, I put my letter in 15211's cubby before I could chicken out of playing twenty questions and answering whatever he asked me. Then I retrieved my assignment from my own cubby and shoved it in my bag, but not before catching sight of my score. A big, fat C-minus stood out on top, so my day kept getting better and better.

At least I had tonight to look forward to, where I was going to research SEO tactics for my mom's site. My friends thought I was weird, but hey, it was interesting. Hopefully speech practice wouldn't be too bad either. Ah, who was I kidding. I'd come in eighth place at the opening tournament. Practice today wasn't going to be great. A week had passed since then, but because Coach was out of town, we hadn't had practices. Maybe enough time had passed that people would forget. But probably not.

Naomi came over to where I was waiting and I was glad for the distraction from my thoughts.

"I hope you wrote him something scandalous," she said, slinging her bag over her shoulder and craning her neck to look at the cubby I'd just placed a letter in. "It's about time you two moved things to the next level."

"Oh, you mean writing in cursive? I'm not sure we're ready for that. Or are you talking about dedicated stationary?" I waggled my eyebrows and Naomi pushed me away playfully.

"I mean exchanging digits or letting each other know who you are. Though cursive would be a nice touch, I won't lie. Or maybe you can go old school and spritz some perfume on the paper or something."

"The only perfume in my apartment is my mom's," I said.

"Well, that'd just be wrong."

"Oh, come on." I nudged her shoulder. "You don't think he'd like old lady perfume?"

"I dare you to try it."

"I'll let you do the honors the next time you're at my place." I laughed. "Then I can tell him it was all your idea."

"Won't I see you tonight? I thought we were doing pizza and stalking some bands on Instagram."

With everything else that had been going on, I'd completely forgotten about our plans.

"Right. Six o'clock? Oh, and I can show you everything I've put together for my mom's site so far. It's got a rotating banner and everything."

"Well, look at you go." Her smile stretched across her face. "I can't wait. I feel like we haven't had a chance to hang out and talk lately."

"That's because I have nothing worth talking about," I said, pushing her out the doorway. "Unless you want to go over my oh-so-amazing speech tournament where I tanked so spectacularly I now need to write something on an entirely new topic."

Not to mention, my own mother hadn't really loved my topic all that much. When I'd presented it to her, her lips had scrunched to the side and she'd said, *So glad to know I make your life miserable. Guess I'm doing my job right.* Apparently my humor kept coming across the wrong way, and I needed to work on that.

"Right, right," Naomi said. "Always with the speech and debate. You need to get yourself a boyfriend already."

"Speak for yourself," I countered.

"I have."

I stopped short in the hallway and turned to face her. "And you didn't tell me?" I asked, disbelief coloring my tone.

She smiled slyly. "I wanted to make sure we were official before I said anything."

"Who? How?" I asked. Students passed me on either side and one of them bumped into me. I barely noticed. Naomi hooked her arm through mine and walked me toward the stairs.

"Remember two weeks ago when Dax asked me to the fall fling?"

I nodded and allowed myself to be pulled along in a daze. Dax was sporty like Naomi. They made sense together. Except for one thing.

"He's shorter than you," I said, the realization causing me to speak without thinking.

Naomi shrugged. "If I only dated guys who were taller than me, I'd be limited to Grant Benson or McKay Williams."

We'd made it to the stairs and Naomi dropped my arm.

"You'll tell me all about it tonight?" I asked, only going up a step.

"I promise. I even promise to listen to as much 5 Seconds of Summer as you want." That was the only band we disagreed about. She was completely wrong, by the way.

"You should be so lucky," I said, playfully shoving her shoulder.

We waved, then went our separate ways.

The speech room was busy, with everyone passing around score sheets from the previous meet. Mine were safely stored away in my locker, where they'd never get to see the light of day ever again. I'd gone over them on the bus ride home, and I'd spent my time since then trying to figure out where the nearest shredder was.

Coach Bates waved me over.

"Could you help Linley with her blocking?" she asked. I nodded and made my way there.

That's what I did for the rest of practice. And I gave it 110 percent so that no one would claim I didn't deserve to be co–team captain.

When I wasn't busy with the JV team, I worked on memorizing my own speech. I had a week to do it, so time was tight. I was desperate enough that I even let Grayson help me. If he could pretend to be friendly with me just so he could crush me in the competition, then I could use him too for practice.

He held my notecards so I couldn't rely on them, and prompted me when I got lost. He cracked a joke about being "lost at sea" because I was talking about whales and I couldn't help but snort. That was what we were doing in the back of the classroom when Coach stood up at the front and clapped her hands for everyone's attention.

"They had to cancel the Twin Falls High tournament," she said to a chorus of boos and the occasional cheer. As for myself, my shoulders felt lighter already. The Twin Falls meet was the one in a week. That meant I had almost an entire month to polish up my performance before competing again. That was completely doable, even with everything else going on. I could get my grades up, spend more time with Naomi, and not let this fall to the side.

"They couldn't get enough food sponsors, so even though the state tournament is still months away, I want to make sure we're on top of things since we're hosting it. Grayson and Quinn, have you two worked out any preliminary details?"

I chewed my lower lip. When I looked at Grayson, it was obvious this was a surprise to him too. With our own tournament being so late in the school year, I hadn't even considered finding sponsors this early.

Coach Bates shook her head. "Well then, put it on your agendas please. It's state, so it needs to run smoothly. We'll need enough food to feed all the volunteer judges lunch for two days, plus the coaches in the tabulation room."

I hastily nodded, and next to me, I felt Grayson do the same. Of course we'd have things organized by the state tournament, but that didn't mean it was on our radar now.

Coach kept talking about what to expect at the next meet, and I tuned her out. Grayson leaned over to whisper in my ear.

"So the Twin Falls tournament was canceled." His breath tickled my skin and I rubbed the goose bumps on my arms.

"Looks like it," I murmured, hoping Coach wouldn't catch us talking.

"You know what that means, right?"

I furrowed my brow. "That the meet was canceled, I'm guessing." This meant, in addition to working on the whale speech, I'd also have time to start something new. Something real for the following tournament.

Grayson smiled like I was missing the point. "The meet was scheduled at the same time as the fall fling. We can all go. Problem is, everyone has dates but the people who were planning on going to the speech meet."

My breath caught, the realization sinking in. I looked around the room, mentally calculating my options. There weren't many. Maybe I wouldn't go. I could claim to be busy. Except, everyone would know that was a lie since I'd been free for the tournament, which was now canceled.

Would Carter be willing to go as just friends? Whether I liked it or not, he was probably my best bet, so I started brainstorming ways to bring it up with him.

"We should go together," Grayson whispered.

My head whipped around to face him.

"What?" I asked the question more loudly than I was intending. My voice echoed around the room and Grayson's eyes got wide.

Everyone looked at me, including Coach Bates.

"I didn't think my remarks on bus etiquette were that surprising," Coach said. I scrambled through my memory to think of what she'd been saying. Something about bus etiquette, apparently.

"But we can't listen to music?" I asked, latching on to the one thing my subconscious could remember.

"Not through speakers, Quinn. But personal headphones are completely fine."

"Oh," I mumbled. Heat rushed to my cheeks and I zipped my hoodie up and down. "I guess that's okay, then. Thanks."

Everyone turned away from me then, except Grayson, who was obviously trying to hide the fact that he was laughing behind his hand. At least he found this situation funny. Because there were a lot of other things he could have felt about my outburst. Maybe laughing was his coping mechanism. I knew *I* was struggling to cope with what was happening.

What. Was. Happening?

Had Grayson just asked me to the fall fling? He had. I was 90 percent sure of it. He'd probably only asked because he was limited to the people in this room. So it wasn't like I should feel flattered. Was this a sign that Carter was right, and Grayson really was trying to do the same thing to me that he'd done last year to Zara to be class president? I really couldn't trust him. But did that mean I couldn't play at his game?

Okay, so one, I could go with Grayson to the fall fling. Two, I could go with Carter, which could give him the wrong idea. Three, I could maybe ask 15211 if he already had a date, but hello, *that* was desperate. Because asking him would mean letting him in on the fact that I wasn't exactly popular and didn't have a date yet.

No matter what, it wasn't like I had a whole lot of time to think things through.

"Don't read too much into it," Grayson whispered. "You know what they say. Keep your friends close . . ."

"And your enemies closer," I finished, holding out my hand for him to shake. Luckily for me, it was steady, even though I had no idea what I was doing.

He took my hand in his. It was warm, and for some bizarre reason, it made my pulse pick up speed.

"I'll pick you up at five for dinner," he said.

I nodded.

I was going to the fall fling with Grayson, and that was that.

Chapter Ten

It was weird how knowing I'd be going to the dance with Grayson made it so we completely avoided each other for the whole week leading up to it. He was at practice of course, and we nodded to each other from across the room. But I was always careful to make the bus on time and I felt too unsure to go up and say anything.

Had he only asked me because of limited options? Because he was setting me up for failure later? It wasn't clear. So we circled around each other like the loading/refresh loop on my phone that continuously circled without ever going anywhere.

There wasn't speech practice on the day of the dance, so I went home to be ready by five o'clock. Thankfully, Naomi was really good at updos, so I was letting her take the reins on that one. When she'd heard Grayson had asked me, she'd insisted we get ready together. It was easier to agree than to argue, so I'd caved under the pressure.

My mom knocked on the door, then opened it as Naomi finished spraying practically an entire can of hairspray around my head.

"How're things coming?" She had to speak loudly to be heard over the music, so I turned it down.

My mom had traded work shifts in order to take pictures for us. She was all smiles as she leaned on the doorframe. Her brown hair was tied back in a bun like usual, but she wasn't wearing her work uniform. I'd almost forgotten she had other clothes. It reminded me why I wanted her photography business to take off. That was her real passion, and she deserved happiness.

I turned from the mirror so she could see the final result. Her eyes crinkled at the edges as she smiled.

"You look so beautiful, Quinn."

Naomi showed me off with her hands in a grand "ta-da" motion. "Her hair is so thick! I had to use like thirty bobby pins."

We both looked good. In contrast to my pinned-back look, Naomi's hair was wild and free, her curls like a black halo around her head. It was my favorite look of hers.

"You're both so grown-up," my mom said. Which was proof that parents can't help but say embarrassing things around their kids' friends. "I want a few pictures of just you two before your dates come."

I put a hand over my stomach as we walked to the front room, but it did nothing to calm my nerves. My lips felt dry, and while I wanted to blame the lipstick for that, I knew better. The fact was, I'd be spending the next hour or so alone with Grayson, and that caused my head and heart to do funny things lately. They were currently in a cage match, and it was anyone's guess who'd win.

Naomi's date was vegan, so we were meeting up at the dance. Vegan was all well and good, but I personally wanted something more substantial. After all, I didn't want to face tonight on an empty stomach. Even the pictures my mom wanted were enough to make me anxious.

There wasn't really a good picture spot in our apartment, so we went outside to use the black brick as a backdrop. That was where we were when Naomi's date showed up. Dax drove a dark gray truck that looked freshly cleaned. For some reason, that only made me more nervous. Like this dance was more important than I'd realized. It was just the fall fling. It wasn't homecoming or prom. People went with friends all the time, and asking someone as a date didn't mean much.

That's what I told myself. So why did it feel like tonight was some kind of tipping point?

I shouldn't like Grayson. I didn't. I was pretty sure. But it seemed like my heart rate picked up anytime he was in the room, and the reasons behind that were getting fuzzy. He never sugarcoated things around me, which I liked, but how real could a guy be when everyone said he used people to get what he wanted? He had an annoying habit of getting in my way and derailing my plans, showing up with his too-good looks and too-smug grin. He knew exactly how to push my buttons and get a reaction out of me, making me all flustered because I never knew how to react.

No matter what Naomi said, that wasn't attraction. That was a thorn in my side.

Dax hopped out of his truck and walked to where we were standing. He whistled at Naomi, who twirled her skirt and acted bashful, even though we all knew she was anything but.

"Naomi's parents will never forgive me if I don't get some pictures of you two," my mom said, motioning for Dax to join Naomi by the brick wall. I stepped out of the frame and joined my mom.

Because I didn't know Dax well, it was still weird to see them as a couple. But they certainly acted like it. Dax kissed her cheek, and Naomi giggled in response. At our girls' night the other night, Naomi couldn't stop blushing as she'd told me all about how Dax had admitted he wanted to be more than friends and how awkward he'd been. I'd hardly seen her since they'd become official, but that was the way things were sometimes. If she was happy, that's what mattered.

"Okay, enough with the PDA," I said when my mom had finished taking pictures. "You two go on already; you're making me sick." Naomi was used to my sense of humor, but it was only after I saw Dax's stricken expression that I worried he'd taken me literally. "No, no, you're fine," I hurried to explain. "I'm kidding."

Naomi bounced over to me. "Of course you were kidding. Because soon your own boy will get here and you'll be doing your own PDA."

I shushed her, like that would somehow erase her comments, or the way my mom's eyebrows rose into her hairline.

"She's joking," I told my mom, waving my hands in the air. "I'm not with Grayson. We're just friends." *Friends* was such a weird thing to call whatever we were, but it was better than whatever my mom was thinking. Competitors-trying-to-get-the-upper-hand didn't have a great ring to it.

Naomi laughed, slinging an arm over my shoulders. "Okay, yes, but, Ms. Edwards—sorry, I mean Lindsey—they'd totally make a cute couple if Quinn would just take her head out of her butt." Even though my mom always preferred people calling her by her first name, my friends still slipped up.

My mom's face relaxed and she handed her camera over to Naomi so she could look at the pictures. "I'm sure they would. Quinn could use some more fun in her life."

"Traitor!" I gasped at my mom, who was supposed to be the one person in the world who never wanted to see me date.

Of course, that was when Grayson pulled up in his car. So when he stepped out and asked what we were all talking about, everyone burst into laughter.

Everyone but me.

I was too busy trying not to ogle Grayson in his button-up shirt and dress pants. Everything about his outfit was perfectly tailored and too flattering for his own good. Or mine. His dark hair was ruffled the same way it was for speech tournaments—like he woke up looking that casually sophisticated and didn't even have to try. He was like a model who'd escaped the runway to stroll casually into my life. How come he had to be so attractive? Life wasn't fair.

"Mom, this is Grayson, Grayson, this is my mom," I said when he'd walked up to us.

"Nice to meet you, Ms. Edwards," Grayson said politely, extending his hand.

"Please, call me Lindsey."

I could already tell my mom liked him. She didn't just shake his hand; she practically cradled it in hers like a caress. So that wasn't embarrassing at all. I put my hand on her arm, signaling that bonding time was officially over. She dropped Grayson's hand and pushed us together.

"Picture time! Let's do the whole group now." My mom arranged us in front of the wall, Naomi and Dax to my side with Grayson's arm around my waist. This was the closest we'd ever been, and by far the longest we'd ever touched. His hand rested on my hip, every part of me burning under his touch. My mom seemed to take forever fiddling with the adjustments on her camera. She looked up for the briefest of moments and my jaw dropped at her expression. She was totally doing this on purpose.

Traitor, indeed.

"Any day now, Mom," I said. My hand was resting on Grayson's arm and I was pretty sure I was starting to sweat, which I was sure Grayson would find super attractive.

"What's the matter, Quinn?" Grayson whispered in my ear. I hated that. It sent shivers down my spine and made me feel all . . . confused. "Do I make you nervous?"

Yes.

"No."

He chuckled, and I pinched his arm.

"You wish," I said.

"Maybe I do."

What was that supposed to mean? I was going to spend the rest of the night thinking about it. He could be saying he liked me, which wasn't likely. Or he could be saying he liked the attention, which I already knew. Or, worst of all, Carter could have been right about him all along.

One thing was for sure, in that moment I was 100 percent glad he'd said it low enough that no one else could have possibly heard it, especially my mom who was busy snapping pictures and then looking at them with much too big of a smile taking over her face.

"Okay, I think we've got it," she said, holding out the camera for us to see. I escaped from Grayson's arm with relief.

The pictures were cute. It didn't even look like I hated Grayson. I was smiling and happy, so I deserved some kind of award. Really, I was just glad they were over with and I wouldn't have to do it again.

"Now I need to get only Grayson and Quinn," my mom said, bursting my bubble. Already, my hands started to get clammy. Why couldn't I be one of those girls who never sweats? "Naomi, you and Dax can go to dinner now. I hope you have a lovely night."

Naomi hugged me, then waved goodbye without looking back. How could she leave me like this, without any backup? Some best friend she was. They took off in Dax's truck and suddenly I was alone with Grayson. And my mom.

Awesome.

"Quinn, let's do one where you're behind him looking over his shoulder. No, you have to be closer than that."

I wanted to remind my mom that we weren't a real couple, but something told me she wouldn't care. Instead, I let her pose us in fifty different ways until she was completely satisfied; then Grayson and I got out of there as quickly as possible.

"Sorry about my mom," I said as we buckled our seat belts. If I could have melted from embarrassment right there in his car, I'd be a puddle right about now.

"Yeah, geez. A photographer doing her job? Talk about torture," Grayson said. I tried to get a read on his emotions, but he was hiding whatever he was thinking under a smile. He started the engine. "No worries. My mom micromanaged everything tonight too. She picked out my outfit and made the dinner reservations for us without any of my input. So you can't be mad at me if it all goes downhill from here."

"Oh?" I turned to face him. "Where are we going to dinner?"

"I don't even know," he said.

I brought a hand to my chest and pretended to look shocked. "You mean there's something you don't know? And you're willing to admit it?"

He laughed, and everything he'd said caught up in my brain.

"Wait a second, how do you not know? You're driving there right now."

He tapped his car's dashboard, which had Google Maps opened.

"She input directions on how to get there. Apparently she had to pull some strings since it's a hot new place and they were completely booked because of the fall fling. But since we only found out we'd be going a week ago, she had to call the owner."

Life as the governor's son sure came with its perks. I used to think Grayson simply got his way all the time because of his charm and presence, but I guess it didn't hurt to have powerful parents.

"I usually hate it when she throws around her position like that, but I'll let it slide tonight if it means we won't starve." He smiled, and I stared at him, stunned.

I opened my mouth, then shut it. I always assumed Grayson liked the attention he got from his mom's position, but looking back now, I realized how rarely he even brought her up in our conversations. He didn't capitalize on it at all. If he enjoyed the attention, wouldn't he bring it up more?

Sometimes I judged people harshly. I knew this. The question was, had I done that to Grayson?

Chapter Eleven

We pulled into the parking lot, and I hit the locks on the doors. "We can't go in there," I said, pushing Grayson back when he'd gone for the handle.

"What?" He glanced down at my arm, which was still pressed against his chest. I dropped it hurriedly.

"That's the same restaurant where Dax and Naomi are eating tonight. The vegan place. If we go in now, they'll wonder why we didn't want to sit with them."

"Are you sure you just don't want to be seen with me in public?"

I sighed exaggeratedly. "You got me."

Grayson laughed and tapped the steering wheel. "Okay, we can go somewhere else," he said. He put the car in reverse and I sagged against my seat in gratitude.

"Where do you want to go? Most of the good places are probably full," he said.

I chewed my lip. "Fast food?" I suggested.

He looked at me. "And you won't call me a cheapskate to all your friends tomorrow?"

I held up my hands in surrender. "No promises," I said sarcastically. "Hey, I might even insist on paying my half, then where would you be?"

Grayson laughed. "I knew I liked you. Fast food it is."

I swallowed. Grayson didn't seem aware of what he'd just said. But his words repeated over and over in my head like one of those breaking news alerts at the bottom of a TV screen. *I knew I liked you. I knew I liked you. I knew I liked you.*

"So, Mexican, Chinese, American, Thai, or some other type of food you're particularly craving? Your wish is my command."

"I like hamburgers," I said as nonchalantly as possible. No need to clue him in that all his suave moves were messing with my mind. What was wrong with me?

After a moment, I got brave enough to look over. It was getting darker and I couldn't quite read his expression. He nodded, then pulled out of the parking lot, turning left.

"I know what we're going to do then," he said.

When we pulled into a Five Guys, I could have kissed him in gratitude. Hamburgers were a thousand times better than any vegan place.

We ordered our food, and Grayson got it to go. True to my word, I insisted on paying for half, even when he put up a fight. Then again, fighting was nothing new to us. When we got to the car, Grayson placed the bags on the back seat.

"What if I'm hungry now?" I asked, reaching behind us and snagging a fry from the bag before clipping my seat belt.

"You'll have to wait and see." He grinned, clearly pleased with whatever he had planned next.

We drove farther and farther from the city, up into the hills of Boise. Soon we were on a dirt road going nowhere and I briefly considered whether Grayson might be a serial killer or something sinister, luring me away from civilization and witnesses. Maybe he wasn't trying to seduce me and sabotage my chances at beating him. Maybe he'd just kill me and be done with it. It'd give a whole new meaning to the phrase *taking her out*.

Grayson turned off the road into a pullout that overlooked the city lights and my stomach flopped, unsure of what to feel. Excited? Anxious? How was I supposed to navigate this situation? If Grayson was only playing a game, and wasn't actually interested in me, then this was sure a long way for him to go to do it. My certainty wavered. I'd always pictured Grayson as the enemy in my story, and usually he fit the part perfectly. But lately all his barbs had been less pointed, more flirty, and I couldn't help but wonder what he was playing at. It was maddening, waiting for the other shoe to drop. Because while I was waiting, I couldn't help but wonder if maybe, maybe I was getting too close to the enemy?

Grayson grabbed the bags of food and motioned for me to stay put while he got out to get my door. That gesture alone made my head spin. Then he led me to a bench and I joined him, smoothing my skirt before I sat. It was a good thing to keep my hands busy, because suddenly I had no idea what to do with them. Thankfully, Grayson handed me my bag of food so I wouldn't have to feel so hopelessly awkward.

Grayson had left the radio running in his car, and the music drifted to where we were sitting on the bench, overlooking the city lights. The stars were starting to come out, and all I could think about was how it could have been romantic—if I were with anyone else. Someone who didn't tease me mercilessly or get in my way every step of every day.

"How're the whales treating you?" Grayson asked. He'd put his bag of food on the other side of the bench so we were sitting side by side. It was relatively warm tonight, the air like a caress on my skin. "Is your speech going *swimmingly*?"

I chewed a bite of hamburger before responding.

"I'm killing it," I said with a chuckle. "Get it? Killer whales? Oh, never mind." He was looking at me with pity, like he couldn't believe such a lame joke had escaped my lips. "You're the one that started with the bad puns."

He scoffed. "Me? A bad pun? That would never happen and you know it."

"What?" The word burst out of me. "You are the king of bad jokes. And bad . . . I don't know. Everything." I waved my hand in the air, gesturing to all of Grayson.

He raised his eyebrows. "Says the girl who lost to me in the last competition."

I set my hamburger down and crossed my arms. "I lost because the judges can't resist a pretty face. Just because you're cute doesn't mean you're talented."

Grayson held his hands up and waggled his eyebrows. "All I hear is that you think I'm cute."

I shook my head, but already I could feel the heat creeping up my neck. "Yeah, well, I think a pangolin is cute, and they look like a walking artichoke, so clearly the bar isn't that high."

Grayson nudged my shoulder. "Still," he said, his voice barely above a whisper, "you think I'm cute."

I scoffed, then picked up a wad of napkins and threw them at him. "You're the worst."

He took another one off the top of the pile and threw it back. "*You're* the worst," he repeated.

I swatted the napkin away from my face and tried to stare him down.

Grayson gave a short laugh. "You're so . . . infuriating sometimes." He ran a hand through his hair. "I don't know whether to—to shake you, or to—" He shook his head in frustration, the words seemingly getting lost in his throat. Then turned to me, his eyes burning.

Grayson brought his hand behind my neck and closed the distance between us.

He kissed me.

It was unexpected and overpowering, and without realizing it, a small gasp escaped my lips. I'd never felt so much heat in a kiss before.

I was too shocked to react. All of me was running on instinct, trying to process what was happening.

Was this some kind of a game? Why now? Was he hoping to break my concentration before the state championship?

And why did I get pickles and onions on my hamburger?

What I should have done was gotten a mint shake.

I couldn't think of anything more substantial than that, because literally nothing made sense anymore.

Grayson's lips softened, and I relaxed almost against my will, running my fingers through the hair at the nape of his neck. He caught my lower lip in his and I placed my other hand on his chest to keep from falling.

He tasted like salt. I'd never known I'd liked salt so much before. I'd thought that his glasses might make things awkward, but he either had a lot of practice, which I didn't really want to think about, or I'd been wrong, because his glasses didn't get in the way.

His kiss made me dizzy. And confused. Very, very confused. Because I thought Grayson hated me. But he seemed to be enjoying it as much as I was, which couldn't be right. Everything around me dulled to a buzz and I couldn't help but get lost in the moment.

Until I saw flashes of red and blue light behind my closed eyelids.

With a snap, I opened them and pulled back. There, directly next to Grayson's, was a cop car with its lights flashing.

"Oh no," I breathed. Grayson turned on the bench to face the lights, so I couldn't see his face, though I desperately wanted to. What had he been thinking? I felt wild and full of energy. Surely my face was flushed, but with the flashing lights all around us, I doubted anyone could tell. Had cop lights always been so blindingly bright? Since when had it gotten so dark? How long had I been here with Grayson?

We were going to jail. For what, I wasn't sure, but I was certain of it.

Cops didn't show up with their lights going if they weren't ready to lay down some law. Served me right for fraternizing with the enemy, even if I had liked it.

The police officer got out of her car and shut the door. She walked to the bench where we were sitting, and from her expression, it was obvious she found this whole situation humorous, which it so was not.

"Grayson Hawks."

Oh great. She knew who he was. This kept getting better and better.

I shrunk back and tried to hide in the shadows. My mom was going to kill me.

"What would your mother think?" the cop asked, and it took me a full twenty seconds to realize she was talking to Grayson, not reading my thoughts. Which meant the police officer didn't know him because Grayson did this a lot, but because she knew the governor, and that made a whole lot more sense than anything else I'd been thinking.

Grayson cleared his throat. "I'm hoping you won't tell her?" he said. It sounded more like a question. "I'd kind of like to tell her myself." Grayson pulled at the collar of his shirt and put his hand to the back of his neck.

The police officer smiled. "Well, since you haven't done anything illegal, you're off the hook."

My brows furrowed and I couldn't help but speak up.

"If we've done nothing illegal, why did you stop here?" And why was there a bench if people weren't supposed to use it?

The officer motioned to the surrounding area. "On certain holidays and school events we make the rounds at popular, ummm, canoodling places," she responded. Who said *canoodling* anymore? Even she seemed uncomfortable with the word, crossing her arms and shrugging at the same time. "If there's some public indecency going on, then we need to step in."

"Public indecency?" I asked.

Then my thoughts caught up to what we were talking about and I wished I hadn't said a thing.

"If anyone was naked," Grayson said, explaining what I already had figured out. Despite the growing darkness, I was pretty sure my face was flaming so much it could light up the sky. In my defense, I still wasn't thinking clearly. Obviously. My better judgment seemed to have taken a vacation.

The police officer nodded, then motioned back to her car, where the lights still flashed. "I'll be on my way. You two don't stay long, all right? I don't want to have to bust you for real."

I'd thought I'd been blushing before, but that was nothing compared to now. I actually thought Grayson might be able to feel the heat coming off my face.

He saluted the police officer, who nodded and walked back to her car. Grayson and I didn't say anything until she'd driven off. Then her headlights disappeared around the curve and I couldn't help it. I burst into laughter.

"I thought we were going to jail," I said between wheezes. "Seriously."

The stress had finally gotten to me. The confusion. The complete and utter inability to know how to react to the situation. It was either laugh or . . . well, there was no *or*. Laughing was my only option.

Grayson seemed to agree, because he had his head in his hands and was laughing so hard it filled the space around us. He tilted his head back and laughed at the sky. Neither of us stopped for quite some time.

I finally got control of myself and took a few deep breaths. That's when Grayson looked at me and we burst into laughter again. When we finally stopped, all we did was sit there for a while, breathing. Of course, that was when my thoughts started flooding back.

What was *that*? What had possessed me? Us?

Grayson looked at me without saying anything. Then he leaned over and kissed me again, catching me by surprise.

It was a good surprise. Maybe. The jury was still out, but I no longer knew what to think anymore.

Grayson pulled back, gave his token half smile, then stood up.

"We should probably get to the dance," he said.

I nodded emphatically. Yes, other people. I needed other people around me, otherwise I'd be tempted to try kissing Grayson again, to see if it'd been a fluke. I mean, I hadn't hated it. Kind of the opposite, really.

We walked back to the car without saying anything.

When Grayson closed my door and walked around back to his side, I let out a whoosh of air. By the time he opened his side, I was perfectly in control again, but my head was still reeling.

With what had just happened, I wasn't sure if the reeling would ever stop.

Chapter Twelve

*G*rayson and I texted on Sunday. We never mentioned The Kiss (yes, it deserved capital letters), but I sent him the pictures my mom had taken before the dance and we ... flirted ... over the phone. And by flirting, I mean he drove me to distraction trying to analyze the meaning behind all his texts. But it was obvious that *something* had changed between us. If only I could figure out exactly *what*.

Nothing unexpected had happened at the fall fling. (Unless you counted the zings of electricity between us whenever we danced or the way he stole glances at me all evening. It was enough to drive me batty.)

He hadn't tried kissing me again.

Somehow a few less-than-sober friends from school had ended up in his car at the end of the night, so it wasn't like we had much opportunity. I didn't know whether to be disappointed or relieved—saved from myself. Because the fact of the matter was, I *wanted* it to happen again, and that was mind-boggling. The only emotion I seemed to settle on with any consistency was bewilderment.

I thought I hated Grayson. But then he kissed me, and I realized maybe I didn't hate him after all. I hadn't been fooling anyone else, but I'd fallen for my own charade plenty. Now I knew I actually . . . *liked* him? I needed his attention. I needed his validation. For him to really *see* me. All those barbs I threw in his direction were a distraction from my own feelings. It was a startling realization to come to. That attraction had been masquerading as hate all along.

The question was whether he felt the same way. But if he didn't . . . Then what had possessed him to kiss me?

I don't know whether to—to shake you, or to—

His words from that night made a perfect kind of strange sense. Well, *if* he really felt that way.

The problem was, I had no idea what he was thinking. Seeing him in person was going to change that, because I needed answers, stat. If this was all some kind of game, like Carter suggested, then I needed to talk to Grayson. In person. No more texts that could mean one thing or another. Maybe Grayson was as confused as I was, but all this tiptoeing around the situation wasn't doing my mental health any favors. I needed to know what that kiss meant, and I needed to know now.

But the rest of the weekend was eternally long. I threw myself into finishing my mom's site, but even that wasn't enough to distract me. It looked amazing, though. Even I was impressed with myself. My mom was over the moon and took me out for ice cream when we officially pushed it live, which was the best feeling ever.

I uploaded some of the pre-dance pictures to her Instagram and obsessed over all the comments saying things like "Couple Goals," "I'm obsessed," or "SO CUTE, I DIE." Like that wasn't enough to give me a complex.

By the time Monday rolled around, I was so anxious I tore out of my seat when the final bell rang in AP Government. I placed my latest reply to 15211 in his cubby, but I hadn't given my response much thought. It wasn't like he'd said anything especially noteworthy that had demanded all my attention.

I returned to the seats, because Naomi was still there. She seemed to take an eternity to gather her things, and I bounced on my heels while I waited for her so we could walk to our lockers.

"Well, someone's in a hurry to get to speech practice today," she said, slinging her bag over one shoulder. "I wonder why that could be?"

She'd been at the dance. I'd told her what had happened. I didn't have classes with Grayson this year, so Naomi had to know things were still the way we'd left them on Saturday night. Wherever that was.

"You know why." I tried not to roll my eyes.

She laughed and we walked to my locker. I shoved things in as fast as I could and grabbed the books I needed. My phone buzzed in my pocket and I pulled it out to see a text from Carter.

You coming to speech practice today?

I checked the time at the top of my phone. I wasn't even close to being late, so I had no idea why Carter would be asking. I quickly texted him back.

Of course. Why?

The three dots showed up on my screen to tell me he was writing something.

I need your help with my transitions between paragraphs.
It's too clunky. Grayson is here now, so I'll ask him until
you can get here. You're better at that kind of thing than
he is, though. What's your ETA?

Grayson was already there. Suddenly I wasn't sure whether I should go to speech practice or hide out in the girl's bathroom. I was hit with an unexplainable apprehension and inability to act. As much as I wanted answers, I didn't know if he'd give me the answers I wanted. Sure, I *wanted* Grayson to like me, but the fear of him using me, or of this being some kind of a game, was like a strong cologne that drenched everything around me in stink, spoiling the entire situation. It was better to keep my expectations low. Like, Mariana Trench low.

While the bathroom seemed like an appealing option, I forced myself to type out my response.

I'll be there in five minutes.

That was how long it took me to get from my locker to the speech room if I didn't stop to talk to anyone, and it was time I figured out what on earth was going on. No more excuses.

I slammed my locker shut and spun to face Naomi. She must have read the trepidation on my face, because she placed her hands on my shoulders.

"I'll be here for you either way. With celebratory cake or depressed ice cream. Go on already. I'll FaceTime you tonight."

I gave her a hug and she pushed me away, giving me a little wave as she went off.

I turned with a sigh and made my way down the hallway. I couldn't have read the situation wrong, could I have? I mean, he'd been the one to kiss me. I'd just reciprocated. Rather enthusiastically.

I took the stairs two at a time, but stopped when I heard Grayson's voice a few feet away. There was only one more bend around the stairway, so I paused to apply some lip balm. Mint flavor.

Just in case.

"What is it you want me to say about her?" Grayson asked. My breath caught, a smile overtaking my face. I didn't know who he was talking to or whether he was on the phone, but I wasn't about to peer around the corner to find out. If Grayson was talking about me, I wanted to know everything he was going to say. Sure, maybe he wasn't talking about me, but come on, the chances were at least fifty-fifty.

I plastered myself against the wall and tried to quiet my breathing. There was nothing I could do about the fact that I'd clomped up the stairs to this point, but since he hadn't said anything, I didn't think he'd noticed.

"You seemed pretty interested when you were telling me about her a couple of weeks ago." It was Carter's voice. Grayson was talking to Carter. But I couldn't puzzle out Carter's comment. Was he saying Grayson actually wasn't interested in me? Or was he simply plying him for more details because he cared entirely too much about my love life and I could finally see it?

Carter kept talking and I stayed frozen. "So are you still? Do you like her?"

"Well, yeah, I guess." Grayson sounded confused, and I smiled. So Grayson did like me. Not only that, but he'd liked me for a few weeks now, apparently. All that meant Carter was wrong to think Grayson had been using me. Bubbles rose up in my stomach and I felt lighter than I had in forever. All those scenarios I'd refused to dream up were now a real possibility.

Grayson kept talking and I tried to stop my clothes from rustling against the wall.

"I feel like I can tell her anything."

I bit my lower lip to keep my smile from going full-on supersonic.

"Let me get this straight," Carter said. "Weeks ago you told me how you liked this girl, and you thought she might be the perfect girl for you, but you didn't ask her to the dance? Quinn deserves better than you."

My smile dropped.

The hallway was closing in. I'd been right to be cautious. Because if it wasn't me they were talking about, then Grayson was definitely toying with me. Playing mind games with a frightening level of skill. I should have learned from Zara's mistakes.

As someone interested in marketing, I knew all too well how a picture could lie. Sure, people might have called us couple goals, but the truth was, we were the furthest thing from a couple. Grayson was trying to get close to me only so he could ruin my chances at winning state. Talk about low. I sagged against the wall and closed my eyes.

I wasn't going to cry, here in the hallway where anyone could see. Especially Grayson. Maybe I'd cry later, but I wasn't about to give Grayson the satisfaction of knowing he'd made me believe, even for a minute, that he liked me. My eyes started to burn and I breathed in slowly through my nose. I took stock of the emotions raging through me right now. No, I wasn't sad. I was *angry*. Angry at myself and that I'd fallen for it.

"I didn't know if she'd say yes," Grayson said. His voice sounded small. I winced.

I was so foolish. The most humiliating part of everything was that it had felt so real. But it hadn't been real. It'd been a game. A ruse. A pitiful ploy that I'd fallen for, all too easily. The worst part was, I'd been warned. I knew Grayson had done this before. I shook my head as my vision blurred in front of me.

Another realization hit me then. Carter had asked me when I was coming to speech and debate because he'd wanted to set this up. He'd *planned* for me to hear this. He didn't need my help with his speech. He'd wanted to humiliate me.

No. He was being a friend. Friends let friends know when the guy they liked was messing around. He said it himself: *Quinn deserves better than you.* He was trying to look out for me. Just like he had all the years of us growing up. That was what friends did.

But knowing that didn't make it easier to swallow. Half of me was mad at Carter, while the other half wanted to crawl into a hole and never show my face here again. To anyone, but least of all Grayson *or* Carter.

Why did boys have to be such jerks? I'd tried playing by their stupid rules. I'd gone on the date. I'd followed his lead. So how come I was the one who was getting ambushed? Nothing bad happened to them, but I had my heart ripped apart. How was that fair?

I didn't have many options. One, I could walk away and pretend I hadn't heard anything. I could come back a few minutes later for speech practice and walk past Grayson like he meant nothing to me. Option two, I could confront him. True, that thought was scarier than a pop test in AP Government, but it meant things would be out in the open between Grayson and me. It wasn't like we were strangers to conflict.

I couldn't take this lying down. That would mean he'd won. And I was never going to let Grayson win at anything ever again. I didn't care if it killed me. I was going to beat him at the state competition, and every competition leading up to it if I had my way. That all started with putting him on the defensive.

I straightened my spine and took the remaining steps around the corner so I was facing them directly. They were sitting on a step near the top, and Grayson sat up when he saw me. Surprise was written all over his face, but Carter looked apologetic.

I shook my head and put a hand on my hip. "Hello, boys."

Grayson swallowed and I allowed myself a small smile as vindication burned through my veins. Served him right for looking uncomfortable. He should be 110 percent miserable.

"Grayson, it's so nice to hear how much you wanted to take someone else to the dance," I said. Grayson stood up, holding his hands out in front of him like that would somehow smooth things over.

"Quinn, you're twisting my words." He reached to touch my arm, but I stepped out of the way.

"Really? Because you're the one who said them." I raised my eyebrows, waiting for his excuse. I was very conscious of every movement my face made. I wasn't about to let him see how much this hurt when I could pretend indifference. Carter stood up too and I transferred my withering stare to him.

This seemed to surprise him, when really, what did he expect? That I'd be happy he interfered?

"Quinn, I tried to warn you—"

I held my hands out in front of me, staving off his comments. "We'll talk about your part in this later, Carter."

He made a wounded face and I felt my resolve weaken. I softened my expression, but crossed my arms. "Right now I need to talk to Grayson."

Grayson inhaled and tried once again to reach out for my hand. I kept my arms where they were and he dropped his.

"I know I can be a jerk, but this isn't one of those times, Quinn. I asked *you* to the dance. I . . . I *care*. I just didn't realize it earlier." He had the audacity to look like the admission had cost him. I scoffed.

Sure, he cared. Cared about winning. Rather than making me feel better, the weight of his words crushed me from the inside. I forced myself to stand tall, just like 15211 had told me to. Appearing confident was more important now than ever. No way was I letting Grayson get the upper hand here. Carter shuffled his feet and looked down at the floor, maybe realizing for the first time what a big mistake he'd made. I didn't look at him.

"You know what?" I shrugged at Grayson. "If you really cared, then none of this"—I made a circle in the air to encompass the scene taking place—"would have happened."

Then I walked into the speech room, away from both of them.

Chapter Thirteen

*T*hanksgiving break was only a week away. We'd had four speech tournaments since the big blowup between Grayson and me, and somehow I'd managed to pretty much avoid him all that time. It'd been almost two months and I still couldn't believe I'd nearly fallen for his game.

I'd still presented the whale speech for one competition, out of spite. It was more to prove that I could still beat Grayson, even with an awful topic. I'd been surprised when he'd presented his anti-feminist speech on women in the workforce. He'd looked apologetic the whole time, shooting me looks that were surely supposed to make me forgive him. But I knew now he was trying to set me up for failure later, when it really counted, and I wasn't going to fall for it.

Of course, I'd won. But even that victory felt cheap because it wasn't really a fair fight.

After that, our competitions had evened out. I won some, I lost some. That irked me more than anything, because I really wanted Grayson to lose. Every time. Karma owed it to me. Was that really so much to ask? Sure, I'd been doing better than I had in the start of the year, but it wasn't enough for me.

Naomi had gone full-on bestie, meaning she iced out Grayson in the hallways and kept encouraging me to see where things went with 15211. Not only did she keep up with our letters, she thought he was the best thing to happen to me. Ever. She was enthusiastic and supportive, and I had to give her points for that.

She ran interference with me and Grayson whenever she could, but since she wasn't in speech and debate, there was only so much she could do. Unfortunately, Grayson and I had to plan the Thanksgiving potluck in a few days, plus the food vendors for the state tournament coming up that we were hosting, so I had to actually talk to him. Today.

I was putting off the moment for as long as possible, hanging out in the AP Government room even though class had ended a while ago. Naomi had left, eager to see Dax before she had to go to volleyball practice. Her team had made the playoffs, so she hadn't had a whole lot of time with him lately. I couldn't fault her for it, even if I missed my friend. Luckily, in the last couple of months I'd had dozens of notes with 15211 to keep me company.

I'd practically thrown myself headlong into that friendship, knowing that he, at least, wouldn't do something like what Grayson had done to me. Without me knowing how, a lot of our interactions turned flirtier, and the attention was exactly what I needed to boost my ego. He became my crutch, the person I turned to for advice and comfort. It was seamless how it happened, and I didn't even understand it.

My favorite letters were stored in my desk drawer at home in my bedroom, where I actually kept them under lock and key so my mom wouldn't read them. Whenever things weren't going my way in speech and debate, I pulled them out to make myself feel better.

Now that the classroom was practically empty, I finished packing my things in my bag and made my way over to the cubby wall to see if 15211 had written me back. I kept my hopes low because I'd only put a letter in this morning and he might not have had time during Ms. Navarrete's lecture today.

But there it was, sitting in my otherwise-empty cubby. My pulse kicked up a notch as I picked it up and opened it.

> *Dear 15511,*
>
> *I'm not sure what unpleasant thing it is that you mentioned having to do later today, but I'm sure you'll be completely fine. You're tough like that. Well, from what I can tell from your letters at least.*
>
> *Okay, see, here's something I've been wanting to ask you about. I've thought about this a lot lately.*
>
> *I have a really hard time letting people into my inner circle. I've told you that. I've told you so much about myself now that I'm actually a little terrified of you ever finding out who I am. But even without knowing who you are, you've become one of my closest friends. Is it weird to admit that?*
>
> *I think it's time. I'm not really saying we should meet, because chances are, we've probably already met. But I think we should tell each other who we are.*

I stopped reading. I stopped breathing. I'd been dreading this letter, knowing it would come eventually. After exchanging so many, it was really only a matter of time. But I still hadn't thought about how I was going to respond. The only thing in my favor was that the ball was now in my court and I didn't have to respond right away. I should at least read the rest of the letter so I could mull things over.

I'm not going to tell you who I am in this letter. Because then you could say no, and I'd be out of luck. So I think we should meet up, agree on a time and place, so we can actually talk. In person. (Novel concept, huh? Communicating in real time, instead of hours apart? I know, I know, bananas!)

So I guess, actually, I am saying we should meet. What do you think? I can't be the only one who's thought about it. You have to know that you've become the person I rely on the most, even though I don't know you.

But I do know you. I know you as a person, even if I don't know your name. I could quote Romeo with his whole "what's in a name" thing here, but I think I've already gotten sappier than I'd ever want to admit, so let's leave it at that.

Now I'm babbling. I'm nervous. Even writing this, my hand is shaking. Can you see it in my handwriting?

I want to know who you are. I think we could really mesh in real life. Please tell me you think so too.

15211

I was shaking simply reading it. Of course, I agreed with some of his points. We *could* mesh in real life.

But.

People could disappoint you. I'd learned that firsthand lately. My heart still hurt.

I folded the paper, put it in my bag, and walked up the stairs to speech practice, trying to put 15211's proposition out of my mind.

Now I had two things to *not* look forward to.

Chapter Fourteen

Every year, the captain of the speech and debate team was in charge of setting up the food sponsors for the home meet. Supposedly, it was to build our leadership skills or something like that. But really, everyone knew it was because Coach hated the task.

Usually, this wasn't a problem because the captain called the same people every year and set up the same thing each time. It was supposed to be a piece of cake.

Unless you were paired with a team captain who insisted on making everything as difficult as it possibly could be.

Grayson sat across the table in the library, an intent expression on his face.

"Their pizza tastes like cardboard, and you know it." He shook his head. "Actually, it's worse."

"Of course I know that. It's why it's so cheap."

"We can do better."

I sighed. "Why do you have to make everything a competition?"

He raised his eyebrows but didn't answer. I supposed he didn't really need to. That was just who Grayson was. It was what we did.

"Listen," I tried again. "If we call the pizza place, we can be done with this in a few minutes and then we don't have to deal with each other."

"What if that's not what I want?"

He was infuriating. Was he saying he wanted to prolong this torture? Or that he simply didn't want pizza? As if he knew his statement could be read two ways, he smiled.

I narrowed my eyes. "You're not going to find anything else within budget."

He pulled out his phone and opened his browser. "It's nice to know you have so little faith in me."

Well. I didn't need to answer that.

He took out a piece of paper and started writing places and phone numbers down, separating it into two lists with our names on top. When he had about ten on each side, he punched a number in his phone, then held it up to his ear. He motioned for me to start on my list, but I didn't move.

Cold calls were the worst thing in the world. Worse than nuts in baked goods. Worse than spam emails with no way to unsubscribe. What if the person who answered the call couldn't hear me clearly and I had to shout here in the library? What if the person on the other end of the line asked me something I didn't know the answer to?

I didn't pick up my phone because I needed to hear what Grayson said, so that I could perfectly parrot back the same thing to the people on my list.

"Hello," Grayson said into his phone. "Is there a manager or someone I could speak to about catering an event?"

I replayed his words in my mind, committing them to memory.

He paused while someone else presumably came to the phone.

"Hi, my name is Grayson Hawks and I'm with BHS's speech and

debate team. We're hosting a tournament in early March and I was wondering about your prices for catering and what size group you can accommodate."

That was a lot of information to try to remember, and I felt the words slipping in my mind. I was focusing so intently, I missed what Grayson said next. How was he so good at this? How was he so good at everything? It wasn't fair for him to always be the best. Didn't he know that it made the rest of us look bad?

I didn't even want to call all these places in the first place, and now I was going to look like a fool in front of Grayson. Again.

"And what does that include?" Grayson asked after a moment of silence. It broke my concentration and I forgot everything he'd said previously. My hands started to sweat.

Why didn't businesses have a texting option? They'd get a whole lot more business that way.

"Great, thank you. We'll be in touch."

Grayson hung up his phone and crossed the top name on his list off. "They'd be four times more expensive." He turned to face me. "Aren't you going to call too?"

I looked at him with wide eyes, my tongue already feeling dry in my mouth.

"What's the matter, Edwards?" he asked, taking in my expression. "You're not scared of a phone call, are you?" One corner of his mouth lifted up in a smile.

Smug jerk. I couldn't let him have the upper hand again.

I clutched my phone and forced myself to dial the number at the top of my list, trying not to let my hand shake.

"Thank you for calling Boise Bagels," a female voice said in my ear. "How can I help you today?"

I struggled to remember what Grayson had said. Something about food. Obviously. Oh!

"Hi, I need to talk to your manager." My words came out in a rush, the relief over remembering my line making my words sharper than I intended.

"Oh!" Her voice sounded startled. "Did you have a complaint you needed to file?"

What? No. Where'd she get that idea? This was precisely why phone calls were so awful.

Grayson was watching me with his eyebrows raised and I tried to focus my attention back on the conversation at hand.

"No, nothing's wrong with you. I mean, I need help, but—" I realized my comment could have been interpreted in multiple ways, and Grayson's resulting laughter scrambled my thoughts even further. This was not going well.

"I'm sorry?" the girl on the other line said. "How can I help you?"

Focus, Quinn.

"Yes. Sorry." I took a deep breath, but my mind was blank. Completely empty. "Uh. Food! My school needs food."

"Are you part of a government-assisted program?" Honestly, she sounded just as confused as I was, so at least I wasn't the only one uncomfortable here.

"No, it's for our speech and debate team." Finally, the first sentence I said that made any kind of sense.

She paused before answering. Then she said, "*You're* on speech and debate?" It was obvious Grayson heard her reply through my earpiece, because he was shaking with silent laughter. I slugged him in the arm, but this only made him laugh harder. This was all his fault. If he'd just stuck with the cheap pizza, I wouldn't be in this mess.

Really, there was nothing I could do to salvage this conversation. I wanted to hang up, but I couldn't give Grayson the satisfaction. Then again, maybe if I hung up, he'd see that I'd been right all along and he'd go along with the pizza plan.

I realized I'd been silent for entirely too long, and I panicked again.

"You know what?" the girl asked. "My manager's not in the store at the moment, so how about you call back tomorrow between eight and five o'clock?"

Relief coursed through my veins. I could finally put this conversation out if its misery.

"Yes, okay. Thank you." I hung up.

Grayson couldn't hold it back anymore and he laughed out loud. I put my head on the table and covered it with my arms. I needed this day to be over. I couldn't plan this state tournament anymore. Not like this. This was why I didn't want to share captaining responsibilities in the first place. If I could have done this all my way, I'd be done by now.

"Please can we just do the pizza?" I mumbled through my arms. They were already expecting our call, so it wouldn't be half as awkward. In fact, I was pretty sure I could do it all through email, which was even better.

Grayson poked my arm, but I didn't raise my head.

"Wow, Quinn, I've never known you to be a quitter."

This made me sit up.

"It's not quitting to do things the expected way." I could feel the heat creeping higher on my neck. "Besides, pizza is something most people can agree on. Half these places on your list aren't going to go over well with a majority of people. Especially if they're already expecting a large cheese with breadsticks."

I was gaining steam now and motioned in the air with my hands. "What if the judges don't like spicy food? We have to go with safer options. Most the places you have listed are specialized. Like when you're in a specific mood. And there's no way those places will be any cheaper."

He nodded slowly like he was actually considering my argument. Miracle of miracles. I pulled up the pizza website on my phone so I could find their email. Grayson put a hand on my arm and I tried not to react.

"Don't call them yet." He withdrew his hand. "I have an idea. Would you say most people like sandwiches?" He had one eyebrow arched, like he was obviously up to something.

"I guess," I said, squirming. I didn't like not knowing what to expect, and clearly Grayson had an end goal in mind.

"And chicken? Like fried chicken or grilled?"

I nodded hesitantly. I could already feel myself losing, but there wasn't anything I could do about it.

"What if I were to say we could get a *variety* of safe choices that people can pick from, and probably for cheaper than the pizza?"

This actually made me snort.

"I'd say it wasn't likely. Any place that caters a variety of food will charge you for the convenience."

He nodded. "Unless that place wasn't a caterer. Unless that place was . . ." He paused dramatically. "A grocery store."

I frowned, but Grayson kept talking. "Think about it. The deli counter at Albertson's could easily handle it, and they'd probably give us a killer discount."

I hated that he was right. Pizza would probably be cheaper overall, but the deli counter would have more variety and wouldn't cost a whole lot more.

"Fine." I pushed the paper back toward him. "You call them. I'm going to input all the specifics into the tab room website so we can start organizing all the volunteer judges."

"We don't need to do that yet," Grayson said. "I think you're trying to get out of making phone calls."

In response, I opened the email Ms. Bates had sent us both that morning and put my phone in front of him.

"See the part where she says other teams are already asking her about judges? That's her subtle way of saying we're dropping the ball."

He scrunched up his face. "I think you're reading into it. We should probably wait until the tournament gets closer. No one's going to sign up this early."

I tried to make my smile light, but it probably came across as patronizing anyway.

"Maybe other people know a good thing when they see it and they like to lock it down early," I said. I couldn't help it.

He tilted his head. "Or maybe they think too much and analyze a few words to death."

I sucked in a breath but didn't reply. If he was implying I'd overanalyzed what he'd said to Carter, well, there was no way I'd misinterpreted that.

He shook his head. "Sorry. That was a jerky thing to say." He ran a hand through his hair. "Fine. How about you organize that while I call Albertson's."

I nodded stiffly, then tried to ignore him while he punched the numbers into his phone. I pulled out my laptop and went to the tab room site to input everything. It was hard to focus on the details of the state tournament when I couldn't help fuming over Grayson's comment. What had happened between us wasn't my fault. None of it.

I plugged the dates into the database and tuned out Grayson while he talked on the phone. It really didn't even take long to put everything up, so I didn't know why he was so against getting it done early. I always liked checking things off my list rather than worrying about them later, but did that mean I took things too seriously, as Grayson sometimes implied?

I hit submit, then breathed a sigh of relief. One less thing for me to remember later.

"Yes, two separate days," Grayson said. "Friday and Saturday." He paused, then said, "Good question, I'm not actually sure."

That was what I hated about phone calls. You couldn't prepare for every possibility, and chances were, the other person was going to put you on the spot. That was why I preferred memorized speech events. We should have had Carter make these phone calls. He was the one who could speak whatever was on his mind without worrying about the repercussions.

I felt a pang just thinking about him. We'd barely spoken since that that day in the stairwell. I missed the way he took over the spotlight in any conversation so that I could melt into the background. It took the pressure off to know he'd willingly jump in and shoulder that social responsibility.

Then I could avoid awkward situations like this one with Grayson, where I had no idea what to say.

Grayson hung up the phone and turned to me.

"I think that will actually work." He looked entirely too smug about his victory. "I'll confirm payment and all that with Coach."

"Great," I mumbled, putting my laptop away, standing up from the table, and shouldering my bag. "I'll send around a sign-up for the Thanksgiving potluck, and I'll be sure to separate it by food types so that we don't end up with twenty desserts like last year."

He looked wounded, but I needed to get out of here. If he wasn't going to care about my feelings, then I shouldn't care about his either.

Chapter Fifteen

I expected this Thanksgiving potluck to crash and burn at any moment. Things don't exactly go according to plan when you can't even stand being around someone long enough to, you know, plan.

Carter came into Coach Bates's kitchen and saw me standing behind the counter. The rest of the team was gathering in the living room, but I couldn't sit still.

Carter put his hands in his pockets and hunched his shoulders.

"So," he said.

That was it. So.

I rearranged the dishes that had already arrived, organizing them by main meals and desserts.

"So?" I asked back, not really looking up to meet his eyes.

"I know I suck at apologizing. I'm trying to get better."

I gave a short laugh. "You know that still wasn't an apology, right?" After a couple months of giving him the cold shoulder, I'd hoped he'd catch a clue. That, more than anything, was why our disagreement had gone on so long. Because I refused to forgive someone who wouldn't even recognize they did something wrong.

The silence had almost killed me. I could feel our friendship slipping, and I desperately wanted everything back the way it was. I didn't have that many friends. I couldn't afford to lose Carter over a stupid fight.

Carter nodded. "I was getting there." He gave a rueful smile and ducked his head. "Quinn, I'm really sorry. I didn't want to see you get hurt, but then I was the one who hurt you. I promise I won't interfere with Grayson again, if that's what you want."

I sighed. No, that wasn't what I wanted. Without Carter's interference, who knew what might have happened with Grayson. Maybe I'd have fallen for his tricks and been in an even worse situation. None of this was really Carter's fault, but I'd been treating him like it was.

Besides, as far as apologies went, that one wasn't half bad. He'd been direct, shouldered the blame, and promised to do better. Wasn't that almost exactly what I'd told 15211 to do when apologizing to girls? How could I stay mad at Carter when I couldn't have asked for anything better?

I fingered the edge of a pie, turning it this way and that. "I'm sorry too, Carter."

I looked up. Carter was watching me intently, perhaps sensing to see the truth of my words. Then he took a hesitant step forward. When I didn't stop him, he came all the way over, and opened his arms for a hug. I stepped into his embrace and let my head rest against his chest. I could feel it when he relaxed.

"I think that's the longest we've been in a fight for like ten years," he said. I felt his words rumble beneath my cheek. He was probably right, which was why I didn't share much boy stuff with him in the first place. I nodded, being careful not to get makeup on his freshly pressed shirt.

Coach always made us dress up for the Thanksgiving potluck. Like we didn't have to do that for all the tournaments. At least this time I wasn't forced into a pair of pantyhose. "I've missed you."

Someone coughed by the door, and Carter and I froze. I ducked my head under his arm to see who was there.

Grayson.

Of course.

Carter allowed me out of his arms and I needlessly adjusted my shirt because I couldn't help but be awkward.

"I just wanted to make sure you had everything under control in here, but it looks like you have all the help you need." Grayson's arms were crossed as he leaned against the doorframe. Like he had any right to be upset. Carter was my friend since childhood. Grayson was just someone who got in my way.

Indignation flared in my chest and I straightened my spine.

"Got it covered," I said, keeping my voice cool. "Thanks."

Grayson nodded once, then turned to leave. Before he did, he turned back and met my eyes. "You know, Quinn, I was honest with you when I said I wasn't playing games."

I couldn't help myself. "You mean it's honest to kiss me when you like someone else?"

To lead me on all so you could dump me before the state championship? I didn't say it, but I wanted to.

At my side, Carter stiffened. Apparently he hadn't known that little fact about our kiss, and I immediately felt bad for letting him know this way. Some friend I was.

I could see Grayson breathe in and out, but he didn't say anything for a minute. So softly I almost didn't hear him, he said, "Yeah well, maybe it took me a while to realize how I feel about you."

Then he walked out the door.

I'd heard him correctly. He'd said "feel," not "felt." As in, he still liked me. Or was pretending he did? Refusing to stop playing his game even when he got caught? I sucked in a breath while I processed what had just happened. My stomach still felt all fluttery, but now I couldn't tell if it was from my nervousness over making up with Carter, or being in the same room as Grayson, listening to him say things like that.

Then my eyes narrowed. It didn't matter. Grayson was still the top person on my hit list. He'd proven once how easily he could play with my heart, so I shouldn't be surprised to find him still at it.

Carter leaned back against the kitchen counter, resting his elbows next to the pie. He shook his head.

"You always keep me guessing, Quinn."

That wasn't intentional. I tried to be very clear with Carter, especially lately. But it was hard to be friendly toward a guy without them thinking you meant something more by your actions.

I needed a rulebook for relationships. Something that could tell me exactly what to do to get the results I wanted. Just because I was a pro at public speaking didn't mean I had the first clue about how to speak boy.

I sighed and handed Carter a towel, pointing to a spot on the counter he could clean up. "I never know what I'm doing, Carter. So really, I'm guessing as much as you are."

"Well, not knowing is half the fun," Carter said. "Keeps life interesting."

I froze. That was almost exactly the same thing 15211 had written back when we'd first started exchanging letters. Maybe it was a common enough phrase, but really, I doubted it. First the apology that followed my formula, and now this?

Carter shrugged, cleaned up the spilled sauce, and passed me back the towel.

He left me alone in the kitchen, but the room wasn't empty. It was full of questions.

* * *

I CALLED AN emergency meeting with Naomi later that night. She was babysitting and couldn't come over even though her younger brother was asleep, so we video chatted. Her face and curls filled my phone's screen, her eyes wide after hearing my news.

"You think it could be *Carter?*"

I shrugged. "I'm not saying I *want* it to be Carter. Just that it's a possibility." I held up the papers with all the students in AP Government. "He has Ms. Navarrete in the morning."

Naomi whistled slowly, then scrunched her eyebrows. "I don't know, though, Carter is so impulsive and says whatever is on his mind. Your letter guy seems much more deliberate."

"Yeah, well, people always think about what they write more than what they say."

"Not true. Think of all the internet trolls you just offended."

I didn't feel much like laughing, even though it was obvious Naomi was trying her best. She sighed.

"Okay, how about you read all the letters to me and we'll go through them for clues."

"That would take the entire night. We've been writing since the beginning of September." Naomi still read a lot of the letters, so it wasn't like this should come as a surprise.

Naomi raised her eyebrows. "Has it really been that long? Look at you go."

"Focus." I snapped my fingers. "What I need to know is, do you think it could be Carter?"

She deliberated, then bit her lip. "I mean, I guess?"

That was *so* not what I wanted to hear. I groaned and flopped back on my bed, dropping my phone to my side. Naomi's voice floated up to me.

"Anything's possible. But you have to admit the odds aren't very good."

I sat up and brought my phone back in front of me. "Well, it has to be *someone.* Some guy who's a senior. And someone who's in AP Government and Politics. That means the odds are pretty good actually."

Naomi winced. "Well, when you put it that way."

Both of us were silent for a while, thinking over the ramifications.

"I was all for having you move on with this guy, but maybe . . ." Naomi paused. "Maybe just put the flirting on hold for a while? At least until you know for sure it's not Carter? Because that would just be awkward."

"You're telling me," I muttered.

"Especially after things went south with Grayson. It's not like you need any more drama right now."

The reminder sent a pang through my chest. Wasn't time supposed to make it hurt less? How come I could still feel the embarrassment and betrayal like it was yesterday?

I didn't say anything and Naomi pushed forward.

"You know I've been a huge fan of this one-five-whatever guy all along, and I honestly don't think it's Carter, and you have nothing to worry about. Just give it time. Once we find out who it is, we'll both look back and laugh at this."

"I really, really hope you're right," I said. "Anyway." I waved my hand in the air. "Enough about boys. We still good for our girls' night tomorrow? Or do you think it will physically hurt you to be without Dax for that long?"

She knew I was teasing. Dax was actually pretty great as far as boyfriends went. He didn't mind when I stole my best friend for a much-needed girls-only outing. Tomorrow, Naomi and I had tickets to a concert that we'd won off the radio. Neither of us knew the band, but hey, free tickets.

"You know it." She gave me a pretend fist bump through the phone. "I'm bringing ear plugs, just in case they're awful."

"Smart. Bring me some too."

She laughed and nodded.

We disconnected the FaceTime call and I fell back against my pillows again. I felt a little better. But it wasn't enough to make me forget that Carter could be the one behind all of 15211's letters.

I didn't think that was something I could ever forget.

Chapter Sixteen

Dear 15211,

I'm not sure meeting each other would be the best thing. It would change . . . a lot. For starters, what if we do know each other?

What if we're friends?

What if we're not?

What if we can't stand each other?

What if you're my cousin? You gotta admit, that'd be creepy.

What if you once dated my best friend?

What if you once dated me? (I mean, I'm pretty sure I'd remember if I'd dated someone who was all the *things you described. That'd be awful if I didn't know those things about someone I dated. But still. What if?)*

Once we know, we can't not know. We can never go back. But we can wait, and we can see where things go.

There's too many what-ifs.

15511

I wasn't really worried about most of those things. Okay, yeah, maybe a little bit. But on the whole, I was now worried 15211 was Carter. Ever since that comment he'd made. The more I thought about it, the more I was convinced. His parents were still married, plus they expected him to become a doctor, or lawyer, or something else important. He played video games too, like 15211 had mentioned. I had no idea if he liked programming them, though. But he had AP Government in the morning, so there was that too.

If I was right, and he found out that I was 15511, then that would change everything. What was frustrating was how different someone could be on paper versus real life. The facts were all the same, but I'd read into them. I'd built 15211 up, turning him into some kind of fantasy, when I should have known better. True, Carter was my friend and I thought he was a great guy. But in the letters, I'd made him into more than just a friend.

I had a letter waiting for me the next day. I couldn't read it right away, so I shoved it in my pocket to read later. Then I transferred it to my suit jacket pocket when I changed after school for parents' night. Parents' night was basically where we all ate spaghetti in the school cafeteria but pretended it was something fancier because we drank water out of plastic cups shaped like champagne flutes. Our top-ranking students performed for the parents and sponsors who did a good job pretending not to be bored even though we all knew the truth. Making things more uncomfortable, we had to dress up.

Grayson and I would both be giving our speeches tonight, along with a Duo Interpretation pair and a staged debate between two people from our Lincoln-Douglas team.

Now, completely ready for my performance with time to spare, I stole away to the hallway to read 15211's response.

People passed me to get into the cafeteria, but I carefully shielded the letter from anyone's eyes, sliding down the wall until I sat cross-legged on the floor.

> *Dear 15511,*
>
> *I understand you're scared. I'm scared too. But it's the things that scare us the most that have the best rewards, right? Didn't someone famous say that once? If not, they should have, because it's rather smart, if I do say so myself.*
>
> *Don't worry. I'm pretty sure all your what-ifs will disappear. I don't have any cousins my age. As for the other things you mentioned, I'd remember if I dated someone like you.*
>
> *15211*

How could his letters still make me smile when I knew, well, *probably* knew that he was totally not someone I should be crushing on?

Carter walked through the cafeteria doors in that moment and I quickly shoved the letter under my leg. The absolute *last* thing I wanted was for Carter to see me reading this letter if it really was from him. I still needed time to sort everything out, especially my emotions.

Carter turned, saw me, and came over to where I was sitting, a smile overtaking his face.

"I dunno, Edwards, there's all these people here, think you'll cave under the pressure?" He sat down next to me and nudged me with his elbow.

"You wish. I've been killing it at competitions, or haven't you noticed? That state championship scholarship is calling my name." By "killing it" I really only meant I'd won two tournaments in a row, but I was all about celebrating little victories.

"Oh, I've noticed," Carter said. His shoulders slumped a little. "You'll get that scholarship and be out of here without even looking back." Carter gave me a sad smile and I rolled my eyes. Part of me regretted letting him think I was so interested in the scholarship, but then he said things like that and I remembered why I'd done it in the first place.

"Whatever. You know we'll keep up with each other online."

This didn't seem to make him any happier. He looked away, toward the main doors where more people were entering for parents' night.

I looked over too and saw my mom laughing with another parent in the lobby.

While we were both looking that way and Carter's head was turned, I tucked the letter back into my pocket.

"Mom!" I called, waving her over. Yes, I wanted to distract Carter. Distracting him was better than facing him. I was such a coward sometimes.

When my mom saw me, her face split into a smile. She parted ways with the parent and came to where we were sitting.

"There's the star of the evening," she said, and I rolled my eyes.

"Hardly," I replied.

"Hi, Lindsey," Carter said. "I'm trying to convince Quinn here to stick around Idaho for college. You're on my side, right?"

Of course, my mom knew all about my plans to go to Boise State. She routinely told me how guilty she felt that she was part of my reasoning for wanting to stay. I didn't want my mom's puzzled frown to give me away, so I quickly interjected.

"Want to save us seats?" I asked. "I'll be there in a second."

"Sure." My mom drew out the word. "And, Quinn, you know you can go wherever you want for school, right?"

That was one of the best things about my mom. She supported me 100 percent, and she always made sure I knew it. Sometimes to the point of embarrassment, like when I was thirteen and she proudly announced to an entire grocery store that we were buying my first period supplies.

I nodded hastily, hoping she'd get the hint now. Also hoping that this wouldn't fuel another debate where she tried to convince me she could live without me. I knew she could. That wasn't the point. The point was, I *wanted* to go to Boise State.

She patted my head and walked away.

"There's your big competition," Carter said, nodding to the doors. "Grayson just got here with his family."

I didn't want to look. Looking meant I was weak. But I totally looked anyway.

Grayson was flanked on either side by his mom and dad. His younger sister, I assumed, walked to the right of their group. She could have been Grayson's twin separated by five or so years. She had the same light brown skin, easy smile, and wavy dark hair. She even wore the same style of glasses.

I'd seen Governor Hawks before, of course, a few times. But I'd never actually met her in person, and suddenly I wasn't sure what to expect.

Her picture had been plastered everywhere over the last couple of months because she'd been campaigning for reelection. *A Name You Know. Vote for Nasha.* Apparently winning was a family trait, because she'd won by a landslide.

Behind their family, two men in suits hovered nearby, obviously security. They weren't wearing uniforms, so they probably were trying to look like school faculty or something, but I knew all the faculty here, and neither of them were familiar.

I stood up and straightened my slacks. For some reason, this felt like a standing occasion. Carter followed, and we both stood awkwardly in the hallway while we waited for Grayson's family to pass.

But they didn't pass. They stopped.

Governor Hawks's billboards made it clear she was confident, but in person, Grayson's mom seemed even more imposing. It was obvious she was the one used to giving directions, not receiving them. Not that she looked mean. Just *powerful*. Her stance was the exact pose I tried to mimic whenever I gave a speech. She was born to be a public figure.

Her black hair was pulled back and she wore a suit that looked simultaneously professional yet feminine. Her brown skin was flawless, like she'd had a professional apply her makeup just for this occasion. Either that or she was just one of those lucky women who had nonexistent pores and dangerously long lashes. But it wasn't her appearance that demanded attention. It was her presence. Her sheer force that both intimidated and fascinated me.

I wanted to be her when I grew up.

His dad's hair was graying on the sides and he kind of looked like Chris Pine, with the same warm smile. He was fit for his age, and tall, with broad shoulders and a relaxed pose.

"Quinn, right?" Grayson's dad asked, extending his hand. He must have seen my shock because he hurried to add, "I saw the pictures from the fall fling. It's nice to finally meet you."

"Right," I choked out, hoping he couldn't see how much my hand shook when I stretched it out. How were you supposed to behave when you met the parents of a boy who you'd crushed on? "Nice to meet you, Mr. Hawks."

How much had Grayson told them? Or, *oh no*. The police officer? What if she told the governor about our kiss?

Mortification. That was the only word that could describe what I was feeling. I knew that night would come back to haunt me. Sure, I still dreamed about it sometimes. Dreamed about things ending differently because I liked to torture myself. But this was a whole new level of torment.

"I hear you'll be performing tonight?" Governor Hawks asked.

I nodded. Then I figured maybe I was supposed to actually say something, like nodding was somehow rude. People wouldn't just nod to the president, would they? "Yes, that's right," I said, after it had already been too long. Ten points for awkwardness.

"You've beat my son at quite a few tournaments lately," she said with a smile. "Your speech must be quite something. I'm looking forward to hearing it."

"I . . . I'll do my best."

No pressure or anything.

I looked at the ground, feeling completely inadequate in this moment. This woman had accomplished so much. There was no way she'd be impressed with my little presentation.

"Quinn's speech is amazing," Grayson said. My head whipped up, surprised. His shoulders were back and his expression was earnest. From the way he looked at his mother, it was obvious he looked up to her and wanted to impress her. I just had no idea why he'd think I was a good way to do that, or why he'd want her to be impressed with me just as badly as I wanted that to happen.

I hadn't been nervous before, but now my tongue stuck to the roof of my mouth and my stomach twisted into knots. Carter put an arm around my shoulders. "Yeah, my girl Quinn here is one of the best."

Nasha's eyes moved from Carter, to his arm, to Grayson, and back again. Her eyebrows raised, and I was too nervous to try and explain, even as I shrugged out of Carter's arm. Grayson didn't seem concerned about it or the way Carter had said "my girl Quinn." As well he shouldn't be. Grayson's mouth lifted up in a smile and I wanted to roll my eyes at the lot of them.

Mr. Hawk's eyebrows drew together in confusion.

"Didn't you two go to the fall fling together, though?" he asked Grayson.

I shared an uncomfortable look with Grayson. Apparently his dad didn't know not to ask questions like that. Either that or he was completely clueless about teenagers in general. Grayson cleared his throat.

"Well, yeah, but we're just friends."

Ha. We were not friends. Not anymore.

Even though I wished we were.

"Friends who go on dates?" His dad was not taking a hint.

Carter was enjoying this immensely. His smile was so big, he looked like he was competing for a spot in a toothpaste commercial.

"Yeah," Carter said. "Like we're going on a date tomorrow, right, Quinn?"

I whipped around so fast Carter took a step back. "What?"

Grayson's dad couldn't catch up to this conversation. "You all are? All of you together? Grayson too?"

Grayson dragged his hand through his hair. His expression was pained, like this hadn't been on his agenda today. I, however, was not going to get roped into a solo date with Carter simply to save face in front of Grayson's parents. If I could make Grayson suffer too, all the better.

"Yes, all of us," I said, keeping my voice cheery. "Grayson is bringing someone too. A group date. We're all going as *friends*." That last part was for Carter's benefit. I stared him down as I said it, but Carter didn't even look sorry. I wasn't surprised. This was exactly the type of thing he'd pull to get me to be more social. But this time, I wasn't secretly looking forward to it.

"Well, that sounds like fun," Grayson's dad said. He seemed proud of himself, like he'd finally cracked the teenager code and knew what we were talking about.

The governor's face was hesitant. She likely wouldn't contradict her husband in public, but we all knew "fun" wasn't the best descriptor.

"Who are you going with?" Grayson's dad asked him. Everyone turned to face Grayson, and I felt a surge of satisfaction for how uncomfortable he looked.

"Uh, I haven't asked anyone yet." Grayson adjusted the collar of his dress shirt.

"Well, it's tomorrow," his dad said. "That's not giving the poor girl much notice. I thought we'd raised you to be more of a gentleman than that."

Carter was eating this up. I elbowed him in the side to keep him from actually laughing out loud.

Governor Hawks looked like she was going to weigh in on the conversation, but I didn't want her to have to explain things to her husband in front of everyone.

"Well, if you'll excuse me." I took a step away from the group. "I really should go get ready for my speech tonight." Why'd the governor have to be so intimidating? How was I supposed to get through tonight with her watching?

She opened her mouth like she was going to respond, but I turned and made my way around the group.

Then, like the coward I was, I practically ran away.

Chapter Seventeen

I just had to make it through tonight's date with my dignity intact. That was all.

I'd been all for canceling this farce, but I was a woman of my word. Besides, I wasn't about to back out and have Grayson know he'd scared me away or somehow gotten the upper hand.

So, here I was. Doing the thing I wanted to do least because I had too much stinking pride. But I could do hard things. That was what I'd proven last night at the spaghetti dinner performing in front of Grayson's mom. I'd rocked that performance. She'd even been smiling while she clapped.

My mom had been so proud I had to stop her from telling every person we met on the way out that I was her daughter. Then she'd gone out of her way to introduce herself to Grayson's parents, and I'd about died right then and there. As if by some unspoken signal, Grayson and I had both steered our parents away from each other as soon as we could while still abiding by polite social norms.

This should be easy-peasy in comparison, but instead I was sitting in the diner booth and stress sweating while I tore a breadstick into little tiny pieces. Carter was beside me to my right, like we usually sat whenever we came to my mom's diner. Naomi usually sat across from us, her long legs requiring a whole side to herself. An old One Direction song came on over the speakers, making her absence all the more noticeable, because she would have been fangirling over it. I really could have used her as backup right about now, because this was all kinds of awkward. Carter seemed to recognize this, because he kept cracking jokes to make me feel more comfortable.

Across from us, the other side of the table was still empty. Grayson and his date weren't here yet, and part of me wondered if he'd be a no-show. If someone had roped me into something like this, I wouldn't have come. I'd say "See ya," and let them deal with the consequences themselves, thank you very much.

But Grayson was a better person than I was, because at that moment, he walked through the doors of the diner with his date. She was walking slightly behind him, so it wasn't until they made it to our table that I recognized Grayson's ex-girlfriend Zara Hayer. He smirked as he sat down.

Maybe he wasn't the better person after all. Maybe tonight was about to get a whole lot worse.

Grayson and Zara settled into their seats and I tried to smile politely. I didn't know Zara well. She was one of those gorgeous people who didn't really mix with anyone I knew. She had jet-black hair that bounced whenever she moved and perfect full lips that made it look like she was always flirting. She seemed nice enough, but why on earth had Grayson invited her tonight? What did it mean? And why did I care? Okay, if I was being honest with myself, I knew why I cared. I just didn't like it. I was determined not to let Grayson under my skin, but somehow he managed to do it anyway.

Still though, I wondered how Grayson had gotten an ex to say yes. Did that mean they were dating again? Or just that they were part of the 1 percent of people who could actually stay friends after a breakup? And how could she still stand to be around him when he'd done what he had to her? He'd dumped her right before the class elections so she'd lose. Talk about awful. How had she forgiven him?

"Hey, thanks for inviting us tonight," Grayson said. I couldn't tell if he was being sarcastic or not. There was no way he was actually grateful to have been bullied into coming. I passed the menu to Zara without saying anything. She shared it with Grayson, and they had to get close to read everything. I forced myself to look away. I wanted to shout that only two months ago, he'd been kissing me, even if it had been a game to him. But I bit my lip and focused on all the holiday decor they'd started putting up around the diner. The stuffed Santa figurine on the counter was slowly falling over and giving up, a live enactment of how well this night was going.

My mom arrived then to take our orders. Saved by Mom.

"Hi, kids." She reached over and knuckled Carter's hair. "Oh, hey, I know you." Then she put an arm over my shoulder in a half hug. "How's it going, sweetie?" She nodded at Grayson. "Nice to see you again, Grayson. You haven't been around."

Please, let me die. Is that too much to ask?

"Hi, Mom." I handed her our menu. "I'm guessing you know what I want."

She winked. "Loaded nachos coming right up. And what about the rest of you?" She poised her pen to write it all down. Carter ordered his usual fettuccini Alfredo and Zara got the house salad. My mom turned to Grayson.

"Is it too late to order breakfast?" he asked.

She smiled. "I'm sure we can work something out. What would you like?"

He ordered the pancake stack and my mom left. I turned to Grayson.

"You know, it says right there on the menu they don't serve breakfast after eleven o'clock."

"That's why I asked if it'd be okay. Your mom seemed fine with it."

"Yeah, well, that's because she likes you."

As soon as I said it, I knew it was a mistake. Grayson's eyebrows raised and a smirk overtook his face. Zara sipped her water quietly, her eyes darting back and forth between Grayson and me.

"So the mother likes me while the daughter hates me. That's interesting." Grayson leaned back and crossed his arms all smug like. Again, I wondered what the story was between him and Zara. Would he act this way if they were back together?

"I don't hate you," I scoffed.

I hated that I liked him. Those were two very different things. I hated that I'd fallen so easily for his ploy, and even worse, that I still thought about him. And okay, I hated that he'd done that to me when I knew better. But if Zara's friendship with him was any indication, maybe I'd gotten things wrong. Then again, that was probably wishful thinking talking.

"Could've fooled me," Grayson said. I rolled my eyes and ate a piece of my breadstick. Guys were clueless. I offered the basket of bread to Zara, who took a piece hesitantly. Was she always this quiet? Maybe that's why Grayson had dated her. Was dating her? So he could hear himself talk all the time. He certainly seemed to like the sound of his own voice.

"Stop acting so naive. You know I don't hate you."

"Yeah, she kissed you, didn't she?" Carter spoke up.

I choked on my bread and grabbed my water glass to chug it. I'd almost forgotten Carter was even there. Now here he was trying to kill me.

"Yes, she did."

Grayson didn't have to sound so conceited about it. Insufferable jerk. Besides, why did we have to talk about this now?

As an added bonus, that was when my mom walked up to see if our waters needed topping off. So that was excellent.

Zara's eyes had gotten really wide.

"Wait, you two kissed?" she asked, her voice raised, pointing between

Grayson and me. It was the first thing she'd said all night. And she'd said it loud enough for the entire freaking diner to hear.

I was *so glad* my mom was here to witness it. Like everyone in the diner who'd turned in their seats to stare at our booth, it was clear she'd heard everything, because she was biting her lip and trying not to laugh. Awesome.

She didn't top off our drinks. She turned and kept walking, like that had been her goal all along, to pause at our table, laugh, and then veer to a different one. I noticed she didn't go far. She hovered close enough to hear our conversation, and she didn't even try to be sneaky about it. That was great.

My entire face was hot enough to roast a marshmallow. If the earth opened up a giant sinkhole beneath my feet, I wouldn't even be mad about it. I'd welcome it with open arms.

Forget about making it through this date with my dignity intact. I just wanted to make it out of here alive.

"Congratulations," someone called out. I looked over to see it was the diner manager, Mr. Porter, who was beaming like he found this whole thing incredibly entertaining.

Grayson kicked Carter under the table. I could tell because I felt his foot brush mine on his way to Carter, and Carter yelped and jumped in his seat.

"Not cool, man," Grayson said.

"What, you're embarrassed about the kiss?" Carter taunted.

Grayson's voice was still as smooth as ever when he replied, "No. But Quinn is, obviously. What a way to treat your friend."

I looked over to see Carter actually seemed shocked by this accusation. For my part, I was still trying to process Grayson's words and why he thought I was embarrassed over kissing him, rather than this whole episode in front of my mom. I figured it was obvious that *this* was what I was embarrassed about.

But why had he come to my defense? That wasn't what we did. We were like cats and dogs forced into close proximity, at each other's throats whenever possible.

Of course, that was when I realized that Grayson hadn't been. Ever since our kiss. Even at competitions, he'd kept everything friendly. It was me that brought the frost. I'd attributed his behavior to him trying to weasel his way into my good graces so he could still play his little game, but could there be more to it?

Zara stood up and fidgeted at the side of the table. "I think I should probably go." She tucked a piece of hair behind her ear. "I mean, I owe you, Grayson, but it's pretty clear I don't really need to be part of whatever is going on between the rest of you."

I didn't know it was possible to feel worse about tonight's events, but that statement did it. Zara was an innocent bystander. None of this was her fault. Unless she was dating Grayson again, and then a spiteful part of me wanted her to feel uncomfortable anyway. And what had she meant about owing Grayson? If anything, he owed *her*.

Grayson stood up, looking guilty. "Sorry, yeah, I'll take you home." He grabbed his coat and put his arms through the sleeves, then reached into his pocket and pulled out some cash, putting it on the table. "That should cover ours, but let me know if I owe you more when the check comes."

There was absolutely no way I was going to stay all the way through dinner until the check came. If Grayson and Zara were bailing, I was on my way out the door right after them.

They left and I turned in my seat to catch my mom's eye. She'd been waiting. Of course.

She came over and put a hand on my shoulder. "Don't worry, I'll cancel your orders if you'd like. Mike hasn't gotten to them yet in the kitchen, I'm sure." Her face was full of compassion, and that, more than anything, made me feel like crying. My eyes were tight and prickly, and I could feel the blotchiness creeping over my skin like a disease. I nodded and she squeezed my shoulder before walking away toward the kitchen.

Then I turned to Carter and anger hit me like a linebacker. "What was that?"

I expected him to feign innocence. Like he had no idea he'd behaved badly. But he hung his head and wiped a hand across his face.

"Wasn't my best moment," he answered.

"Yeah, well, it certainly wasn't a great moment for me either. Did you think of that?" I threw a sugar packet at him. It bounced off his cheek and landed on the table. "What got into you?"

He ran a hand through his hair and looked intently at me. "Do you really want me to answer that?"

I crossed my arms and stared him down.

Carter swallowed.

"Jealousy."

It was one simple word, but it made me stop in my tracks.

"I'm sorry, I know I said I wouldn't interfere with you and Grayson anymore. But just because he's being nice to you, I don't want you to fall for it."

I stayed silent. I didn't want to admit that Carter was right. I'd been questioning things again, and Carter was the only one who seemed to see things properly. Some friend I was.

"That was still a sucky way to get your message across," I said. "I appreciate you looking out for me, but we've got to develop some kind of secret signal or something you could give me whenever you think Grayson is up to something shady."

This made Carter smile. He reached out, took my hand in his, and gave it a squeeze. "You mean like this?"

I pulled my hand from his and put it in my sweater pocket.

Carter's smile faltered, but then he shrugged and stood up, grabbing his jacket in one hand.

"We can avoid it for however long you want, but don't expect me to give up." He motioned for me to stand too. His face had softened a little bit and he didn't seem upset. Just certain. "Come on, I'll take you home."

It was the most direct he'd been about his feelings, and I didn't want to face it yet.

I shook my head. "I'll get a ride with my mom." She didn't get off for another hour, but waiting here was better than the alternative. Even with the entire diner watching me right now.

Carter released a breath, then nodded. His smile was kind of sad, so I stood up to give him a hug.

I watched him leave, then slumped back to the booth bench with a loud exhale. My mom came to sit on the opposite side of the table.

"You okay?" She reached her hand out and I placed mine in it.

"I will be." At least I hoped so. Tonight had dipped way into the negative numbers, but things had to turn around eventually. That's what everyone always said, and I didn't want to think about the possibilities if it weren't true.

"So, you kissed Grayson, huh?" She raised her eyebrows. "Or so I hear."

I rolled my eyes. "It was two months ago, Mom." And I didn't want to talk about it.

She nodded and pursed her lips together like she was trying not to say anything else. Eventually, she sucked in a breath.

"Do you really want to go to Boise State? Are you sure?" Her voice was small, and I hated that she trusted Carter's word more than mine. "I don't want you to feel like you don't have a choice. You have so much going for you, kiddo. So much to experience. I can't be the thing holding you back." Her voice cracked, and I knew why. Those words were loaded with meaning.

When I was a baby and my dad left, that had been what he'd told her. He'd said she was only holding him back, and that he had so much more to experience in life than simply being a family man. Sometimes I really hated him for that. It wasn't like I knew the guy well. He never fought for parental rights, so I only saw him once every few years when he happened to be in town. But I hated what he'd done to my mom's esteem. That was half the reason it'd taken her so long to really believe in this photography goal of hers, and I wasn't about to let her give up on it now.

"Mom." I squeezed her hand. "You know how much I've been looking forward to their marketing program. Their business school is internationally accredited. Carter's the one I've been lying to."

Her expression went soft, and her eyes scrunched up. "You mean that? You're telling your mom the truth and not your friends? Because from all the parenting books I've read, it's supposed to go the other way around."

I smiled. "You're a closer friend than Carter will ever be."

She wiped at her eyes, then took a deep breath in and out. "Okay, enough with the sappy stuff. I love you, but I have an image here to maintain."

We laughed and I let go of her hand.

Mr. Porter came by then and I thought he'd get mad at my mom for slacking on the job, but he put two pieces of apple pie on the table.

"On the house," the restaurant manager said. "You need it."

That was the truth. He smiled as he left, and Mom passed me a fork.

"You know," she said, cutting off a piece. "I've seen a lot of dates here, but that was probably the fastest I've ever seen one implode." She chuckled as she dug into her pie.

"Yeah," I said, taking a bite. "I have a knack for that."

A knack for ruining dates, relationships, and anything in between. What a knack to have.

Chapter Eighteen

Naomi often joked about me being antisocial, but it wasn't like I did it on purpose. Not right now at least.

Carter'd been out of town all of winter break, skiing in Utah with his family. Naomi spent all her time with Dax, which I wasn't even mad about. I wanted her to be happy and I didn't want to use my "best friend card" too many times in begging for her company.

Sure, I had other people I was friends with, but they were more like acquaintances. Not the type of people I could text at midnight to ask them if they were binging the same Netflix show as me. No one to stop me from fixating on my mom's Instagram and rereading all the comments on the picture of Grayson and me. In all honesty, sometimes our followers seemed more real than was probably healthy. I really did need more friends. It seemed like all of mine lately were either online, or mostly in my head, like 15211.

I got out of bed and got the little key from its hiding place so I could open the drawer where I saved all of 15211's letters. I fanned them out on the desk in front of me, looking through my favorites.

I wished I could text him. Winter break just ended and I had my first new letter in over a week. But even without the break, it was agony waiting a full day before getting a response. I'd never appreciated modern technology as much as I had lately when writing old-fashioned letters with a boy I didn't even know. I briefly considered asking him for his number, but then thought better of it. If it was Carter, he'd already have my number in his phone and that'd be the end of things.

That was a constant debate I had with myself, whether or not 15211 could be Carter. There were so many similarities. So many boxes I could tick. The facts were there, but the essence wasn't. I mean, from what I could tell 15211 was a true gentleman in every sense of the word. Carter, on the other hand, did things like tell someone you kissed their ex when you were on a group date.

True, he could be a gentleman when he tried, and I guess that was what made me question everything. Because obviously 15211 was going to put his best foot forward. He had time to think through his responses and come up with clever replies. In real life Carter was impulsive, always ready for fun, and willing to drag me along, helping me get out of my shell whenever I needed it most. He stretched me and got me out of my comfort zone. Usually I appreciated the gesture. But in a boyfriend? I needed someone who I could be myself around, all the time. Someone who could see my bad and not want to change me. Someone, even, who *liked* those things about me.

The chances that 15211 was Carter were probably one in a million. Right?

What I needed was a sign. Something definite I could point to as proof that 15211 was *not* Carter and I had nothing to worry about. Then I was pretty sure I could meet him. All the other questions were still there: What if we actually knew each other in real life? What if he wanted nothing to do with me once he found out who I was?

But even with those questions, the payoff was starting to sound a lot better than staying in the dark. If I could prove it wasn't Carter, I'd chance it.

Probably.

I found the letter I was looking for and opened it up. It was one of the first ones we'd exchanged, where 15211 had told me all the reasons I should be his friend.

If I was being honest with myself, I could probably use more friends. Carter hadn't even made it back in town until today, so he hadn't been in school. But things had been weird between us, and I wasn't sure how to fix it. Part of me blamed Carter, which wasn't fair. I tried to tell myself it'd get better with time, and all I could do was hope I was right.

Naomi might as well have not been in school, for how distracted she was. It was our first day back from winter break, and the entire week previous had been lonely and silent. I'd spent my time doing college applications, so talk about fun.

I obviously knew 15211 wouldn't contact me over winter break, but without Naomi or Carter to talk to, it seemed like everyone had better things to do. None of my mom's siblings were in town this year, so Christmas had just been her and me, with our little pile of gifts and our traditional platter of peppermint bark, which we'd finished off in less than a day, a new record.

I fingered the letter in my hand, rereading the parts that made me laugh. I picked up another one, all about how he thought moms always liked him. Then there was the one where he mentioned cooking for his younger siblings.

I sat up straight. *15211 liked to cook for his younger siblings.*

Carter's skills in the kitchen went as far as pouring a bowl of cereal. If he was feeling extra ambitious, he might get fancy and add milk. When his parents left him in charge, he ordered pizza. As far as I knew, he didn't know the difference between a teaspoon and tablespoon.

I couldn't help the smile that stretched across my face.

Now I had other options besides a frustrating boy who didn't even like me back or the friend who I didn't want to hurt. I could invest my time and attention into someone who was now a real possibility—one I could actually see playing out. I could picture meeting this mystery guy and maybe hitting it off. He was funny and considerate, and he always made me feel good about myself in our letters. I'd introduce him to Naomi and we could go on double dates without me being a third wheel to her couple bliss. We'd talk about all these expectations other people had for our futures and bond over the fact that we both liked Chinese takeout.

I brought out my phone to text Naomi.

My letter writer—it's not Carter.

Please let her be awake. And not busy with Dax.

I couldn't even blame her entirely, since speech and debate had practically taken over my life. Planning the state tournament was a lot more difficult than I'd anticipated. Because our food would be more expensive this year, we had to have a fundraiser to cover the extra costs. It wasn't a whole lot, and we probably would have had to do a fundraiser anyway, but with all the stress from AP Government and everything else going on in my life, it wasn't like I was looking forward to it.

Luckily, Grayson had given in to my fundraiser idea—after making a big fuss about it. He kept suggesting selling things like candy or donuts. Basically, all the things that would be a lot of work and would take a portion of our profits. He didn't think the school administration would go for my idea. But then I dragged him into the office and spoken directly with the principal and shown Grayson that sometimes the simplest solution really was the best one.

Normally we couldn't wear hats at our school. But the principal had allowed us to plan a hat day, where students could pay a couple bucks for the privilege, and we'd get to pocket all the profits.

Eat that, Grayson.

All that to say I'd been spending more time on speech and debate stuff than I'd wanted lately, and I was feeling like my friendships were paying the price.

My phone chimed with a text from Naomi.

> How do you know it's not Carter?

I hurried in my response.

> Because 15211 said he likes to cook for his younger siblings.

She texted back right away.

> Oh! And Carter only knows how to order pizza! Yes!

She sent a GIF of a girl wiping her brow in relief, which I totally related to.

> That means Mr. Note Guy isn't off-limits anymore. Go get him, girl!

I smiled at her response and put my phone down on my desk. I replaced the letters and locked them up. My mom already knew more about my romantic life than I was comfortable with.

I took the lists out, the ones that had all the students listed that were in AP Government. Then I crossed Carter's name off with a bold slash of my pen. There were still too many possibilities, mostly because I simply didn't know enough of the guys on the list well enough to know for sure one way or the other. It wasn't like I could go up to people I barely knew and ask them if their parents were still together, and oh, by the way, do you know how to pronounce *Worcestershire?*

But it was one less person to be concerned about.

Now if I could get my grades up in AP Government, everything would finally be working out. I'd been winning at speech tournaments, but the more time I devoted to that, the more my grades suffered.

I fell back on my bed in an exhausted whoosh. Grown-ups always thought high school was so easy. But all they had to worry about was a job they already knew how to do. They had their established group of friends, and a lot of them didn't even have to worry about dating because they were in long-term relationships. They didn't have to learn new information all the time and balance that with new relationships or anything like that. They simply did their usual thing every day and kept things the status quo.

The status quo was easy. It was change that was paralyzing.

Change, like wondering whether I should meet 15211 in person or not.

* * *

THIS WEEKEND WAS a huge national forensics tournament in Arizona. It wasn't Nationals with a capital *N*. You didn't have to qualify to compete, and anyone could go. It just happened to be open nationally. But it was still good prep for the later tournaments because most people wouldn't pay for the travel unless they had something to prove. I was one of those people. I needed to crush Grayson into dust.

Our team was only bringing four students, which meant we were actually able to fly instead of drive, thankfully. It was Thursday morning and we were meeting at school, but not actually going to classes. Even with flying, we'd miss two days of school, right after winter break.

I already felt stressed knowing how much work the teachers would assign while we were gone to catch up on everything. Especially my AP Government teacher, who loved essays more than life itself.

I was stressing about all the work, but worse was the idea of being seated on a confined airplane next to Grayson. Our Duo Interpretation team, Aisha and Landon were coming too, but they listened to their headphones all the time at meets, and I didn't think this trip would be any different. Besides being a duo pair, they were also a couple, and I was pretty sure they'd be in their own little world the whole time. But the flight wasn't that long, so hopefully I could ignore Grayson. Besides, it wasn't like he'd say much with our coach right there. Hopefully.

I paced the school hallway outside the speech room while I waited for everyone else to show up. The trip made me so anxious, I'd shown up a full half hour early to our meeting time. Students and teachers weren't even here yet, so the school was eerily silent.

I walked downstairs to the AP Government room. I wasn't sure if the room was open, but I wanted to see if 15211 happened to leave me another note.

He hadn't.

But I did have my latest test in my cubby. It was facedown, and I debated whether to look or not. On the plus side, it'd put me out of my misery so I wouldn't have to wonder the whole trip whether all my studying had helped at all. But on the down side, if I got a bad grade, it might put me in a funk for the tournament, so competing could be rocky.

I flipped the test over and stared at the grade scratched across the top.

I'd failed. Literally. Not just, wow, that was a bad score, but an actual F was marked in red, like a beacon for my inadequacy for the whole world to see.

I wasn't sure how it was possible. How could I be so bad at something even when I tried my hardest?

I leaned against the cubbies and sank down until I was sitting on the floor, holding the test in front of me between my knees. The cherry on top was that I'd put in the effort. I needed actual help, like from a tutor or something. But I'd never be able to afford a tutor when I could barely afford pantyhose.

Tears pooled at the corners of my eyes and the F swam in front of my vision. It shouldn't have mattered this much. This sharp pain in my gut shouldn't have been there. But I was helpless against the sheer enormity of it all. *Helpless.* That was a good word for it. Because it didn't feel like there was anything I could do that would make any kind of difference. Plus, the fact that I'd come here for something to boost me up but only got torn down wasn't making it any easier to swallow.

I knew I shouldn't compare, but I couldn't help it—I climbed back to my feet and walked to 15211's cubby. I had to know his score. Was I the only one who struggled so much with the class? Or had everyone bombed the test? Maybe it'd been impossibly difficult and everyone going to class today would hear all about how Ms. Navarrete had decided to grade it on a curve.

I flipped over his test and groaned. Of course he'd gotten an A. There was even a plus mark next to it, rubbing my failure in for good measure. Putting his test back the way it was, I looked at my own to see what I'd missed.

Practically everything. They were little details and dates I couldn't help but mix up. How could someone possibly keep all these facts straight? How did 15211 do it?

My chest hitched. If we met in person, maybe he could tutor me and I wouldn't have to pay someone money I didn't have. He'd probably say yes. He was nice like that. Plus, he obviously knew what he was talking about. I doubted there was someone in all of Ms. Navarrete's classes who was getting a better grade. At least, not someone who'd be willing to help me.

I fingered the edge of my paper while I thought things over.

Pros and cons. There were so many of each and I was running out of time to decide. Pretty soon, other students would start showing up; plus, I needed to get back upstairs.

My heart hammered in my rib cage. My hands were sweaty on my paper and I bit my lip. There'd be no turning back from this. The pressure was building in my chest, making it difficult to breathe.

Tearing the blank lower section of my test off, I pulled out a pen and scribbled a hasty note.

I shoved the note in his cubby before I could talk myself out of it.

You still want to meet?

Chapter Nineteen

I thought the flight down to the Arizona competition would be the worst part of the trip. But that'd been over before I'd even finished listening to my audiobook, and Grayson had sat on the other side of Coach. No, sharing a room with Aisha was worse. Especially getting back to the hotel the first night of the competition to find Aisha and Landon all tangled on her bed while they watched a movie and I somehow had to find somewhere else to go for a couple of hours. They said I could stay and watch the movie with them, but yeah, that wasn't happening.

Coach had given us a whole spiel on proper conduct since we only had two people per room and she didn't want a scandal on her hands. So I didn't think anything was going to happen, but I didn't want to be a third wheel either.

I didn't have a lot of options. The hotel lobby only had two chairs in it, and they were taken by a petite older woman and her very large dog, who took up a chair all on his own. The receptionist kept giving the woman a disapproving glare, but didn't say anything, so I was out of luck there.

Coach Bates had her own room. But somehow I didn't think Aisha would like it if I went there to hang out.

It was much warmer here in Phoenix than it was in Boise, so I could go outside. My stomach kept clenching angrily, demanding food. I didn't think there were any restaurants nearby, though, and my feet were already protesting from walking around all day in heels. Students were on their own for dinner at all the meets. Usually there was something at the tournament itself, like what we were planning for the state meet, but this one was too large to accommodate that many people.

I could order food and have it delivered. But to do that, I'd need to look up the phone numbers for those places, and my data plan had already run out for the month. I walked over to the receptionist, who was still staring at the woman and her dog like she could telepathically move them with the force of her gaze.

"Excuse me, do you have Wi-Fi here?" I asked.

The receptionist didn't even look at me as she answered. "Yes. A credit card is required, though." She tapped a sign to her right, which had all the fees written out. I let out a breath. It figured.

"Okay, well, do you have any takeout menus or anything from some close food places?"

The receptionist finally looked at me. "No. Sorry."

She was so helpful. I tried not to roll my eyes. "Do you have room service?"

Room service was expensive. But I was running out of options.

She handed me a paper menu. "You can take it to your room."

That was the other downside with room service. You had to have a room they could deliver it to. I guessed I could hang out outside my own room, but that seemed all kinds of pathetic.

My stomach clenched again and I knew I'd need to act fast before I reached my hangry point.

My room was down the hall to the right.

I turned left instead.

I walked to room 223 and stood outside, my hand raised to knock, hovering right near the surface. My stomach gurgled and I was pretty sure it was loud enough to hear even behind the closed door.

I knocked, and my hand only shook a little.

I could hear shuffling behind the door. Then it opened and Grayson was standing there in pajama bottoms and a T-shirt that was tight around his arms. I tried not to stare. I failed.

"Quinn." He leaned against the doorframe. "To what do I owe the honor?"

"Can I borrow your phone?" I blurted.

I was too tired and hungry to banter around. I wanted to order food and get out of here.

His eyebrows drew together and he processed what I said. I fidgeted with the hem of my shirt, twisting a loose thread around my finger until it nearly lost all circulation. Realization dawned on his face, and he grinned.

"So . . . what you're saying is, you need *my help*." He looked entirely too smug about it.

I bit back the retort on the tip of my tongue, as much as it physically pained me to do so. I hated when Grayson was right.

"Why?" he asked. The word seemed to take up all the space between us. Why? I wanted to ask him the same thing. Why don't you like me? Why'd you have to kiss me and make me realize my own feelings only to set me up?

"Because my data is up, the hotel charges for Wi-Fi, and if I don't find a place for food soon, I'm pretty sure I might eat the furniture."

One side of his mouth quirked up in a smile and he held the door open for me to come in. "Well, we can't have that, now can we?"

I hesitated before stepping in. Really, I could use his phone in the hallway, so I didn't need to go in there. I didn't need to tempt fate.

Grayson walked to the small table where his phone was sitting and he handed it to me after unlocking it. I immediately sat on the side of his bed and started looking up fast food places.

"I'm guessing my roommate is now in your room?" Grayson asked, sitting down too. He was only a foot away from me, his back against the headboard as he brought his legs up under him.

I nodded, trying not to think about how close we sat or how I could smell the soap on his skin. He must have showered right after getting back from the competition. His soap had a nice clean yet spicy scent to it that I really liked. Ugh. Why couldn't he have been gross? It'd be so much easier to hate him. Instead he smelled, and looked, like an Old Spice commercial.

Nope. Not thinking about it. It was all part of his trap.

"Why are there no good food places close to us?" I asked, scrolling through the options. "The closest pizza place is still a half-hour wait." I sighed in resignation. "At least they deliver." I clicked on one of the search results, then pulled out my own phone to dial the number. Pizza places often added the number you called from to the order, and I didn't want to wait around here in case they called. My nerves were already fried enough.

Grayson leaned over and plucked his phone and the room service menu from my hands. My breath hitched at the close proximity and I sat very still until he leaned back.

"Or we could order room service," he said, like he hadn't just caused me to go into shock. "It'd be faster." I'd hoped that time would make it easier to be around Grayson. Unfortunately, the universe had it out for me. Sure, I acted all tough on the outside, but inside, I was still vulnerable. I hated that.

"Since when did you weasel your way into my dinner plans?" I asked.

"Since you knocked on my door." He turned the paper around so it was facing me. "They have hamburgers. I know how much you like those."

He smirked.

I narrowed my eyes.

"I'll get the mac and cheese, thanks." I made sure to keep my voice level.

He was right that room service would be faster, and with how my stomach was trying to eat me from the inside out, that might not be the worst thing in the world. It sounded better than pizza anyway.

Grayson picked up the room phone, pushed a button, and spoke into the receiver. "Room service, please."

Grayson proceeded to order multiple things off the menu, like he planned on feeding the entire hotel, or at least every member of our speech team. He asked to pay with his credit card rather than putting it on the room, then gave them the number.

"I'll pay you back," I said after he hung up.

He shrugged like it wasn't a big deal, but the last thing I wanted was to be in Grayson's debt. I didn't need him to be nice.

Grayson cleared his throat. "Quinn." He reached out and put his hand over mine briefly before pulling back. "I really want us to be friends."

I looked up to find his dark brown eyes focusing intently on me. Now was the time to be strong. To not fall for his tricks the way I had before.

"We . . . are . . . ?" I stumbled over my words, feeling their insincerity even as I said them. Grayson was shaking his head.

"No, we hardly speak to one another. And even if things can't be more between us, I still think we work really well together, and we have fun. I think we could not just be friends, but be really good friends, if you give us a chance."

People didn't say stuff like that. Bare their soul and say the truth they're thinking. But Grayson did, and as much as I hated to admit it, I liked that about him.

If he was being honest. I couldn't help but hear Carter's voice in my head, saying that Grayson couldn't be trusted.

I had too many emotions to process, so I simply sat there and watched Grayson swallow.

"I'm sorry about everything. If that makes it any better," he said.

I fiddled with the ends of my hair as I considered what to say.

I really had missed talking with him. Grayson knew exactly how to tease a response out of me. But being "friendly" came with some pretty big red flags. Now that months had passed, though, I was relatively sure I could handle it. *Relatively* being the key word.

After the silence got to be too much, I sighed.

"I honestly don't know if I can trust you." I was surprised when the truth fell from my lips. I was outright telling him I was onto his game, and that could maybe give him the upper hand somehow. But what if I'd been wrong, and whatever had happened with Zara wasn't what I thought? "I don't want you to say you're my friend, then have you turn around and hurt me when you get a chance. And I don't know if you will."

Grayson sat back, clearly not expecting what I'd just said. "You don't trust me," he repeated. Then he sighed. "I guess that's fair, after what happened."

It wasn't just what had happened between us, but with other girls as well. But I didn't feel like airing his dirty laundry right now. Especially if I didn't have all the facts.

The silence now filled the room and I fidgeted with the awkwardness of everything. I didn't like where things were with Grayson, and I wished they were different. I *wanted* to believe him. Life had been better back when we bantered and riled each other up. It'd been fun. I hadn't even realized what we had until it was taken away. Eventually I sighed.

"Okay, yeah, let's try to be friends. I'll try to trust you. And in the name of friendship and being totally honest, I guess I should say I understand what you were going through because I'm pretty sure I like someone else now too." I wasn't 100 percent sure why I'd said that. Maybe so Grayson would stop trying to play me. Maybe so I wouldn't feel like such a loser.

I didn't know where things stood with 15211. But I wanted to believe he could be the guy for me. Because maybe then I could forget about Grayson. Grayson, who leaned over and nudged my knee.

"Yeah?" He settled back against the headboard. I thought he looked disappointed, but that was probably wishful thinking. Or his mind games at work. "Who's the lucky guy?"

I shook my head. "Nope, we're not that good of friends yet."

"Yet," he repeated, a small smile on his face. "We'll get there."

I smiled, and I tried to make sure it didn't look wistful. "Okay, so you should break the silence first then—who were you crushing on and how're things going there?" I didn't really want to ask, but it'd be better to know. Maybe then I could warn her if she was competing with Grayson in any way. Or maybe it'd teach my heart to move on already.

He shook his head. "I'm still working on it. But let's just say that before we left, I got some really good news in that area of my life."

"Yeah?" I asked. "Like, good news that she likes you back?"

"Can't say for sure. She's, uh, really hard to read." He let out a chuckle.

"Okay, well, maybe when you tell me about your mystery crush, I'll think about telling you about mine."

Grayson looked away and I took the opportunity to study his features.

Maybe he didn't like me scrutinizing him because he took his glasses off and wiped them on the hem of his shirt. He put them back on and adjusted them.

"Glasses suit you," I said without thinking. I wanted to take the words back, but they were out, so I kept stammering one word after another, like that might somehow erase what I'd said. "I mean, they look right on you. Like, you look good. Ummm, wow, I should stop talking."

"Nah," Grayson said with a smile. "I think you should keep talking."

He was insufferable. I reached over and snatched one of the pillows, then hit him with it.

"Oh, no you didn't." He grabbed the pillow from behind his back and then he whacked me across the face. He didn't hold back either. It knocked me back off the bed so I fell to the floor in a tangle of limbs, laughing so hard I couldn't move for a minute.

"You are so going to pay for that," I said between fits of laughter, standing up on still-shaking legs. I gripped the end of the pillow for better leverage and rocked my weight back on my heels. Grayson held his hands in front of his face.

"Wait, wait!" He took his glasses off and put them on the nightstand. "Okay, contin—"

I didn't wait for him to finish before I smacked him full-on in the face.

It was cathartic. Freeing. Surprisingly fun and all I could have wanted in that moment.

He lunged from the bed and tackled me back onto it, his fingers finding the sensitive skin at my waist and squeezing until I squealed.

I was suddenly breathless. Breathless from laughing, yes, but more so because his hands were on my waist and I could feel the heat of his fingertips on my skin. Either he was very good at playing games, or he was very bad at being just friends. How did he expect me to think of him that way when his face was only inches away from my own? I sucked in a breath and bit my lip—and that was when someone knocked on the door.

"That must be room service." My voice sounded wispy even to my own ears. Funny, but I hadn't even considered how hungry I was once I got in the same room with Grayson.

I crawled out from under him and slid off the bed. He was laughing behind me as I walked up to the door and flung it open.

It was not room service.

It was our coach.

And she seemed as surprised to see me there as I was to see her.

It was too late to smooth down my hair, which was staticky after our pillow fight. It didn't help when Grayson came up to the door, still putting on his glasses with one side of his hair all smooshed in a way that totally made it look like we'd been doing something else.

Coach Bates opened her mouth, but no words came out.

Then Grayson burst out laughing again and it was easier to join in than to dwell on what must be going through my coach's head. I started out with a chuckle, but soon, Grayson and I were full-on cry-laughing while our coach watched us concerned.

"Sorry," Grayson gasped. "I promise nothing is going on here. I hit her with a pillow is all."

Coach's eyes raised up, but this time when she opened her mouth, she actually spoke.

"I'll need you to go back to your own room now, Quinn, and I'll walk with you to ensure Landon returns here."

"Can she at least wait until our food gets here?" Grayson asked.

I was resigned to go hungry for the night rather than risk my coach's wrath, but in that moment, I was infinitely glad he'd asked. Because I was pretty sure I'd faint from hunger here pretty soon. My stomach grumbled, but Coach's expression didn't soften. She looked down at her watch.

"How much longer will that be?"

At that moment, a hotel employee rounded the corner with a cart of food.

Coach sighed.

"Fifteen minutes to eat your dinner, then you need to return to your own room. I'll be back to check."

I nodded emphatically, knowing the only reason she wasn't yelling right now was because Grayson had clout. I hated to see how she'd react when she went to check on Aisha and Landon, which she was sure to do right after leaving here. I'd text them a warning after Coach left, but it'd probably be too late.

She nodded once. "I didn't expect this of either of you. Tomorrow I anticipate you'll both focus extra hard." Her disapproval was written all over her face. It was a good reminder that really I should avoid Grayson for my own benefit. If I had, my coach wouldn't be so disappointed right now. That, and I wouldn't feel so confused and conflicted.

We each nodded again, staying silent.

"See that you do." She took a step back and gave a cold stare. "I'll be back. Think about your choices."

Oh, I'd be thinking about them all right. But probably not the choices she was talking about.

Chapter Twenty

We got back from the meet Sunday night. I'd sat by Grayson on the flight back, and we'd even shared an armrest. I still didn't know how to feel about it. But he was super supportive of my win at the tournament, and it was hard to be negative about anything with that kind of adrenaline running through my veins, so I tried not to question things.

There was a letter in my cubby Monday morning. I felt a little bad for writing 15211 about setting up a meeting and then skipping out of town for the rest of the week. He'd probably gone bananas waiting for my reply. At least, I kind of hoped he had.

Now I stood in front of the Idaho state capitol building and wondered if agreeing to meet him had been a mistake. The building stood in front of me, all stoic, and formal, and *pillar-y*. Why did government buildings have so many pillars? And they always had a dome top. What was that about? Like we couldn't do official things unless the building had a stick up its butt? There were approximately a bazillion stairs between me and the front doors, but I didn't move.

Meeting at the capitol building had been his idea, and he'd set it a few days out so I'd have a chance to back out if I wanted. I'd told him the only reason I was agreeing to meet with him was because I needed serious help in AP Government, so he suggested this as the place to go. He wanted me to watch a session to really get a grasp of how things worked, and even though that sounded like the most boring thing I could possibly be doing with my Wednesday evening, I was desperate enough to try. Plus, it didn't hurt that I'd be learning who 15211 was soon. So there was that to look forward to.

Naomi had practically pushed me out the door when she saw his response. After she helped me with my hair, of course. Then she'd done the pushing. She'd offered to drive me here, but I didn't want her staking out the parking lot and spying on us, so I took the bus. Not that I'd put it past her anyway, since she was all for me taking things to the next level, ASAP.

Now, though, now I couldn't take a step. True, taking a step would mean I was that much closer to finding out 15211's identity, but the downside was, he'd then know who I was too. It worked both ways.

The steps went on forever, reaching up into a fortress of marble and stone.

When I'd written my acceptance of 15211's plan, I'd been all hyped up over my win from the Arizona competition. I'd been on top of my game. On top of the world. Now I was at the bottom of a very long stairway, and I wasn't sure about anything at all.

All along, 15211 had been this figment in my mind, like he didn't actually exist. I'd imagine the way he'd look or act, and everything was in my control. But I couldn't control a real boy. I could barely even talk to one. He'd have his own opinions, his own way of thinking and acting, and he'd no longer be this fantasy I could turn to whenever I needed it.

He could stop writing me once he figured out who I was. He could disappoint me. He could hurt me. He could do all those things if I walked up the steps. But he couldn't if I stayed where I was.

My heart banged in my chest as I heavily placed my foot on the first stair. Had someone stolen into my room and filled all my limbs with cement overnight? I took one step after another until I'd made my way to the front doors. Then I pulled them open and walked inside, refusing to look back and see if 15211 might already be there in the parking lot.

I tried to ignore all the grown-ups in suits watching me as I walked the length of the marble floor and found a chair placed to the side. It was better to wait inside where it was warm than outside in the January air. I crossed my legs and prepared to wait, but then I saw him.

Not 15211.

Grayson.

Here.

A huge potted plant was to the right of the bench where I sat, and I ducked behind the branches to peer from behind the fronds. Grayson was laughing with an older man, both of them standing toward the back of the lobby. They clearly knew each other, and people passing by all waved at them. Grayson was no stranger to the state capitol building, apparently, which shouldn't have surprised me since he looked like he was here on some kind of business. The man gave Grayson a sticky note and Grayson put it in his pocket before turning with a wave. They parted ways and Grayson started walking toward the main entrance.

He was leaving, thank all that was good in the world.

He was leaving, which meant Grayson was not 15211. He just happened to be here around the same time, and now he was going someplace else. It was only a coincidence. My mind was going full-on hummingbird speed, but I took in a shaky breath.

I was wearing a black-and-white-striped shirt, like I'd specified in my letter so 15211 would know who I was. He was supposed to be wearing a hat, which Grayson clearly wasn't.

I let go of the plant branches I'd been holding on to and the bush made a rustling sound, teetering in its pot. I put my hands to the base of the pot, but it was too late.

Grayson turned and saw me.

"Quinn?"

He looked just as surprised to see me as I had been to see him. Or maybe his expression was more one of confusion. It was kind of hard to tell. His eyebrows were pulled together, but one corner of his mouth was pulled up in a smile.

There wasn't enough air in this place. Every inch of my skin was tingling and all I could do was sit there and think through all the letters I had sitting in my drawer at home.

Grayson had been leaving, walking toward the main doors with purpose. He couldn't be 15211. I knew it for the same reason I knew Carter wasn't. 15211 said he liked to cook dinner for his younger siblings. Siblings, as in, plural little brothers or sisters. Grayson only had a little sister. I'd met her at parents' night. Plus, 15211 was witty and flirty—Grayson was nothing but trouble. And he wasn't wearing a hat.

He came to where I was sitting and I stopped fussing with the potted plant. "What are you doing here?" he asked me, which was also something he wouldn't have had to ask me if he were 15211. He sounded hesitant, his voice betraying his confusion.

I fiddled with the sleeve of my shirt. "I don't want to say." I could barely meet his gaze. If he knew the truth behind why I was here, he'd judge me. Would he think I was a hopeless romantic or something, to be crushing on someone I'd never even met? Or would he figure out I'd only shifted my feelings to the letter writer when he'd rejected me?

Besides, Grayson probably knew everything and then some about politics—what would he think if he knew how much I struggled in AP

Government and how that had been the reason 15211 had suggested we meet here?

Grayson ran a hand through his hair and came to sit on the bench next to me. "Why won't you tell me?"

"Because knowing my luck, you'd use the information against me." *Or you'll mock me.*

He considered my words with a slow nod. "You really don't trust me, do you?"

That was it, and it wasn't. But I wasn't sure how to put into words the complete and utter embarrassment I was feeling. Like giving a speech in only my underwear.

Actually, I think I'd take the underwear speech, thank you very much.

"What are you doing here?" I asked instead.

He looked around, as if seeming to realize we were in a big, fancy government building made of marble, and not the linoleum halls of our school.

"Uh, my mom asked me to bring her some paperwork from home," he said.

Oh. He really, certainly, definitely wasn't 15211 after all. I tried not to let my ping-ponging emotions show on my face.

"So you really won't tell me why you're here?" His voice took on a teasing tone and he nudged my shoulder. I felt my resolve crack a little bit. "Pretty please?" He batted his eyelashes dramatically and I heaved a sigh.

"You have to promise not to laugh."

I guessed if we were going to give friendship a shot, then it could start here.

Grayson smiled a blinding smile and I couldn't turn back now. I pursed my lips together and thought of the best way to tell him without looking like a fool.

Grayson held up his fingers in what I guessed was the scout oath. "I won't laugh," he said.

I still didn't say anything, and Grayson exhaled. "You still don't believe me? Fine, I pinkie promise." He caught my hand in his and intertwined our pinkie fingers. My skin burned at the contact and I stared down at our fingers. How could he be so casual about touching me when I overanalyzed every single thing I did in his presence to replay in my mind later?

"I won't laugh, and I won't tell a soul. I promise I won't judge either."

He certainly seemed sure of himself. He always did. But how could he know it wasn't something he'd laugh at?

He still hadn't dropped my hand, and I tried not to read anything into it. It was getting harder and harder to remember why crushing on Grayson was a bad idea. Not so long ago it'd been so easy to hate him. I hadn't even realized my own feelings. Then he kissed me, and my world shifted. Adding that to the fact that I still had no idea what was going on with him and Zara, or what *had* gone down. Plus, he'd said things were going well with some other girl, so really, I didn't know which way was up right now.

"Okay, I'll tell you, but not here, surrounded by all these strangers."

He pulled me up, still holding my hand as he towed me after him.

"Wait," I said. "I need to watch this main lobby." I wasn't about to miss meeting 15211 because I couldn't keep my head on straight. But it wasn't like I wanted 15211 to come and find me talking to some other guy either, so maybe it was for the best that we go somewhere else. Grayson nodded, but still kept pulling me along.

The lobby was an enormous circular room, with pillars reaching up several floors surrounding it. Each floor looked down on the red-and-black marble star on the bottom floor, a short guardrail going around the pillars on every level. We went all the way to the fourth floor, the dome above us filling the space with its fancy filigree ornamentation. The star was actually below the main level, but when you walked in, there was a circular overlook and chairs that looked down on it. That main waiting area was where I was supposed to meet 15211, but from here on the top floor, I could clearly see everyone milling around below, so my shoulders relaxed.

Grayson leaned back against the railing and crossed his arms, looking at me intently. I avoided his gaze and scanned the people below. 15211 would be here any minute. I was running out of time to explain things to Grayson without leaving him here to find out for himself. Then who knew what he'd do. If he learned about 15211 without me explaining it first, he might . . . I don't know. Say something to him or something. I didn't want to wait to find out.

"So I'm supposed to meet someone here," I said, drumming my fingers lightly against the marble railing and looking down.

"I figured." Grayson turned so we were facing the same way, our shoulders touching. "Who?"

I sucked in a breath. "I don't know." It was freeing to finally say it aloud. Here on the top floor, we were all alone. Just Grayson, and me, and the secret I'd been holding on to all school year. Well, that and the Winged Victory replica and creepy horseback dude statues.

"You don't know," he repeated.

I nodded.

"Like a blind date? Because the state capitol building is so romantic." His voice was dripping with sarcasm. We were speaking in kind of hushed tones since the marble made everything echo, and Grayson gestured around us. "All these politicians making shady deals and getting hyped up over their own importance. I know I'm feeling the love."

He elbowed me lightly in the side and I scoffed.

"Not like a date. Well, I don't know, but I don't think so."

"Shouldn't that be something you know?" Grayson was outright smirking now, and I punched him in the arm.

"You promised not to make fun of me."

He held up his hands in surrender. "Okay, okay, I'll be good. So, you're meeting someone you don't know, for what could maybe be a date, but could also be a regular traipse through the Idaho state capitol building. As one does."

I rolled my eyes and he continued.

"I mean, I come here all the time to hang out. All the cool kids are doing it. It's *the* place to be these days."

"He was going to help me with AP Government and Politics," I said, laughing. "So yes, this is the place to do that."

"Like a tutor?"

I took a deep breath before nodding. Admitting there was one more thing Grayson beat me at wasn't easy. But it wasn't like it was a fair fight. His mom was in politics. He had politics in his DNA. "Our assignments got swapped in our cubbies way back in the beginning of the school year, so we started exchanging letters. He's really good in that class and I'm pretty much failing, so I finally agreed to meet him under the condition that he share some of his knowledge."

Grayson drew back and looked at me.

"And you didn't ask me for help? I'm offended. I happen to know a lot about government stuff, you know."

"I know." I looked at the floor. My worn-out shoes were so out of place among all the grandeur. "But it's not exactly easy for me to admit that I suck at something. To say I'm stupid."

He tilted his head. "You are the furthest thing from stupid. You don't understand something. There's a big difference." He then peered over the railing. "So what time is your mystery man supposed to meet you?"

Grayson hadn't mocked me. An unfamiliar emotion bloomed in my chest and I struggled to make sense of it. Grayson had once accused me of always making him into the bad guy. It was easy to do when you constantly competed with someone. But now I wondered how many of my interactions of him were colored by my *expecting* him to play the villain, because right now he was acting downright heroic.

I looked back over the foyer. Still no one under the age of forty. The time to meet had come and gone and I didn't quite know what to make of it. My palms were sticky with sweat and I wiped them on my jeans, but that didn't stop them from shaking. What if 15211 had seen me waiting in the foyer, figured out who I was, and then left? What if he was one of those people who cared about popularity, or what if he simply didn't care enough to show up in the first place? I could have built this whole thing out of nothing when, to him, it was something he did to pass the time.

Grayson took my silence for his answer and he turned away from the balcony to look at me. His scrutiny made me self-conscious and I bit my lip.

"You're really upset by this, aren't you?" he asked. I sighed and moved to walk away, but he put his hand on my arm. "Why?"

"Why?" I folded my arms. "Why do you think? I've been stood up." I turned away from him to look back out again. He joined me at the railing, placing his forearms on the marble and leaning out.

"Well, he's the stupid one for letting you go when he had the opportunity." He said it so certainly, looking deep into my eyes until I had to look away. "Really stupid."

I gave him a sad smile, my chest feeling tight and stiff. "You want to know why I care so much?"

"I already said I did."

I sighed. "Remember how I told you I liked someone?" I turned around so I was facing Grayson. His eyes were wide with surprise.

"You were talking about him." He didn't say it as a question, so I didn't bother replying. I simply stood there, willing the tears not to come. I could feel them on the corners of my vision, stinging as I blinked. That'd now been two guys to reject me. I really knew how to pick them.

"Maybe you wouldn't have liked him," Grayson said. "Maybe you would have been disappointed and it's better that you don't know."

I shrugged. "It's kind of hard to imagine. He was pretty perfect on paper."

Grayson's cheek twitched.

"Perfect is overrated. You turned me down at least."

I scoffed and pushed his shoulder. If I was being honest with myself, though, well, sometimes I regretted that decision.

But that was a secret I was prepared to take to my grave.

Chapter Twenty-One

You know what we should do? We should write this guy a letter."
Grayson started leading me away from the overlook.

"We?" I asked. "There is no we."

I didn't mean for that to sound as harsh as it came out. What I meant
was that I was pretty sure 15211 wouldn't appreciate a letter from some
random person I'd invited into our little secret relationship. But Grayson
winced and I hurried to explain.

"What I mean is—"

"No, I get it. You already told me you don't trust me. I'm going to prove
to you that you can. But now, what I meant is that you should write him
a letter and I'll help you."

"You'll help me," I repeated, still not sure what he was talking about, or
where we were going. I followed Grayson toward the stairwell. I reached
out to stop him, and my hand lingered on his arm against my will. "Where
are we going?"

"My mom's office. We need paper."

My feet were now planted on the ground. I wasn't about to keep walking even if there was a hurricane on the way.

Grayson walked a few more steps before realizing I wasn't following. He turned, then came back and grabbed my hand to tow me along. He had to pull, because I wasn't coming easy.

"What? She doesn't bite."

"I know," I said, still not moving. "But she's so . . . intimidating. She's scary."

This made him chuckle. "Don't I know it. I have to live with her. But don't worry. She's not there right now."

"I thought she asked you to bring her some paperwork?" I said.

"Oh, yeah, well, she had to leave right after I brought it to her," he said. "That's why I know she's not there."

"And they allow anyone to go into the governor's office?" I took one step. "I mean, I guess you're her son, but what about state secrets or something?"

"We'll get the paper from her assistant. Her desk is outside."

He'd thought of answers for everything, and I found my resolve weakening.

"Okay, but why are we writing a letter right now?" I took another step.

"Because you need to tell him what you're really feeling while your emotions are fresh from him ghosting you."

"I can do that on my own, thank you very much."

I was running out of reasons. Once again, Grayson was winning an argument despite my best efforts. I shook my head, but this time somehow found myself smiling.

"That's not as much fun," Grayson said.

We made it to the stairwell and started walking down. He was in front, me still a step behind.

"Besides, I'm a guy and can tell you what will make him feel the worst about it."

"But I don't want to make him feel bad," I said.

"Why not?" Grayson stopped and looked at me. "He stood you up and you don't want to make him even a little uncomfortable?"

"Because I like the guy." I chewed my lower lip. "If I tell him off for today, that might be the end of it. Besides, I'm not that mean. Well, not to most people at least. Just you."

Grayson smiled and it was like the sun was there with us in that stairwell.

"All the more reason to ream him out then," Grayson said, resuming our walk down the stairs. "If you really like the guy, he should treat you right and you shouldn't let him get away with stuff like this. As your friend, I have to make sure he's good enough for you."

"I'm really more concerned about my grade in AP Government than anything," I said. That was a half lie. I was probably fifty-fifty on my reasons for wanting to meet 15211.

"Don't be. I'll tutor you." He said it like it was a done deal. Like he totally didn't mind all the extra time it'd take or the fact that I really had no idea what I was doing in that class.

"I think you're underestimating how bad I am at AP Government," I said, trailing my fingers along the stair railing. "I can't ask you to do that for me. I mean, it could take up a lot of your time. My grades are really that low."

"That's what friends are for, right? Besides, maybe then you'll see I'm not such a bad guy after all and I can prove it to you. Your grades will prove it." Grayson led me down a hall, then turned right. "As for time . . ." He turned to face me. "I'm counting on it."

Butterflies the size of elephants were having a dance party in my stomach. How could he act all flirty like that and use the word *friends* in the same breath? Was he doing this on purpose? To build my hopes up only to crush them before state, like Carter implied? I tried to imagine what Naomi would tell me to do since she was much better with guys. But she'd been the one to encourage things with 15211 and that hadn't exactly worked out, so I had no clue what she'd think now. Trying to imagine what Carter would say wasn't any better, because I knew he had definite opinions and I increasingly wasn't sure I agreed with them.

We reached our destination. Or so I was guessing, because the lady at the desk looked up and smiled when she saw Grayson. We were in some kind of a foyer, the large desk taking more than its fair share of space. There was a door to the side, and I stared at it in awe. I was 90 percent sure that was his mom's office, and I could still feel the glimmer of her presence, like even the door was affected by her aura.

The receptionist's eyes crinkled at the corners. "Grayson! How nice to see you."

Grayson returned her smile. "We wondered if you had some paper we could borrow. And a pen too, please."

"Of course." She handed him a notebook with the instruction that he could keep it. Grayson took it with a smile and then passed over the sticky note he'd had in his pocket from earlier.

"Oh, I'm supposed to give this to you too," he said. "I wasn't sure I'd have time today, but here you go."

I remembered that Grayson had been walking toward the main doors when he'd seen me and I wondered where he'd been going, and what I was keeping him from.

Grayson walked me over to one of the benches surrounding the star in the floor, giving me the notebook. He sat close to me, and even though I promised I wouldn't read into those kinds of things anymore, I couldn't help it.

"Okay, so how do you usually start your letters?" Grayson asked.

I wrote *Dear 15211* at the top of the paper.

"Well, that's no good," he said, reading over my shoulder. "You need to start with 'Hey, dirtbag,' or something so he knows you're mad at him."

I laughed, which seemed impossible in this situation. He was right. I should have been mad. But with Grayson here to soften the blow, I'd almost forgotten all those negative emotions.

He reached over and scratched out my words, leaving the notepad in my hands.

"Try again. *Hey, Loser*," he said, motioning for me to start writing.

"Don't call me a loser," I retorted with a laugh. He rolled his eyes.

"I'm dictating. Write *Hey, Loser* already."

I sighed, but started writing as Grayson kept talking. Might as well get this out of my system, because it was obvious Grayson wasn't going to give up.

"*You have no idea what you're missing because I'm the best thing that's ever happened to you*," Grayson dictated.

I smacked his arm, but Grayson talked over me. "*Seriously. I'm witty, gorgeous, talented, and smart, so it's your loss.*"

I stopped writing, swallowed the lump in my throat, and bit my lip. Grayson wasn't saying he believed all those things about me. He was trying to be funny. To take my mind off things, to prove he was a real friend. But I couldn't stop my pulse from reacting, speeding up and taking flight in a fit of happiness. I wrote the words slowly, shaking my head the whole time. Grayson waited for me to finish before continuing.

"*You probably smell bad and cheat on all your AP Government tests anyway, so I've found myself a better tutor who showers regularly and also happens to be a really good kisser.*"

By now I was laughing so hard I couldn't write if I tried.

"Here, I'll write it if you won't," he responded, capturing the notebook from me despite my best attempts to hold on to it. "He needs to know I kissed you first." He scribbled the words on the page, his handwriting a mess from the way I pulled on his arm.

"You sure think a lot of yourself, don't you?" I said, tugging on the page. Grayson didn't let go, and held it away from me so I had to practically drape myself over his lap to even reach it.

"Watch it," Grayson said, laughing with me. "Remember, I still know where you're ticklish."

That was all the warning he gave me. My side was unguarded as I reached across him, and Grayson took the opportunity to lightly squeeze my waist. I yipped and backed off, but not before several adults walking in the area turned to stare. My face heated up and I scooted to the far other side of the bench, keeping a good two feet between us. Grayson was laughing hard, hardly caring at all what everyone around us thought.

I, on the other hand, hid my face behind my hands, trying to stop from laughing because I knew this was the kind of place where people would get disproportionately upset over this type of thing. I wasn't overly successful at curbing my laughter, though, so eventually I dropped my hands.

That was when I saw Grayson's mom striding toward us. Grayson must have seen her too, because he stopped laughing and sat up straight.

"I thought you said she wasn't here," I hissed. I'd planned on meeting 15211 and then sneaking away to some dusty corner where Nasha Hawks couldn't see my insignificance. I wouldn't have hung out in the main lobby, essentially with a sign above my head that said, *Here I am flirting with your son even though I know it can only end badly. Come get me!*

Grayson didn't answer. He waited for his mom to reach us, then stood up. I did the same, because what else was I supposed to do?

"Hello, Grayson, Quinn." She tilted her head to one side, and I tried to read her expression. Was she upset? Disappointed? My palms were sweaty and I hated that she'd seen me acting so disrespectful at the state capitol building.

"Hey, Mom." Grayson cleared his throat. "I thought you had a meeting."

She raised her eyebrows. "It was canceled."

Grayson nodded, bobbing his head up and down like a buoy in the water. Governor Hawks turned to me.

"Nice to see you, Quinn. I was hoping I'd get a chance to run into you again."

I was willing to bet this wasn't the kind of run-in she'd been thinking about.

"What brings you to the Idaho state capitol building?" Governor Hawks asked.

Okay, so option one, I could tell her I needed tutoring help, which would make her think I was lacking in an area that was her expertise. Option two, I could confess I liked another boy and she didn't have to worry about me not being good enough for her family, which I obviously wasn't. Or, option three, I could lie. None of those seemed like good options, so I stood there like a gaping fish. Luckily, Grayson stepped in.

"I invited her. She's in AP Government too and she wanted to know more."

A half-truth I could get behind. Yes, I wanted to know more, but only for the sake of my grade. As for inviting me, well, I was surprised Grayson could lie so smoothly to his mother. His voice didn't waver even a little bit.

The governor assessed me and a small smile crossed her face. "Yes, it certainly looked like you were both very studious just now, in my place of work."

I had no response for that. All I could do was hope she didn't ask to see the notebook Grayson was holding, because if she read the line about her son being a good kisser, I was 100 percent sure I would die on the spot.

"I hate to be a dictator, but please make sure you aren't a distraction for people working here." She uncrossed her arms and half turned to go. "I need to get back to work, but I'm guessing you aren't staying long?"

Grayson saluted. I nodded. Both of us stayed rooted to the spot, spines straight like good little soldiers. We didn't breathe until she turned a corner and walked out of sight; then we collapsed onto the bench like deflated balloons.

"Your mom must hate me."

Grayson shook his head. "Hardly. She worries about me and anything that might interfere with 'the plan,' but trust me, she's not as strict as she seems."

I gave him a skeptical look. "Are you sure you're okay with tutoring me? Your mom might disown you. I can find someone else." I looked down at the floor, hoping he might not recognize how hard the words were for me to say. Even though he'd only made the offer minutes ago, I already depended on it like oxygen.

Grayson reached out and grasped my chin, turning my head so I was forced to look directly at him. My skin tingled underneath his fingers.

"I wouldn't have it any other way."

He said it with such conviction, I couldn't help but believe him.

Chapter Twenty-Two

Dear 15211,

I don't know why you weren't there yesterday. Maybe you decided not to come because, like me, you were scared. Or maybe you came in, saw who I was, and then left. I really hope it wasn't that, because that would be pretty awful. Not for me, because I'll get over it. But for you, because that would mean you are a judgmental and petty human being, and that's not something that's easy to change.

I've never thought that about you, though, so I really hope you have a good excuse for not showing up. I'm not sure whether to keep writing you, or forget about you entirely. So I guess this is me giving you one last chance, even though I'm not sure you deserve it.

15511

Naomi helped me write it, since I wasn't sure what to say. She kept giving him the benefit of the doubt, and was convinced he'd been hit by a bus or something, which, even if it gave him an excuse not for showing up, I really hoped hadn't happened.

I'd left the note in his cubby this morning, but he didn't reply by my class time. Now it was after speech practice, and I checked again, even though I should have been hightailing it to the bus. We had another speech tournament tomorrow, so I'd be MIA from school to see if 15211 wrote back this week. Just my luck.

Of course, I thought about never writing 15211 ever again. But I was doing better in speech and debate with his help. All his tips made it so I had the edge in competition for once. Not to mention, writing 15211 got my mind off . . . other people.

I sighed and turned around to find Grayson in the doorway watching me.

My hands hung awkwardly at my sides and I shifted back on my heels, unsure of what to do. I tried to play it cool by hooking my thumb through my belt loop and pretending I'd known he was there all along. Smooth. That was me.

"Spying on me, Hawks?" I picked my bag up from where I'd left it on the floor and came to stand by his side. "Maybe you're hoping to see which cubby I was at so you could read my messages to . . ." I was about to say 15211, but then that'd give Grayson the number of the cubby, so I finished by saying, "Him."

Then another thought hit me. Grayson had already seen the number when I wrote it on the fake letter he'd tried to make me write. "Or did you already memorize it?" I gasped, and took a step away from him. He laughed at my expression and leaned against the doorframe.

"I promise I didn't memorize it when you showed me his number."

His smile still made me think he was hiding something. I narrowed my eyes at him, but this only made him laugh harder. I looked back at the cubbies, debating my options.

"Listen." He reached out to touch my arm and turned me to face him.

If only Grayson weren't so touchy, then it'd be easier to get over him. But every time it happened, it was like a jolt of electricity buzzed through my veins and I couldn't help the way my body responded. He was too good at this game.

"I wanted to check your schedule," he said. My pulse picked up and my brain went into hyperdrive.

"Why? What for?"

His hand was still on my elbow. How did he expect me to think rationally when he was so casually touching me like that?

"For tutoring," he responded. He finally dropped his hand and I focused on bringing my breathing back to normal.

"Is there a good time for you when we could get together?" he asked.

I wanted to read into his comment, but I resisted. I chewed my lip. "We have the tournament this weekend and a test first thing when we get back." My stomach dropped at the realization. That was one more test I was bound to fail because I simply didn't understand the subject.

"Today then," he said, undeterred.

"The last bus leaves in a few minutes," I said, already scooting past him to exit through the door. "And they lock the school soon."

"I could drive you. We could study at your apartment. Or my house."

I raised my eyebrows. "Are civilians allowed at your house since it's where the governor lives?"

He smiled. "You'd be fine since you'd be with me."

With me. Why did so much of what he'd been saying have a double meaning? Or maybe not exactly a double meaning, but a different way to interpret it if Grayson was flirting. Which he wasn't. Because he wanted to be friends (maybe), his mom didn't approve of me (probably), and we'd already gone there once (kind of). Plus, there was the whole "possibility of him setting me up to fail" thing I couldn't forget about. And the other girl he liked. So many reasons for me to back off and accept things for the way they were, but it didn't stop me from wanting something I could never have. Why'd he have to kiss me? Why couldn't I move on? It shouldn't have been this hard.

"Also, my mom left for Idaho Falls this morning for work, so she's not even in Boise. In case you wanted to know. Even though I've already told you she has nothing against you." It was like he knew everything I was thinking and could anticipate whatever I'd say next. I hated that he knew me so well, when I felt like he was this giant enigma I had no hope of ever understanding.

But I really did need the help in AP Government, which was why I found myself saying the words "Your house it is."

* * *

HIS HOUSE WAS gated. Like an actual gate with a security code that Grayson had to enter. I'd only seen those in movies.

We drove the rest of the driveway, and Grayson parked his car in the multi-car garage before punching in a code at the door. A cheery electronic voice said the alarm was deactivated; then after we walked inside and closed the door, Grayson reset the alarm.

That was it.

"I thought you'd have guards or something," I said, gently placing my bag on their enormous kitchen table. "Maybe some scary-looking dogs with spiked collars." My entire apartment could have fit inside this one room. With plenty of space to spare.

Everything was white. White counters, white cabinets, white tile backsplash behind a gigantic double oven that was probably made for hosting grand parties. I turned in a slow circle as I took everything in. All the appliances were new and everything was so clean, it was like I'd stepped into a catalog.

"No dogs. The security detail follows my mom," Grayson said. "Since she's out of town, we get to live like normal people for a bit. Even then, they're not here much."

Normal. Ha. This wasn't normal. But I didn't say anything as Grayson unceremoniously dumped his bag and coat on the table.

That was when his little sister traipsed into the kitchen. She was singing to herself and her braids swished around her as she walked. She stopped when she saw me.

"Hey, I know you," she said, tilting her head.

I guess I'd assumed the house was empty, since Grayson had to enter the code. But he'd set the alarm again after we'd entered, so maybe they lived with it on all the time.

If his sister was home, his dad probably was too. I didn't know whether to be disappointed or relieved that Grayson and I weren't alone. Honestly, it was probably a good thing. But my heart didn't seem to get the message.

His dad entered the kitchen a minute after Grayson's sister.

"Quinn, how nice to see you again," he said. I turned to say hi, but that was when I noticed he had a toddler on his hip. A toddler, as in Grayson had multiple siblings.

I was too stunned to say anything back. How could I, when everything was shifting around me?

"Uh, hi, Mr. Hawks," I finally stammered out. "Who's this?" I held my hand out for the little boy to give me a high five, which he did with gusto, making me smile.

"This is Levi," Grayson said, coming to stand by me. "And I don't think you've officially met Ava, even though you saw her at parents' night."

"Yessss," I said, dragging out the word. "I didn't know you had a younger brother too." It probably sounded a bit accusing, but that was the shock talking.

"Levi was sick that night," Mr. Hawks said, walking to the fridge and opening the door. "So his grandma came to watch him."

"Your grandma lives close by?" I asked Grayson, who nodded. Mentally, I was going through all the letters I'd shared with 15211 to remember whether he'd ever mentioned living close to his extended family. Nothing. That made me breathe a little easier.

"Grandma's the best," Ava said. "I wish I'd been sick that night. You both were boring."

"Way to be supportive," Grayson said, sitting at the table and unzipping his backpack. "Dad, Quinn and I are studying for our AP Government test. Is that okay?"

Like he needed to study. Grayson was the king of diplomatic speaking. I wondered if he got that from his mom.

My brain was still going a hundred miles a minute, when my phone chimed in my pocket. I took it out to read the text, hoping that maybe it was something that would ground me. It wasn't.

I vaguely heard Grayson's dad reply, but all my attention was focused on the text I'd just received from Carter.

> Ok, so don't laugh, but I've been taking cooking classes since pretty much the start of the school year.

Cooking classes. Carter was taking cooking classes? So I couldn't rule him out as 15211 either? What was happening? Another text came through and I stared at it numbly.

> So far I've only really cooked for my family. But the class is ending and they say we should each throw a party where we cook for all of our friends. I dunno. Sounded like it might be fun. You in? I was thinking sometime in the next month. You can invite whoever you want as long as I get a head count. My mom's complaining that you haven't been around here enough.

"You okay?" Grayson asked, his voice cutting through my haze. I looked up from my phone and sat down at the table with a thump. Grayson's dad and younger siblings had left the kitchen and I hadn't even noticed.

"What? Oh, yeah, I'm fine." I got out my AP Government notes with jerky robotic movements. "Did you know Carter was taking cooking classes?"

One of Grayson's eyebrows shot up. After a moment, he frowned. "I didn't."

"Yeah, he's throwing some kind of a party sometime. You want to go?"

I didn't know why I asked him. I wasn't even sure what I meant by it. Did I mean to ask him as just a friend? As a date? If I didn't know, how was Grayson supposed to figure it out? Besides, Carter wasn't exactly Grayson's number one fan. In thinking about it more, maybe that could explain my impulsiveness.

"I don't know, I'm not really invited." Grayson flipped through his AP Government book until he found the chapter we were studying.

"Carter said I could invite whoever I wanted, and I want to invite you."

At this, Grayson's frown turned into a smile and he leaned forward to rest his elbows on the table. My heart did a little flip. Traitorous heart. "See, my friendship plan is working. Already you hate me a little less."

"Who said I hate you? The only thing I hate is AP Government."

Grayson chuckled and pulled out some notecards and a pen.

"Okay, let's make some flash cards for you then. This test is going to focus on the Fourteenth Amendment, so we'll do some terms on one side with their definitions and implications on the back. Then we can study them on the bus ride to the tournament."

I sighed, but scooted my chair up to the table and leaned over to see what he wrote. But Grayson wasn't writing anything. His pen hovered over the notecard for a minute; then he dropped the pen to the table.

"You should write it," he said.

Alarm bells rang out in my mind and I narrowed my eyes at him.

"Why? You know the terms better. What if I put the wrong information on the flash cards?"

He picked up the pen and handed it to me. Our fingers brushed and I sucked in a breath.

"I'm not doing the work for you, lazy." He smiled. "If you write it, you'll retain the information better."

His explanation made sense, but I was still suspicious. I gave in and accepted the pen, uncapping it, vowing to catch a glance at his handwriting later. His, and Carter's. For being friends for so long, I'd never paid much attention before now.

"Have you ever taken dance lessons?" I asked abruptly.

Grayson sat back in surprise.

"What? Why?"

I knew it.

"You have, haven't you?" I accused. "I bet you know the waltz."

He chuckled and shook his head, but I wasn't about to let the subject drop.

"Admit it."

He held his hands up in front of him. "I've never taken dance lessons."

I scoffed. "Liar. If we were to call your dad back in here, would he verify your story?"

I expected him to look hesitant, or make excuses, but Grayson leaned back in his chair and put his hands behind his head.

"Go ahead. I don't know why it's so important to you, though."

I narrowed my eyes. "Yeah? I'm going to ask him."

This didn't faze him. He just made an "after you" gesture with his hand, motioning for me to continue.

I couldn't do it. It seemed rude somehow, to involve Grayson's dad to prove my own petty point.

Grayson noticed my indecision and laughed.

"Hey, Dad!" he yelled. My eyes widened.

So that was it, then. If he was calling his dad to verify his claim, he couldn't possibly be 15211. Something inside me twisted with that knowledge.

A minute later, his dad entered the kitchen again.

Grayson looked pointedly at me, waiting for me to say something.

"Uh, Mr. Hawks, has Grayson ever taken dance lessons?" I couldn't bring myself to meet his eyes. I wasn't sure how to categorize what I was feeling, but it wasn't what I'd expected.

Mr. Hawks laughed and clapped Grayson on the shoulder. "Well there's an idea." He shook his head. "No, Grayson's never taken dance lessons, but now that you mention it, I don't think he'd mind going with you."

Grayson coughed. I turned red. Once again, I was struck by how little Mr. Hawks seemed to know about teenagers.

"Thanks," I muttered.

Grayson's dad left again, chuckling the whole time. Soon, it was just Grayson and me, him relaxed and me filling up the room with enough awkwardness for the both of us.

"Why'd you want to know?" he asked.

I fiddled with the cap of the pen.

"No reason."

Grayson made a "hmmm" sound, then pushed the notecards toward me, pulling open his book at the same time.

"Let's start with selective incorporation and then we'll move on to the equal protection clause and *Roe v. Wade*." Grayson was still flipping through his book as I started writing out "selective incorporation"—

whatever that was. I looked up while I waited for Grayson to tell me what to put next. He was bent over his book, his hair falling into his face, framing his dark eyes.

I wasn't sure I'd ever figure him out. And I wasn't sure whether that was something I should even want in the first place.

Chapter Twenty-Three

Dear 15511,

I am so sorry. I mean that. If I could say it a thousand times,
I would.

I'm sorry.

I'm sorry.

I'm sorry.

I'm sorry.

I'm sorry.

I'm sorry.

I'm sorry.

I'm sorry.

I'm sorry.

I'm sorry.

I'm sorry.

I'm sorry.

I'm sorry.

I'm sorry.

I'm sorry.

I think you might get the idea and my hand is getting a cramp. I mean it, though. I really wanted to be there.

Something happened, and I wish I could tell you what. I wish I could explain everything so you wouldn't think I'm a bad person. Just know I wouldn't do anything to purposefully hurt you, and I still think only good things about you. None of that has changed. Can you forgive me? I know it's a lot to ask.

15211

P.S. I can share my AP Government notes with you. If you want.

He was lucky I'd just gotten a good score on my test, otherwise I might have not been in the best mood. But for the first time, with Grayson's help, I'd actually pulled off a miracle, so there wasn't much that could bring me down.

In a way, I had 15211 to thank for my good test result. Because he'd ghosted me, I'd gotten help from Grayson, and that certainly would not have happened without a little push. So I couldn't be mad now.

If anything, I was confused. He said something had happened, but what?

With an aggravated sigh, I folded the letter and put it in my bag before heading up to the speech and debate room. The state tournament was a little over a month away, and there was still so much we had to plan.

Grayson was waiting for me at the door.

"So?" he asked. "How'd you do on the test?"

We'd spent all of the bus ride home memorizing things from the note-cards, so it was no wonder he was curious. He'd helped me make a story out of the terms and civil cases, weaving them together in a way that made sense to my brain. I could memorize stories. That's what I was good at.

I held the paper out in front of me for his inspection. "Solid B," I said with a smile. "So we're getting there."

He held up his hand for a high five, which I gave.

"We can study again tomorrow if you're not sick of me yet. I can give you a ride after practice." He said the last part hesitantly, perhaps remembering all the times in the past I'd been so prickly about his offer.

I was supposed to hang out with Naomi. But I doubted she'd mind getting more Dax time instead. She'd probably give me an earful for hanging on to Grayson when she was rooting for 15211, but right now I was more inclined to ask for forgiveness than permission.

"Sure," I said quickly. Maybe too quickly. I didn't want to sound too eager. But the word was out now and I couldn't take it back. His returning smile made it worth it.

"Okay," he said, walking into the speech and debate room. "Good. So we have all the food figured out for the state meet that we're hosting, but we still need to follow up with them just in case. Plus, we need to make sure we have enough volunteers for judging. Coach Bates has the sign-ups on her computer, and we need to go through and make sure there will be enough when we factor in that a few will probably cancel last minute or forget to show up."

It was funny. Months ago, I'd thought co-captaining with Grayson would be the Worst Thing Ever. But it was nice to share the responsibilities with someone who actually followed through on whatever he promised. He was dependable, and I couldn't help but trust him in that respect. Could I trust him to not do something horrible to win the state tournament? I still had the walls around my heart, but Grayson kept chipping away at them, despite my best intentions.

"If you'll go over the volunteer lists, I'll call and reconfirm the food sponsors," Grayson offered. "Even though you're my competition, I don't want to actually kill you off, and I know how much you hate phone calls."

It was true. But I was still surprised he'd be willing to take that responsibility for himself.

"It's a deal," I said, holding out my hand for him to shake. I held on a little longer than was necessary, hoping Grayson wouldn't notice, before heading to the desk in the back where Coach Bates sat at her computer. Grayson pulled out his phone and left the room, probably so he could make the calls where it wasn't quite as loud.

Coach Bates saw me coming and pulled out a chair for me to sit beside her.

"Look at these numbers," she said, turning the computer screen to face me.

I wasn't sure what I was looking at, so I made a "hmmm" sound in hopes that I looked knowledgeable. She huffed.

"Quinn, these are your speech scores. If you keep performing this well, then that state championship is yours."

My chest squeezed, and I scooted closer to the computer screen.

"Just don't let anything distract you, you hear me?" Coach raised her eyebrows and looked pointedly toward the door, where Grayson had left only moments before. "This is a competition, Quinn. Sometimes it's not nice. Yes, I want you to be friendly with your teammates, but not too friendly, okay? I still remember what happened at the Arizona tournament."

I wanted to say, "You mean the tournament that I won?" but I held my tongue and nodded instead. Coach sighed.

"I know you. And I know you mean well. But I also know how distracted you get when you have too much on your plate, and I want to make sure you put your best foot forward at the state tournament. Not to mention the whole 'save the whales' speech you did. I don't know what kind of thing you had going on with Grayson in order for him to get you to sabotage your odds like that, but it wasn't a good choice for a competition, and you know that. He doesn't have your best interests at heart; he has his. Just like you should have yours." Coach fixed me with a solid stare.

"Now isn't the time for boys. Besides, teachers hear gossip too, and while I'm not going to comment on any of it, let's just say I think you'd be smart to keep your head in the game. Capiche?"

She'd probably meant for this little pep talk to be encouraging, but it was more like a pinprick to a balloon. The only thing I felt was deflated.

She was right. I remembered that first tournament, and how much I'd bombed. I couldn't afford to let that happen again. Not when I was this close. I'd fought so hard to get those scores on her screen. If Grayson wasn't playing fair, then making me lose at state would be his final play. I needed to win now more than ever.

"Capiche," I repeated. She smiled.

"Good girl. Now, here's where the volunteers are listed." She clicked on something and the list popped up on the screen. "Have at it."

I watched her walk away and let out a breath. Nothing was ever easy, it seemed.

I made my way through the list of volunteers, checking it against the time slots available and who said they could come when. When that was over, I walked around the room to see if anyone at practice needed my help. They didn't. We were far enough into the season now that people pretty much knew what they were doing.

I sat at the desk while I waited for Grayson to come back from making phone calls. Coach's words were on an endless loop in my mind. I really did need to focus and stop worrying so much about boys. *All* boys.

I pulled out a paper to write 15211 back. I'd keep it simple.

Dear 15211,

You're forgiven.

Honestly, maybe it's for the best that we didn't meet. I think we should probably keep it that way. I like things the way they are.

For now.

15511

P.S. I got a tutor. So your offer is appreciated, but I'll take it from here.

* * *

MY PHONE DINGED later that night, and I'd never known one little email could hold that much power over me until I saw the notification flash across my screen.

I forgot all about my computer and the homepage banner I was updating for my mom's photography business. I threw my phone down, pushing my chair away from my desk. I didn't even realize I'd yelled until my mom barged through my door with a frying pan, à la Rapunzel in *Tangled*.

"What? What is it?" She looked panicked, her eyes searching the room like she expected to find an intruder hiding behind my curtains.

I pointed to my phone. "I just got an email. From Boise State University."

Her expression changed instantly and she brought the frying pan in front of her, clasping the handle with both hands like a prayer. "What did it say?"

I swallowed.

"I didn't open it."

Opening it would have consequences. It would make their decision—whatever it was—real.

My mom sat on the edge of my bed, setting the frying pan aside and tucking her fingers under her legs.

"Well?" She motioned toward my phone with her chin. "What are you waiting for?"

I held my phone out to her.

"You read it. I can't."

She shook her head. "This is your moment. You can't let your mom steal your thunder."

My outstretched hand shook as I brought it back to my chest. "What if it's a no?"

She pursed her lips, which didn't make me feel any better. "You'll only know if you open it."

My heart hammered in my rib cage as I unlocked my phone and opened my email. My finger hovered over the unopened message uncertainly for a moment before finally clicking down.

"*Congrats, Quinn,*" I read aloud. "*I am so excited to tell you that you've been admitted to Boise State University—*"

My mom started screaming and suffocated me in a hug before I could utter another word.

"Mom, I still need to breathe," I gasped into her hair.

"You're in! You're in!" She jumped up and down, refusing to let go, so I was forced to bob along in my chair or risk losing my head. I wasn't sure whether I was laughing or crying, but my mom was making enough noise for the both of us.

She released me and put her hands on my shoulders. "How does it feel?"

I looked back down at my phone, my eye catching the logo at the top of the email in a way that made everything seem more real. I scanned it again. "It doesn't say anything about financial aid."

She looked at my phone and pointed to the orange button at the bottom of the email. "See, it says 'Next Steps' and I'm sure that will have the information you need. Whatever it is, we'll make it work. But for now, we celebrate!"

I stroked the edge of my phone, the lines of it starting to blur in my vision. It was the good news I needed to hear. With my love life in shambles, the state speech competition looming, and things with Carter being more awkward than a bad *American Idol* contestant, this was a bright spot for sure.

"I can't believe I got in." I smiled up at my mom and she squeezed my shoulder.

"How could you not? You're the most talented kid I know."

"You have to say that; you're my mom."

"Have I mentioned lately that you're my favorite child?"

I shook my head and laughed. "I'm your only child."

She shrugged, like she always did. She brushed my hair back with her hand and leaned down to kiss my forehead.

"It's still true. And it always will be. Now"—she stood up—"let's go eat pie."

Chapter Twenty-Four

Considering that Carter had organized his cooking party to be on Valentine's Day, having Grayson pick me up made it feel very much like a date, which it wasn't. I had to keep reminding myself of that or I'd run away with the idea. As for why Carter had put it on Valentine's Day, well, I had my thoughts about that, and I didn't like them.

Grayson and I walked to his car and I spied a covered dish sitting on the front seat when I opened the door.

"Why are you bringing something?" I asked. "The whole point is that he's supposed to cook for us."

My mom waved from the doorway, and I smiled back. She was *all* for this being a date, as she'd mentioned to me this morning. Several times.

I placed Grayson's dish in my lap so I could sit down and buckle my seat belt. It was covered in foil, so I couldn't see its contents, but I was dying of curiosity.

"Because it's polite to bring something," Grayson said, settling into the driver's seat and starting the engine. "And if he's just learning how to cook, I want to make sure there's at least one edible thing there."

I slapped his arm and he grinned. I wanted to reach out and hold his hand—an impulse I'd been fighting way too much lately during all our study sessions or at speech meets—and I was glad we wouldn't be the only ones at this event tonight. I needed buffers. Naomi and Dax were coming for a bit before they went and did some separate Valentine's Day plans, and Carter had invited a few other friends as well.

I still had Coach's warning firm in my mind. Sometimes it was slippery, was all. But the fact that Coach had seconded Carter's warning, well, that was troubling. I knew what rumors she was talking about. They were the same ones I'd known about all along. Was it too much to hope that maybe I was the exception to Grayson's thirst for winning?

I gave Grayson directions to Carter's house and tried not to worry about what might be awaiting us there. Was I being rude for *not* bringing a side dish? Would Carter make some kind of grand romantic gesture and expect me to finally fall in love with him once and for all? Things had almost been normal between us, and I didn't want to fall backward.

By the time we pulled into Carter's driveway, I'd managed to think myself into a full-on panic. Dax's truck was already there, but I still hesitated in getting out of the car. Grayson took his dish from my hands and we made our way up the front steps. Naomi yanked open the door before we'd even knocked.

"About time," she said. "I've been here for a whole minute and a half already."

"So sorry to keep you waiting." Grayson grinned. "That must have been torture."

I liked that Naomi got along with Grayson. It wasn't like we'd ever become a couple, but as long as we were trying this whole "friends" thing out, it was nice that he got along with my best one. True, he and Carter butted heads sometimes, but that was bound to happen with someone like Carter. Carter was so brash he often polarized people, but usually we evened each other out. I could get him to scale things back, and he got me to think big. It'd been that way as long as I could remember.

"Ooh, what'd you bring?" Naomi reached out and took the dish from Grayson, peeking under the tinfoil as she turned around to walk back inside. We followed, taking our shoes off in the front entryway.

"They're mini quiche," Grayson said nonchalantly, like it was no big deal. Maybe he ate them all the time. The closest I got to mini quiche on a regular basis was Hot Pockets.

"Fancy," I said, following after Naomi.

"Not really," he said, joining us. "It's mostly egg, and I used store-bought pie crusts."

"You made them yourself?" I stopped and turned to face him.

One half of Grayson's mouth quirked up in a smile as he brushed past me toward the kitchen. He turned and walked backward, maintaining eye contact. "I'm a man of many talents." He laughed and turned back around. I followed silently.

"You cook too, Grayson?" Naomi clapped her hands. "You know what this means. A cook-off!"

We'd made it to the kitchen, where Carter was pulling something out of the oven. He straightened quickly, mischief written all over his face. He never did back down from any kind of bet.

"A cook-off?" He put down the tray and the oven mitts he'd been wearing.

Grayson set his dish on the counter and held up his hands. "No worries, man. I only brought the one thing to satisfy my mom's etiquette rules. I'm not planning on stealing your thunder today."

Carter cocked an eyebrow. "Maybe you're scared I'd win."

Grayson folded his arms across his chest. "Is that a challenge?"

Naomi squealed and started rooting through one of the kitchen drawers for something. She came back up with an extra apron, which she started tying around Grayson's waist until he swatted her hands away and took over.

It was an endearing look. Grayson, with a frilly blue apron, rolling his sleeves and pushing up his glasses like this meant war.

Dax was over in the corner with a few other people I recognized from school, and he looked up to see what the fuss was about. They all went back to their conversation a beat later.

"Okay, here's the deal," Carter said. "I'll need two desserts for tonight. We can each do one. Quinn will be the judge. I trust her to be impartial since she's friends with both of us."

This was so not fair. I opened my mouth to say so, but Grayson spoke over me.

"Deal."

I swallowed. This was clearly a no-win situation for me. No matter who I picked as the winner, I would come out the loser.

Naomi came to my side and navigated me to sit at one of the counter barstools. I did so rigidly. She sat on the stool next to me and continued to chat while Grayson and Carter picked out their ingredients. I could barely pay her any attention.

"How're things going with your mystery pen pal?" Grayson asked while cracking eggs into a bowl. I widened my eyes and motioned for him to keep quiet, but it was too late.

"Mystery pen pal?" Carter asked. "You haven't told me anything about a mystery pen pal." His stirring slowed as he put chocolate chips into his bowl.

Grayson looked shocked, then pleased. "You didn't tell Carter?" he asked. His smile was so big it could have split his face in two. He made a zipper motion across his lips, sealing the secret in. Fat lot of good that would do now.

I sighed and tapped my fingers on the counter, debating the best way to spill my secret.

"It's really not a huge deal," I said. It certainly felt less so the more time it went on without going anywhere. Naomi raised her eyebrows, clearly challenging my assessment of the situation.

I considered keeping things under wraps, even now. But then, maybe it'd be good for Carter to think there was someone else on my mind, even if I knew I wasn't going to do anything about it for a while. At least until after the state competition in two weeks. I was all about the focus lately.

"We've been exchanging letters for a while now, but I don't know who he is. Ms. Navarrete switched our assignments once by accident and we just kept writing to each other."

Grayson and Carter were silent as they worked on their desserts, but I could tell they were both listening intently.

"Then we were supposed to meet like a month ago, but that never happened." I shifted my weight on the barstool. "But we still exchange letters and he seems decent."

Carter was watching me. "So you were supposed to meet, and what happened? He didn't show?"

I shook my head.

"What excuse did he give for that?"

Even though Carter hadn't sounded accusing, Naomi jumped to 15211's defense, as she always did whenever I questioned things.

"He said he had something come up. Give him a break. His apology was, like, A-plus material."

"She's seen the letters?" Carter asked, pointing to Naomi. I couldn't read his expression, but I wanted to. If he was 15211, what would he think about Naomi reading the words between us?

Another thought struck me then. If Carter was 15211, then this would let him know I was on the other end of the letters, which was probably brand-new information for him. I analyzed his face for any signs of surprise, acceptance, or even excitement, but it was completely blank, like he was some kind of robot.

"She's seen some of them," I said, as noncommittally as possible. There were some I hadn't coughed up, wanting to keep things more private. Being the best friend she was, she hadn't pushed.

But could 15211 really be Carter? My mystery pen pal had been super flirty, and Carter probably wouldn't be flirting with me in real life if he had a girl he was writing to on the side. Then again, maybe that was why he was dropping hints like the fact that he cooked. Maybe he'd figured out I was on the other end and now he was upping his game. I honestly had no way to tell, and the more I thought about it, the more my head went in circles.

"He's totally boyfriend material," Naomi said, looking meaningfully at me as she said it. Her motive was clear. She knew how much Carter's flirting had bothered me lately, and this was her trying to clue him into the fact. But she hadn't clued into the fact that Carter was back in the running as a potential 15211 candidate since he was here cooking, so saying he was boyfriend material might actually backfire.

"You should ask to meet again," Grayson said. "See what he says."

"I dunno." I chewed on my lower lip. "It didn't work out so well the first time, and I don't want to risk it."

"Wait, are you saying you actually like this guy?" Carter asked. He stopped stirring and the spoon slid into the bowl, but Carter didn't seem to notice.

What I'd give for a mood ring right about now, or something that'd give me some hint of Carter's feelings. I'd have to tread carefully.

Carter looked over at Grayson, perhaps gauging his reaction to my pronouncement, but Grayson was busy cutting apples for his dessert.

"It's . . . it's probably nothing," I stammered. "I mean, he hasn't asked to meet me again, and it's not like anything will come of it if it hasn't already. Honestly, I don't even know anymore." Not to mention I'd been the one trying to hit the brakes on things. I'd only hit the accelerator when things had gone south with Grayson, so 15211 was probably getting whiplash, poor guy.

"Sorry, Carter," Naomi said. "But her heart's taken. As her best friend, I can tell."

I winced, but neither Carter nor Grayson showed much reaction to this statement.

Carter pursed his lips, considering. "What types of things does he write in these letters? Maybe you should show them to me. We could analyze them together."

"We talk about anything and everything," I said, ignoring his hidden request. "Our parents, school, college, whatever happens to be on our minds."

"Speaking of college," Carter said. He looked down at his bowl, slowly scraping some of the batter from the sides with a spatula. "Have you heard back from your dream college?"

Yes, I was a horrible friend who'd kept my acceptance to myself because I knew he'd go off on another rant like he had earlier. I hated that our friendship had gotten so complicated lately. It never used to be like this, but lately, I walked on eggshells anytime he was around.

"I got in."

Carter still didn't know I'd be sticking around this area. I didn't want to get his hopes up. Naomi already knew which school I'd been wanting, and I'd probably tell Grayson later. It was strange to think he actually did feel like a friend, like someone I could share those details with and know they'd only think well of me. It might have been naive, but I couldn't help but trust him, despite what everyone else said.

Carter was my friend too, but the kind that thought he knew what was best for me. Sometimes he was right, like when he pointed out Grayson wasn't being completely honest, so it was hard to discount his opinion all the time.

"Congratulations!" Grayson said, looking up from what he was doing. He seemed genuinely happy for me, the corners of his eyes crinkling behind his glasses and a huge smile in place.

"Yeah, now I need to keep my grade up in AP Government, no biggie. Oh, and secure some financial aid to help. Sorry, Grayson, but I'm totally planning on taking you down at the state competition in two weeks to get that scholarship."

That last part was to change the topic, but it was also for Carter's benefit. I hated doing it, but he wasn't taking any of my hints and I didn't like being outright mean to my friend.

Grayson waved my comment away. "You know that will probably happen anyway. You've been beating me at all the latest tournaments. And you've been doing great in AP Government, so you've got this in the bag."

His comment made me feel all warm and fuzzy, which wasn't a good sign. I had to turn away. I shouldn't rely on him to boost my ego when he was my competitor. I shouldn't care what he thought either.

Naomi tackled me in a side hug, then turned to address everyone else in the room. "Best Valentine's Day ever. My best friend got accepted into her dream college and we're having a cook-off!"

"More like a bake-off," I said, motioning to the counter. "Technically, cooking and baking are different things."

She shrugged, then stole a chocolate chip from Carter's batter. Dax came to where we were sitting and gave me a high five before wrapping his arms around Naomi from behind.

"Way to go, Quinn." He kissed the top of Naomi's head and I was hit with a sudden ache.

I looked up to find Grayson watching me, so I quickly averted my gaze to the desserts they were making. Grayson was making apple crisp while Carter had opted for some kind of giant deep-dish cookie pie that he was going to bake in a skillet. Both of them looked amazing, so that made my life more complicated than it needed to be.

They argued for a bit about whose would go in the oven first, but Grayson eventually won out because his would take longer to bake. He smiled at the victory, the same smile he wore whenever he beat me at something. He obviously loved winning and it didn't matter what it was he won. The question mark in my mind grew a size or two. Was Grayson setting me up to fail?

True, we were competitors. But really, what did that matter if you liked being with someone? Grayson might see things the same way, if I gave him the chance.

Maybe, after the state tournament, I'd know for sure. That wasn't so long from now, only two weeks away.

I chewed on my nail while Grayson put his apple crisp in the oven.

Soon, I'd have to make a choice. About so many things.

Chapter Twenty-Five

*G*rayson was shaking his head at me. "I still can't believe you picked Carter's burnt cookie thing over my dessert. I thought you had good taste."

He turned onto my street and I fingered the edge of the foil that covered his leftover apple crisp. We'd eaten all the mini quiche, so Carter had put the leftover apple crisp in that dish. There wasn't much left, but I still wondered if Grayson would let me take the rest home. It'd been that good. I'd had a hard time keeping all my salivating in check enough to lie through my teeth to proclaim Carter the winner of the bake-off.

"I think this is proof that you still don't really like me all that much," Grayson said, which actually made me laugh out loud. That was so not my problem. Not anymore at least.

"You know yours was better," I said. "You didn't need my verdict to know that."

"Oho!" Grayson abruptly pulled over to the curb and parked his car.

We still weren't in front of my apartment yet. "You're admitting you outright lied to make your friend the winner?"

"You're my friend too."

"Hmmm." He put his hand on my headrest, and turned to face me. I stopped breathing. I wanted so badly to reach over, bring his face close to mine, and kiss him.

But I didn't. Because with the state tournament still looming over us, he was still my biggest competition. He could still break my heart.

I slapped his arm playfully, because I had no idea what I was doing, or what I was *supposed* to be doing right now. Was I supposed to flirt? Push him away? There needed to be some kind of manual for this type of situation.

"You didn't need the ego boost," I told him. "Everyone was pretty unanimous in loving your dessert. But did you see how crushed Carter looked when everyone was agreeing yours was better?"

"Mmmhmm." He was smiling. "Just admit it, I'm growing on you."

A little too much. Apparently all my trying to act cool and distant was about as ineffective as the hand dryers in the school bathrooms. Soon, he'd know about my feelings either way, so I might as well be the one to tell him. Right?

"How're things going with you and that girl you like?" I asked. Such a smooth transition. Could I be more hopeless?

Grayson's smile got even wider. "Pretty good actually." He started the car again and pulled onto the street while I tried not to let my disappointment show on my face. If he really liked this other girl so much, he should stop flirting with me all the time. That was just common courtesy. Maybe I really was right to not trust him. This was the same thing, and same girl, he'd been talking to Carter about months ago, so was I that much a glutton for punishment that I'd put myself in the exact situation for a second time?

Apparently.

"What's her name?" I wasn't even trying to be casual anymore. I knew it was desperate, but really, what was I supposed to do?

Grayson shook his head. "Nope, I'm not saying any names until you can tell me the name of your secret crush."

"But I don't even know his name. You know as much as I do."

This comment made him laugh. I never realized before how much I liked hearing it.

He looked over at me briefly, and I self-consciously tucked a piece of hair behind my ear.

"Back in Arizona . . ." He swallowed. "You said you didn't trust me."

I bit my lower lip, but didn't say anything.

Grayson's voice was low as he said, "Can I ask why? And not just the stunt that Carter pulled to make you hate me. I want the full reason."

I sucked in a breath. This was the moment of truth. If I told him the real reason I didn't trust him, what would he do with that information? How would he take it?

"Sometimes—" I started, but paused. I took a breath. "Sometimes I worry you're only being nice to me to get close to me. Then, right before the finals round at the state meet, you'll do something, I don't know, just something, that will shake my confidence or ruin my chances somehow so that you can win. Like people say you did with Zara."

What had possessed me to say the truth? My hands flew up to my mouth and I stifled a gasp. But I turned to him with open eyes, hoping he'd be able to deny the rumors that had been circulating about him for so long.

But he didn't.

The longer he was silent, the more my confidence in him waned.

He sat there for a full minute without saying a word, and then he nodded. "So to earn your trust, I have to prove to you that I'll still be your friend, even after you beat me at state?"

I gave a low, uncertain laugh.

Grayson nodded. "I can do that. Just you wait. Two weeks. I'll be patient."

His comment made goose bumps rise along my arm. My butterflies came back in full force, but I reminded those butterflies that Grayson had said *friend* and that he was interested in someone else. And so was I. Maybe? I didn't even know anymore.

"I still think you should ask to meet him again," Grayson said, his thoughts obviously following the same path mine had taken.

I sighed.

"Maybe this time will be different."

He pulled up to my apartment complex and parked the car. I didn't open the door, not wanting to leave quite yet. I unbuckled my seat belt and turned to face him.

"I live in the land of reality," I said. "Dreams are great and all, but maybe it's better to accept the facts and move on."

Nothing was working out the way I wanted it to, when it came to my love life at least.

"That's pretty pessimistic, don't you think?"

I shrugged. "Pessimism, optimism, I don't know. I can't help hoping for the happily ever after even though I know it doesn't really happen all that often."

His eyes were soft as he considered me. "I don't think that's true. I mean, you got accepted into your dream college, didn't you?"

It was sweet that he was trying to cheer me up, but the news he'd delivered about things going well with his crush basically made it so I couldn't think positively even if I tried. I shifted my weight so I was leaning against the car door and facing him.

I shrugged. It was time to steer the conversation away from me. I was pretty sure if I let this continue, I'd spill all my feelings for Grayson, even though *that* was a mistake. "Do you know where you're going yet?"

He ran a hand through his hair. "If my mom had her way, I'll be shipped off to Princeton to study politics, literally following in her footsteps."

I waited without saying anything, sensing there was more.

"I haven't heard back from Princeton yet," he said. "But I may or may not have sent in an incredibly awful essay in an attempt to sabotage my chances."

This made me smile. "Really?"

He nodded.

"Why don't you tell your mom you don't want to go there?"

He raised his eyebrows and tilted his head to the side. "You've met her. You try telling her your own plan when she has something else in mind. She's like a force of nature."

I didn't have a response to that, which made Grayson laugh.

"Okay," I said. "So, if you don't want to study politics, what do you want to major in?"

Grayson drew in a breath and let it out. "Maybe one of these days I'll tell you."

I smacked his arm again. "So full of secrets! You never tell me anything."

"That's not true," he said. "I tell you more than I tell anyone else."

My heart grew about twenty sizes with that revelation. I could feel it swell inside me, almost as much as I could feel the blush creeping across my cheeks.

"Really?" I knew my smile was impossibly big, but I didn't care. It was funny how my emotions could go on such a roller coaster within only a few minutes. Well, maybe *funny* wasn't the word for it. "Will you at least tell me where you want to go?"

He paused, then said "Boise State" in a rush.

"No way! That's where I'm going. To study marketing."

Truthfully, I always pictured him in a place like Princeton or Harvard. If you had the money and grades, why wouldn't you take that opportunity?

"Really?" Grayson brought a hand to the back of his neck. "I've never wanted to go to school in the east. I've visited a few times with my mom, and everything is so different. The culture, education, everything. I think if anything, my mom's taught me to love Idaho a little too much, because I can't imagine leaving. I like the pace here. Plus, why waste that much money on an Ivy League education if I don't even want it? Lots of other people would kill for that spot, so I say, let them have it."

"What will you do if you get in to Princeton?" I asked.

"Hide my acceptance letter from my mom." He laughed.

"She seems like the type of parent who'd have access to your email. Maybe she's already set up a filter to forward college emails to her own account."

"She's in meetings enough that hopefully I can delete it before she ever sees it."

"Solid plan." I nodded. "It's not like she'll ask you about it or anything."

He sighed. "I know. Eventually, I'm going to have to face her. It's not that she's unreasonable. She's just . . . well, you said it best. She's intimidating. She has a lot of expectations for me, and I respect her opinion and don't want to let her down. My grandparents came from nothing and my mom expects me to make something of myself just like she has. The American dream and all that. She's worked too hard for me to have a better life for me to throw it all away."

"It's not throwing it away if you have a different dream," I murmured. But I was barely paying attention to the conversation anymore, because I was thinking back to how 15211 had mentioned his parents wanting him to become the next president of the United States. Grayson's mom wanted him to be a politician, and those two things were pretty close. I couldn't remember the rest of the letter off the top of my head, it had been so long ago, but I looked over at Grayson to see if maybe there was something else he wasn't telling me.

Grayson couldn't be 15211. That was wishful thinking. His own father had put the kibosh on that idea when he said Grayson had never taken dancing lessons. You couldn't get more direct than that.

The fact of the matter was, Grayson was my competition, and it was time I started acting like it.

Sometimes coaches really did know what was best.

Chapter Twenty-Six

My brain officially was done. I couldn't have added two and two even if my life depended on it. Naomi and I had crashed at my apartment after finishing the ACT that morning, and I was still experiencing aftershocks of stress. Technically I didn't need to take it, since I'd already gotten my college acceptance letter. But some scholarships required a higher score, and I was hoping to increase my chances at them. Even if I was now brain-dead. I'd made Naomi promise we wouldn't do anything that would involve actual thinking, so now we were sprawled out on my bed, staring at nothing. I could tell it was getting to Naomi, though, because she kept unlocking her phone, like maybe this time there'd be something for her to look at. She'd always been better at testing than me, as was evidenced by the fact that I was still seeing fill-in-the-space bubbles floating in my mind.

"Listen to this," she said, shoving an earbud at me. It was hooked up to her phone, and as I brought it to my ear, she hit play. I wasn't familiar with the music, but it was catchy. Still not catchy enough when my brain was running on empty. I handed the earbud back.

"Nice," I said noncommittally.

"It's this new band from Australia and I think they're going to be huge," she gushed. When I didn't respond right away, she kicked my leg. "Seriously, Quinn, you're boring. We have to do something." She sighed and flopped over so she was lying on her stomach. "Let's get a group together to hang out."

I grunted and barely raised my head from the pillow. "No people. I can't people."

She flounced off my bed and walked over to my desk, sitting down on the chair and flipping through the various papers, books, and magazines I had there. I left her to it, and rearranged the pillow under my head.

"I don't think you showed me this letter," I heard her say. Her voice wasn't accusing, just curious. I sat up to see which one she held.

"Oh, yeah. That's an older one."

I didn't say anything else as she read. I just sat there, suddenly alert and awake despite all the hours of testing I'd had to endure earlier today. My knee bounced up and down, and I was torn between snatching the letter from her hands and waiting with bated breath to see what she thought. I knew the letter she held. It'd been one I'd purposefully kept to myself because it was almost too perfect to be real and I didn't want anyone to burst the bubble.

It was one of my favorites, from when we'd played our own version of twenty questions that didn't lead to only one answer but a wealth of information about 15211 that I occasionally dreamed about. It described his views on education and politics, how he didn't like the color orange because it reminded him of Halloween, and, most importantly, how he thought I was funny.

I totally wasn't funny. I was a neurotic mess sometimes, too much of a control freak, and entirely out of my element 90 percent of the time. But 15211 didn't see all those things. The way he often described me in his letters was like he recognized only the good things and couldn't even see the bad. He thought I was smart and witty, and in the letters, I was. I had time to think up clever responses, while in real life I only thought of the perfect thing to say ten minutes after the conversation had already ended.

Naomi turned to face me and started fanning herself with the letter. "Girl, tell me again why you haven't met this guy yet?"

Our letters weren't *that* spicy that she needed to fan herself. It wasn't like he declared his undying love for me or anything. I sat back against my headrest and let out a breath.

"I guess we haven't had it work out."

Naomi came and practically jumped back on the bed. "You need to change that, ASAP."

"We tried it once, remember? He didn't show up." And the more I thought about things, the more I worried 15211 was a figment of my imagination, that his reality couldn't match up with the fantasy I'd built up in my head. The longer this drew on, the more I was convinced it simply wasn't meant to be. The longer it took, the more Grayson replaced 15211 in my mind, despite the fact I knew he liked someone else and it wouldn't work.

I still liked the idea of 15211. But the reality, well, that was becoming fuzzier with every passing day, and I found it really didn't matter who 15211 was, because he wasn't Grayson.

Naomi waved the letter in my face. "Hello! This guy is practically perfect. I'm in a relationship and even I think so. Why don't you see it? You don't let a guy like that slip through your fingers."

"It's complicated," I said. "And yes, I'm aware that that's the lamest line in all of history, thank you very much."

Naomi rolled her eyes. "Is this about Grayson? You were right to put that on a permanent hiatus, and I totally support that decision. Now you have to stand by it. But this letter guy." She breathed a dreamy sigh. "I don't want to see you mess this one up."

I rolled over and pulled the pillow over my head. Naomi yanked it off, so I covered the back of my head with my arms, as if they'd be any sort of protection against Naomi's truth bombs.

"Come on, you need to stop mooning over Grayson already. It's been months since you two kissed."

"Thanks for the reminder. I *am* moving on. I'm keeping busy. Or did you not see how well my mom's business has been doing on Instagram lately?"

"If anything, that shows how much you *aren't* moving on, because you're just throwing yourself into that as a distraction."

"I thought best friends were supposed to be supportive and helpful and all that," I mumbled through the mouthful of bedding around my face.

"That's what I'm doing," she said. "Being helpful by getting you to realize how perfect 15211 is for you." She poked my side and I jerked away, still keeping my face buried in the sheets.

What was it about people who were in relationships always trying to play matchmaker? Did they think the rest of us were miserable simply because we weren't with someone? I still had my friends, speech and debate, and, you know, my whole life to live. When faced with the idea of getting rejected by 15211 *again*, or simply keeping everything the same, I was quite content to wait this one out. Besides, I had Coach's orders.

Naomi walked to my desk and rooted through everything until she found a notepad and pen. Then she tossed them on the bed, an inch away from my head. I sat up with a sigh.

"You're going to ask him to meet. I'm doing this because I love you," she said, pushing the notebook even closer. "Besides, maybe it'd do Grayson good to see he has some serious competition."

I begrudgingly picked up the pen and wrote another letter to 15211, asking him if maybe he'd want to meet me again.

I didn't plan on giving it to him.

Chapter Twenty-Seven

*T*wo weeks later, I put the letter in 15211's cubby because the suspense was finally getting to me. I did it after speech practice on Thursday, when no one from school, especially Naomi, would see what I'd done. I didn't need Naomi questioning me all the time whether he'd written back. It was easier for her to think I still hadn't given him the letter. And I was still obeying Coach, because there was no way I'd be able to meet him before the state competition was over. I was still waiting for the other shoe to drop with Grayson, but he'd also been pressuring me into meeting 15211, so that meant he really wasn't interested in me. I needed to accept that.

All day Friday, I tried to ignore the urge to check my cubby incessantly, because the state competition was finally here and I needed to focus. I'd promised myself, and Coach.

That first day of the tournament, I was a good girl and I didn't look.

So much was riding on this now. On me. I felt it in every step I took.

Like a bolt of lightning, it infused all my actions with purpose. Each time I presented my speech, I delivered it with precision.

My teammates could tell I was dialed in. No one talked to me once they saw I had earbuds in, which I did anytime I wasn't actively competing. The music drowned everything else out and kept me from dwelling too much on all the possibilities. The possibility of failure. Of defeat. Of all this work amounting to nothing. Those things crept in on the corners of my vision every time I allowed myself a moment to think, so I pretended they didn't exist.

The energy was palpable in the air. The judges were actually excited to be there, and the students more so.

Every student competing was doing their best, so I had to be even better.

I was a torpedo, and nothing could keep me from my target. Not even the knowledge that in all likelihood I had a letter waiting for me. That was another possibility I tried to ignore for as long as possible.

Until it became impossible.

On the second day, I had a round that took place in the AP Government room and I couldn't hold out any longer. *Looking* wasn't disobeying my coach. Because I'd be meeting him after state.

It was *right there*, calling to me. I could see there was something in my cubby. It was there, and I had to read it.

I grabbed the letter and then went to the hallway, where I opened it with shaky fingers, hoping I wasn't making a terrible mistake that would destroy my concentration for the rest of the competition. That had been the whole goal of pushing both 15211 and Grayson away lately, after all.

> Dear Quinn,
>
> Don't freak out.
>
> Whatever you do, please promise me you'll read to the end.
>
> You'll notice I used your name and not your number. Yes, I know

who you are, but I swear I haven't known all that long, and I wanted to tell you. I really, really did.

But I couldn't. Because if I told you who I was, I was pretty sure you'd want nothing to do with me. Maybe that's selfish, but I had to have you in my life, even if only in letters.

We've been writing to each other for months now, and I've been surprised by how much I've come to rely on it—on you. You make me laugh when I'm down, you make me look outside myself, and most importantly, you give me something to look forward to each and every day. Even if it's only a short sentence or two, it makes me smile. I've kept every single letter.

When I got your first note, I had no idea I'd come to fall for the girl writing it. But I'll come right out and say it now so there is no confusion.

I like you.

And I'd hate for you to walk away without knowing that.

Which is why I'm so glad you finally asked to meet me again. I've been waiting for that. Because after I didn't show up last time, I didn't know if you'd ever trust me again. And I had to wait until I at least thought you might give me a chance.

Please give me a chance. To explain everything, and hopefully to change things between us in a more-than-friends kind of way.

Again, don't freak out. I promise I'm not a creep. I just don't know how to say what I've been bottling up for so long now without sounding desperate. I'm trying to put everything into words, but everything I write comes out sounding wrong. Lately *it seems we've been circling around things without ever actually coming right out and saying it.*

I'm tired of circling. I don't want you to have any excuse to mis-interpret what I've said. I need you to hear it. I need to know how you feel. Which is why I'm sounding like a complete fool right now by repeating myself and being so blunt when I'd rather hide away about now.

I know you have the state speech and debate tournament this weekend. All the students here will get out early today so that our school can host it.

Is it weird to say I'm proud of you for making state? That takes a lot of work and it's really impressive.

I want to celebrate with you. In person. I think that's where we should meet, especially since it's here. I can come on Saturday after it's all over and we can go out after. That way I won't be a distraction to you and you can focus on competing, rather than who I am. If we go out after, I'll have time to explain everything and it won't take up time during your tournament.

I'll wear a red scarf so you know who I am. I'll find you.

Please say yes.

15211

The state tournament started yesterday. This was the final day, and he sprung this on me now? He had to know I wouldn't get his letter right away. I hadn't even come into the AP Government room on Fri-day for class because everyone on the speech team got the whole day off instead of only the last couple of hours. I'd avoided this room like my life depended on it.

I knew I shouldn't have looked. Coach had been right. My concentration was nonexistent now.

Here I was, all dressed up, with only a half an hour before the finals round, and this announcement of his was supposed to make me feel *more* focused because we'd be meeting after the awards ceremony? Now was the time I needed to focus more than ever.

I paced the hallway. There was so much to dissect from this letter. The biggest bombshell of all was that 15211 knew who I was. He knew who I was, and he still liked me. That realization made me feel all kinds of fluttery and dread at the same time. My stomach kept flipping over and over and I swallowed hard. This could all go so wrong.

I liked somebody else.

Reading this letter, everything became concrete in my mind. I couldn't meet up with 15211 with him hoping for something more when I had feelings for Grayson. That wasn't fair to 15211, no matter who he was. I still felt something for 15211, but it didn't feel solid. Not in the way Grayson did. No matter what orders I'd been given, it didn't change how I felt. I'd been waiting for finals to be over so I could finally stop listening to everyone else telling me not to trust him, but the fact was, I *did* trust Grayson. I trusted him not to use me, or set me up for failure. I trusted him to put my needs and wants before his own. Because that was what he'd always done.

I sat against the wall and stared down at the floor. It didn't have any answers.

Perhaps the biggest disappointment was that this letter meant 15211 really wasn't Grayson. I already knew that, from when he said he'd never taken dancing lessons, but this was even more evidence. Because of course Grayson knew about the state tournament and wouldn't feel the need to tell me he was proud of me or what a big accomplishment that was. He was here too. How could it be a big accomplishment if he'd done the same thing? Even Carter was here.

Besides, neither of them had been treating me any differently lately. Neither of them came in today wearing a red scarf. And if 15211 was on the speech team, he would have mentioned wearing a tie or something instead. No one wore scarves inside, and if he was planning on being inside all day for the competition, that wouldn't have been on his mind.

Was I reading too much into everything? Probably. But it was what I was best at, and too much was going on for me to stop now.

There wasn't time to process everything before I heard footsteps coming down the hallway. I looked up to see Carter coming my way and I scrambled to my feet, heartbeat still beating overtime in my ribs. The letter was limp and folded up in my hand, but I couldn't bring myself to put it away entirely.

"The lists are up," he said. He was smiling, which could only mean one thing.

"You made it into finals?"

He nodded, then scooped me into a hug, twirling me around in the hallway. I squealed in protest, but didn't put up a fight. He deserved to be happy about this. His position had been iffy, so breaking into finals was a big deal. There was a corner of my mind that said if he was 15211, I shouldn't be leading him on by hugging him right now. But this last letter made all that seem so improbable, I brushed the thought aside.

He put me down and pulled out his phone, showing me the picture he'd saved there. It was the paper with all our competition codes assigned to our finals room. He pointed to his number, which was set to go right before mine. I somehow managed to score the coveted last spot in the lineup, which was great for having judges remember you, but not so great for my nerves. I'd have to spend the entire round wondering who 15211 was, and what I was going to do about Grayson.

I needed to resolve all this sooner rather than later. Coach was wrong. I couldn't handle all the waiting. This was worse. If I had to wait through the whole round, and then the awards ceremony later, all without know-ing? I really might combust.

I couldn't do anything about 15211. Not yet. I couldn't tell him I'd fallen for someone else, no matter how much I wanted to. But I could tell that someone else, and then at least I'd know, one way or another. Like 15211 had mentioned, I was tired of all this circling. I needed to land, even if it was a crash. At least that way I could pick up the pieces and move on once and for all.

If I told Grayson how I felt now, before the finals round, he'd know I trusted him. I needed him to know that.

I needed to talk with Grayson before I met 15211, but most of all, I needed to talk to Grayson before finals started.

I took the letter and shoved it into my bag.

"Can you text me that picture so I have the order and room number?" I asked Carter, slinging the bag over my shoulder. I had to find Grayson. Maybe it wasn't fair to spring this all on him before the finals round, but there wasn't anything I could do about it. Maybe if I'd read 15211's letter earlier, but now I was out of options.

"I'll see you in there," I said, placing my hand on his shoulder as I walked past. "There's something I need to do. If I don't, I won't be able to focus, and then I'd have no chance in there."

His face twisted. "You know you're way too competitive, right?"

I stopped and gave him a look. "It's the state championships. Most people would agree this is all a pretty big deal."

"That's just it, though. The scholarship's not nearly as important as you're making it out to be. You're thinking too far in advance about college and missing everything that's going on in the present, that's your problem."

"No, Carter, your problem is that you don't think ahead enough."

We'd had this same argument several times over the years. He pushed me to be more spontaneous; I tried to make him see the bigger picture.

Usually it wasn't an issue, but lately I was wondering if we were too different to ever really see eye to eye.

I hated to leave on such a bad note, but I was running out of time. I only had half an hour until the final round started, and I needed to get everything in order before then so my mind would be in the right place for the competition. "Text me the picture, please?" I didn't have time to go check the board with all the postings on it. Not if I wanted to talk with Grayson first.

"Fine," Carter said, his face turned down toward his phone.

"Thanks." I squeezed his arm and walked away.

I made my way to the speech room. All the other competitors were in the cafeteria, like the rest of our tournaments. But because we were hosting this meet, our team got to use a separate room. Home-court advantage. By the time I made it up the stairs, I felt my phone vibrate in my suit pocket with Carter's text. That was one less thing to worry about.

Grayson was standing in the far corner, talking with our coach.

I stood in the doorway, debating my options.

I could interrupt, but that was rude.

I could wait, but that was torture.

I walked slowly into the room, meandering in that general direction to see if I could overhear what they were talking about. Maybe it was nothing serious and they wouldn't mind the break. Whatever it was, I didn't get the chance to know because Coach stopped talking when she saw me approach.

I wiped my palms on my skirt and forced myself to breathe regularly. That was hard to do, because suddenly there wasn't enough air in the room. And it was much too hot. The odds of spontaneous combustion were already high, but with the way Grayson was watching me now, it rose to approximately 99 percent.

"Hi, umm, sorry to interrupt." Was I really, though? Right now, I couldn't feel anything. Even my lips were numb. Feeling something like remorse for interrupting wasn't even on my radar. "Grayson, when you get a minute, I'd really like to talk to you. Not here." My eyes cut to my coach, who was watching me with narrowed eyes. It was like she could read my mind and knew what I had planned.

I barreled ahead. "Uh, I'll meet you in the finals room before the round starts, if that's okay with you. It's really important."

It was out there now. There was no going back. It wasn't like I could ask for an important meeting and then chat with him about the weather when he got there.

Who cared what Coach thought? It was my life, and I was tired of living it her way.

Besides, he most definitely was not wearing a red scarf, and so I needed to fix this. Fix *us*.

Grayson's face betrayed no emotion. Curse him and his poker face.

"Sure, I'll be there in a sec."

I nodded once, then turned and quickly walked away so it wouldn't be obvious my legs were shaking.

Because I'd never been more nervous about anything in my life.

Chapter Twenty-Eight

The room was all beige and peeling linoleum. What a great place for a romantic rendezvous. Most of the desks had been pushed to the side so we could have a larger "stage" for performing. The only ones out were for the other competitors and the judges. Occasionally someone brought a friend to watch, but really, who wanted to bore their friends to death? Most of the time, finals rounds felt a lot like any other round of the competition. But with more judges.

I didn't typically get nervous. Even during the finals round. But now I was pretty sure I'd end up in the hospital if I didn't slow my racing heart down. I didn't know what to do with my hands. They kept fluttering around like that would somehow make this situation better, and if I kept chewing on my lower lip like this, all the red Ruby Woo lipstick in the world wouldn't be able to save me.

I checked my phone for the time, and to make sure I was in the right room. Carter's picture had the room number at the top, and I was in the correct place, so I started rearranging the desks so the three judges could sit in the front. It was more to give me something to do, but I was in denial. When that was done, I sat in one of the other desks and pulled my bag on top. I didn't want to look pathetic when Grayson got to the room, so I pulled out my phone again like Grayson wouldn't see right through that. I didn't actually have anything to do on it, so I stared at the home screen and opened random apps only to close them a second later.

Judging from my racing pulse, I was right to try to get this out of the way before the round began. I was like that GIF of Kermit the Frog flailing his arms all around, and I needed to get whatever this was out of my system soon so I could compete.

I watched the time tick by, and I waited.

Grayson's definition of a "sec" must have been much longer than mine. The time stretched on and I forced my hands to stop tapping against the desk. It was impossible not to read into the silence, no matter how much I tried not to. I'd told Grayson it was important, so he had to know to hurry. I estimated the time it would take for him to wrap up his conversation with Coach and then to check the postings to find the room number. Maybe he'd stopped in the bathroom. Even then, he should have been here by now. The round started in ten minutes. Any second now, the other competitors would start to arrive, and then I wouldn't be able to say anything.

Disappointment seeped into my gut. It started because I wouldn't be able to tell Grayson my feelings before the round began. But then it spread, because if Grayson wasn't here, he had to have a reason. The only reason I could think of was that he was trying to let me down gently. It wasn't like I'd been all that great at hiding my emotions. He had to know how I felt. And now he didn't want me to embarrass myself any further. Either that, or Carter had been right all along, and Grayson was using this opportunity to crush me before I got the chance to compete.

I hated even thinking that.

Or maybe Coach had stopped him from coming. Would she do that? Would Grayson have let her? Because if he let something like that stop him, then that was almost as bad as him not showing up because he was trying to let me down easy.

It all came down to this: He knew I had something important to tell him, and he still hadn't shown up. Obviously, he didn't feel the same way about me, or he would have been here by now.

My once-tingling fingertips were now motionless on the desktop, and I stared at my hands, wondering what I was supposed to do now. Before, I'd felt overly alive. Like I'd been full of so much excitement that I might lift up and out of this room. Now the knowledge of Grayson's rejection sat in my stomach like food poisoning, and all I could think about was why he didn't want me.

The minutes kept going by, and still Grayson didn't show up.

No one did.

I heard people pass in the hall, but no one entered this room. Eventually the halls grew quiet again. I checked my phone. The round was supposed to have started five minutes ago. I checked the room number again, even though I already knew I had it right. I texted Carter.

> Where are you? Did the time get pushed back or something? I thought finals were supposed to have started by now. Are you sure it's in room 115, or did they change it?

Sometimes they delayed the rounds if they were having trouble organizing the judges. I hoped that was what had happened here, and I hadn't gotten the memo because I hadn't been in the cafeteria. Because none of the alternatives made any sense.

Three little dots appeared on my screen while I waited for Carter to finish typing.

> Yes. Some of the judges from the last round turned in their ballots late and they're still figuring stuff out in the

tab room. Don't worry, you still have lots of time. You're
in the right place. Stay in 115. I'll let you know when they
say the round is going to start.

My shoulders relaxed. The tab room was where all the judges and
coaches organized things behind the scenes like puppet masters. If they
were still figuring out rooms for certain events or something, then I had
nothing to worry about.

Well, except for the fact that Grayson still wasn't here. Before they'd
been tense, but now my shoulders slumped, and I rested my elbows on the
desk. I didn't have the energy to get all worked up about it or upset. *Upset*
wasn't the right word, because that implied too much investment. I'd with-
drawn. If I pulled away and made myself numb, then it couldn't hurt me.

That was a lie. I could feel the hurt deep in my bones. It was throughout my whole body, making my arms feel heavy and my head clouded.
After this, Grayson probably wouldn't tutor me anymore either. Not only
would I lose the guy, I'd lose the grade. There'd be no more reason for
him to keep up the appearance of being my friend after the finals round
was over. Would Boise State still accept me if my grade point average
dropped? And if I failed the AP Government test, all that work would be
for nothing. No, not nothing. Worse than nothing. My bad grade in that
class would also put my acceptance to college in jeopardy.

My one action of pressuring Grayson into talking now had caused
me to lose everything. Why couldn't I have waited like a normal person?
Why'd I have to get so caught up that I rushed ahead without thinking?
That wasn't like me. I wasn't a risk taker. And this was why.

Or maybe this would have happened anyway. *That* thought was more
depressing than anything else, because it meant I'd been played.

I'd thought meeting 15211 after the awards ceremony would distract
me too much from this final round of competition. I'd thought I'd be able
to blame him when my brain revolted and decided to only focus on boys

instead of the task ahead, so I wanted to get it over with early. But I'd done all this to myself. I'd gone and fallen for a guy who couldn't even be bothered to show up when I told him I had something important to say.

I didn't realize the hallways had been silent for some time until I heard someone running down them. I didn't really care.

Well, I didn't care until I saw Grayson stick his head in the door. Then I cared a whole lot.

I stood up. I didn't know why, but I did. It wasn't like he was the queen of England or anything. But he was just as important to me.

"Hi." He still hovered outside the doorway, half his body obscured by the frame. I remembered how Carter said we still had plenty of time before the round started, and my heart softened a little toward Grayson. Maybe he wasn't trying to send me any subliminal messages after all. Maybe he was just being a clueless guy.

I went to nervously fix a strand of my hair, then remembered it was pulled back in a French twist and there wasn't anything there for me to fiddle with. Why hadn't he come inside the room yet?

Then Grayson finally stepped through the door and I could see what he'd been hiding.

In his hand, he held a red scarf.

Chapter Twenty-Nine

My breath caught in my throat and I took a step forward without realizing it.

"It *was* you?"

He took a few more steps and brought the scarf in front of him, moving the fabric between his fingers like he didn't know what to do with his hands. It was the most endearing thing I'd ever seen, and I found myself striding across the room and throwing my arms around his neck.

The force of my embrace caused him to stumble slightly and it took him a second to encircle his arms around my waist. That one second was torture. But when he finally did, it was like everything was complete and had fallen into place. *This.* This was what was meant to happen. This was who I was supposed to be with, whether on paper or in real life. It had always been Grayson, and I'd simply been too preoccupied to put all the pieces together. And he'd come before the finals round. So he wasn't trying to break my heart so he could win.

His fingers ran up my spine, coming up to my neck and causing me to melt on the spot. But then he pushed aside my suit collar and kissed the skin where my neck met my shoulder and I couldn't have breathed if I tried. He kissed me there once, twice, then pulled back to look me in the eyes.

"Sorry. I couldn't wait until after the awards ceremony to tell you." Using his fingertips, he traced the skin along my hairline and brought his hand to cradle the back of my neck. "I really want to kiss you right now, but I don't want to ruin your lipstick."

I closed the distance between us for him, pushing up on my toes until our lips met in the middle.

I'd missed his lips. How his hair curled at the base of his neck. The way he looked at me whenever he thought I wasn't watching. How could you miss someone when you saw them practically every day? It shouldn't have been possible, but it was true. I'd missed everything about him, but most of all, I'd missed that he wasn't mine.

Now I breathed him in, my fingers in his hair as he pulled me closer. Our lips moved together and my heart hammered against my rib cage.

I didn't care if anyone walked in on us right then, because as far as I was concerned, we were in our own little bubble and nothing could break it. My hands traveled to his chest, pulling his dress shirt closer until there was no space between us at all.

Eventually he pulled back, kissed my forehead, and brought his hand to my face. Even with us no longer kissing, he couldn't seem to stop touching me in some way, and I craved the contact.

Then I stepped back and hit his arm. "Why didn't you tell me sooner?" I crossed my arms and tried to glare. It wasn't really successful. "You weren't even wearing a hat at the capitol building."

He laughed, then brought me into his arms again. I went willingly.

"I'd forgotten my hat in my car and was going to get it." He stroked my arm. "I wanted to tell you earlier, but I didn't know how you'd take it. I honestly thought you hated me after what Carter pulled."

"You mean when he made you admit to liking someone else?" It dawned on me then and I couldn't help but gasp. "That was me! Our letters. You were talking about me."

Grayson nodded. "I just didn't know it yet." He entwined our fingers and walked me back to the desks. I took my seat and he pulled another desk close so he could reach out and hold my hand across the top. "After I figured things out, I went back and reread everything. It all clicked. And don't think I didn't see how you tricked me into telling you all my competition secrets. Well played, Quinn."

Even the way he said my name made goose bumps erupt on my arms. I couldn't help but smile as Grayson continued.

"I'm sorry about lying to you—about the dance lessons. I took them. At the time I was so embarrassed I swore my mom to complete secrecy, even from my dad. That's how I knew he'd back me up."

I shook my head. "Why didn't you tell me when I asked?"

"I wanted you to like *me*. Not just 15211." He took a deep breath. "I needed to change your opinion of me. I liked you almost from the beginning when we started writing. Then I made the mistake of telling Carter long before the actual possibility of us ever started taking its place in real life."

Grayson looked down. "I didn't know how to fix it. Sometimes you seemed to like me, but I didn't know if I was reading into things because that was what I wanted to see. Then you told me you didn't trust me, and I was trying my hardest to wait until after the finals round. I mean, I knew what really happened with Zara, but I didn't know if you'd believe me if I told you then, since the state tournament was still weeks away."

"What happened with Zara?"

Grayson let out a breath. "She dumped me after I won the election. But she didn't want everyone thinking she was actually that petty or jealous, so she told everyone I'd sabotaged her chances before the election speech, trying to make me look bad. She didn't want to admit she'd lost. At the time, I didn't bother correcting the rumors. I didn't really care enough to get involved in any kind of "he said/she said" situation. My mom's always taught me that the best way to avoid drama is to not get involved. But that kind of backfired when you told me you thought I'd do the same thing to you." Grayson chuckled. "But if I told you my side of the story, you could have thought I was lying because the state competition was still weeks away at that point. I was stuck."

I nodded, thinking through everything he'd said. "And that's why Zara said she owed you, because you went along with the rumors, rather than making her out to be the bad guy."

Grayson smiled. "Yeah, but to be honest, I mostly brought her because I was trying to make you jealous. I thought that's what you were trying to do to me with Carter half the time."

"I've never liked Carter as anything more than a friend," I said. "But he doesn't take a hint. Then Coach gave me orders to avoid all guys entirely, so that was when I started pulling away from you and 15211."

He stroked my arm and smiled. "That explains a lot. When you told me you wanted to talk to me before the finals round, I didn't know if it was to say goodbye forever since I knew I'd written a letter telling you, well, almost everything, and I couldn't bear that, so I went and grabbed the scarf. I was so worried I'd pushed our rivalry so far that I'd lost the girl in the process."

His thumb traced patterns along my hand, leaving my skin tingling where he touched.

"The opposite actually," I said. "I was going to tell you that I wanted it to be you and that I trusted you, even before the finals round." I smiled. "So you went to get the scarf. Is that what took you so long?"

He swallowed. "Not exactly." Something in his expression made me wary, and I drew back.

"What aren't you telling me?"

He didn't say anything for a moment; then he inhaled and spoke in a rush. "We're missing the finals round. It started on time. Carter lied."

I didn't respond. I couldn't. Of course, I recognized why he hadn't told me this at the beginning of our conversation. Because it wouldn't have made a difference. If you were late to a round, you didn't get to compete. Sure, some tournaments were a little loose with the rules, but this was the state championships. There was no way they'd let us into that round, so I could see why Grayson hadn't brought me there right away. It wouldn't have changed anything.

How was it possible to feel so happy and so sad, all at the same time? There wasn't room in my body for this many emotions at once, so I sat there dumbfounded. Then my brain caught up to everything Grayson had said.

"Carter lied, and you knew?"

I pulled my hand away, but he grabbed it back.

"No! Well, yes. But I came here as soon as I found out."

My eyebrows furrowed, but I didn't remove my hand. Yet. I wasn't sure I could handle this yo-yoing of emotions, though. Everything was bundled up so tightly I felt like I'd burst into a thousand pieces with a single push. "Explain."

"I went early to the finals round, but you weren't there." He was talking quickly, perhaps sensing my dwindling patience. "I already had the scarf because I'd grabbed it from my bag as soon as you left the speech room. I waited in the finals room until the other competitors started showing up. That waiting was agony, by the way. I didn't know why you weren't there." His smile was rueful, and I gave his hand a squeeze. I knew that feeling all too well.

"When Carter showed up, I asked him if he knew where you were because I was supposed to meet you. I told him you had something you wanted to tell me, and he said . . ." Grayson swallowed. "He said you'd told him you'd changed your mind and that you didn't want to talk to me. Ever again."

"What?" I was too shocked to say anything else. Grayson nodded.

"That was hard to hear." He gave a weak laugh, and I brought his hand up to kiss it. He touched my lips with his thumb, and I momentarily forgot what we were talking about. I even forgot to be sad, because Grayson made everything better.

"So then Carter sat in the seat in front of me and made some kind of joke about how we could be our own little 'rejected by Quinn' group. The first person gave their speech, and that was when you texted Carter. The judges were still writing their critiques of the first speech, so we were all just waiting there." Grayson brought his other hand to mine. "I could see it clearly over his shoulder, and when your name flashed on the screen, I, well, I read your message. I couldn't help it." He shook his head. "That was when you asked him if you had the right room, and I watched as he responded and told you that the round was postponed, and I got so mad, I got up and left. I came right here to find you." He smiled wistfully. "I'm sorry I didn't have the guts to text you earlier and ask where you were."

I let his story sink in, and all the ramifications of it.

I should have seen it earlier. Anyone could adjust a photo to put a different number on top. Carter had told me there was a delay because some judges had been late in turning in their ballots, but the more I thought about it, they couldn't have posted the lists for the final rounds if any of the judges had been late. I'd been too caught up in my own drama to think things through.

Not that it mattered now.

We were out of the running, and Carter had succeeded. All along, I'd been worried that Grayson would ruin my chances, but it was Carter who had put the knife in my back.

I still didn't know why Carter would do this to me. Even with me out of the competition, Carter wouldn't have won. Grayson would have. Well, if he'd stayed.

"You left the round for me?" I asked. "But you could have won."

Grayson shook his head. "You're the one who deserved to win, Quinn, and you know it."

I looked at his intent face, and felt an outpouring of emotion. He'd left the finals round of the state tournament—for me. It didn't really change my position in the standings, but it changed things between us. Because I knew he had my back. And I had to have his.

I wasn't about to let that go without doing something about it.

I dug through my bag until I found my compact, then handed the small mirror to Grayson. He held it uncertainly.

"What's this for?"

"For you to wipe my lipstick off," I said. He smiled.

"I kind of like it there." He leaned over and kissed me again, and I got so caught up I almost forgot my plan. My fingers found their way into his hair again without my knowledge, and I was almost tempted to crawl from my desk onto his lap. But I gently pushed him away instead.

"Don't distract me. I'm on a mission." I was confident and sure. I'd been right all along that knowing was better than not knowing. Hopefully my coach would agree. That was another reason why I had to make this work. Because if I rolled over and accepted defeat now, she'd blame it on Grayson, and I wasn't about to let that happen. Who would have thought I'd be defending Grayson's chances to compete?

Grayson laughed, and opened the mirror to make sure he was good. I took it back and used it to reapply the shade of red that had just been on Grayson's lips. Then I stood. He did so too, uncertainly.

I picked up the scarf that had fallen to the ground and wrapped it behind Grayson's neck, my fingers lingering there for a moment. It was so freeing to be able to actually touch him now, like I'd been wanting to do for so long.

Then I used the scarf to pull him out of the room after me.

"Where are we going?" He took a couple long strides to reach me, then took my hand in his when we were walking side by side. My fingers wove between his and I smiled.

"We're going to the tab room to see if there are any coaches or judges in there. Then we're going to tell them everything and hope they let us compete anyway. This isn't just a case of being late. This was sabotage, and hopefully they'll see it that way too."

After all Grayson had done for me, it was the least I could do.

I hoped it worked.

Chapter Thirty

*T*he look on Carter's face when we went back to the room, two coaches in tow, was so stricken it was almost worth all the trouble he'd caused.

Not really, but it was still vindicating.

It'd taken us some time to explain everything to the coaches, and then they'd all deliberated over what to do. But we were here now and they were letting us compete. That was the important thing.

One of the coaches we'd brought with us addressed the room. "Sorry to interrupt," he said. "Judges, could we see you in the hall for a moment?" They all shuffled outside while Grayson and I took our seats in the back of the room. Far away from Carter. Carter, who turned in his chair and tried to catch my eye. I refused to even look in his direction.

"Quinn," he started.

I held up my hand to stop him. "I don't want to hear it."

This didn't deter him. He got out of his seat and came to stand in front of me.

"Quinn." He put his hands in his pockets. "I—"

"Carter, I need to focus now," I interrupted. I took a shaky breath. It wasn't that I didn't want to talk to Carter right now—it was that I didn't want to talk to him ever again. "Because of you, I nearly lost my chance to compete. I refuse to let you take away my concentration now."

"That's not what—"

"Carter, she asked you to stop." Grayson interjected. His eyes were fire and ice at the same time. I wasn't quite sure how Carter was still standing, to be honest.

Carter swallowed, and looked around the room at all the students watching him. No one bothered to hide their interest. Everyone had to be wondering what was happening, but I didn't feel like explaining.

The door to the room opened again and the judges filed back inside. The coaches who'd accompanied us here stayed by the door.

"Contestant 10720, please come with us. I'm afraid you've been disqualified."

Carter was still standing, but he didn't move.

The coach wasn't having it. "Now." He held the door open. "You've already caused enough of a delay, and your coach is waiting for you in the tab room."

Our coach hadn't been there when Grayson and I had gone, but I was glad to hear she knew about the situation now.

Carter looked back at me one last time before grabbing his things and following the coaches out the door. I expected to feel some relief, but fire still coursed through my veins. There wasn't room for me to feel anything else. The coaches and Carter closed the door behind them, and everyone in the room seemed to hold their breath in the silence.

"Okay." One of the judges turned in her seat. "Sorry for all the drama. It looks like we missed two of the speeches, so we're going to tag them onto the end of the lineup. Since we've heard the others in this room, that means"— she looked down at her paper—"Contestant 91698, you're up next."

I stood up and walked to the front of the room.

This wasn't any different than the other countless times I'd performed this speech.

Except it was.

Everything felt different. *I* was different. So much had changed in just the last hour that I couldn't begin to process it all.

I looked out at my audience and felt their curious glances like a second skin. My gaze skimmed over the people in the room, passing over the contestants and landing on the judges. They were focused, their pens poised over their papers, waiting for me to make all this worth their time. My eyes kept traveling until my gaze stopped on the one person who grounded me.

Grayson smiled reassuringly. Everything I needed to know was right there in his expression. He knew I could do this. He believed in me, probably as much as I believed in myself.

I took a deep breath and began.

Chapter Thirty-One

Now that I'd had a chance to compete and everything was entirely out of my hands, I couldn't help but let the demons in. The high was over, and all that was left was worry, negativity, and buckets of self-doubt.

I had good reason. After interrupting the finals round like that, there was zero hope the judges would treat me fairly in their results. I looked like the entitled diva that demanded everything go her way. They'd penalize me for that reason alone.

More than anything, I was still experiencing aftershocks of Carter's betrayal. When today started, he'd been one of my friends. He'd been the one I turned to when I needed a boost, or the person who'd had my back if someone said something that cut too deep. Then he'd done the unthinkable, and I was still processing the fact that our friendship was officially over. He made the deep cut himself this time, and the shock was slowly being replaced with hurt. It was like I couldn't take a full breath. My mind was cloudy with the weight of it all, still trying to make sense of everything.

I sat on the floor with Grayson, our backs against the wall in the speech and debate room. There was still an hour before the awards ceremony, and our coach was away in the tab room, probably hiding from all my drama. I didn't even blame her.

Grayson held my hand, obviously unsure of how to make me feel better. He knew that Carter had been one of my only friends. But it wasn't a secret that they didn't get along. At the same time, he wasn't likely to speak badly of Carter knowing that we'd been friends either.

Competition, though, *that* he knew something about. It was obvious he felt comfortable on that subject, because he kept reassuring me. "You know you did great," Grayson said again. His thumb made circles on my hand, and if it weren't for my impending doom, I might have been distracted by it.

Okay, full disclosure, I was still pretty distracted by it.

But everything I'd worked so hard for, for an entire year, was slipping from my grasp all because of something someone else did. Now that things had finally, *finally*, worked out with Grayson, I could allow all my headspace to focus on this final tournament, and my stress was taking advantage of it by obsessing nonstop. Plus, the fact that Carter had been the one to do this to me wasn't exactly making it easier to swallow.

Carter was my friend. Well, he had been. If it had been another competitor, I'd have an easier time processing things. I still wouldn't have liked it, but at least I would have understood. *This* was not something I could understand.

My mom always said it was the people closest to us that could hurt us most. It sucked that I had to learn this firsthand. Carter was my personal Peter Pettigrew, betraying me to Voldemort for his own gain.

Of course he'd been disqualified. But his real punishment would have to wait until we went back to school on Monday. That's when Coach said Carter had a meeting with the principal to discuss an in-school suspension for how he'd represented our school at an event. He was currently sitting in the far opposite corner, headphones in and hood up. We hadn't talked yet, and I wasn't sure what to say to him if we had. How do you say, "Gee, thanks for stabbing me in the back, please get out of my life," to someone who once knew all your darkest secrets?

He'd kept his head down when we returned to the room, and I was just fine with that.

I'd been so optimistic then, when the round had just gotten over. I'd still been all vindicated and full of justice. But then the judges left the room, and none of them even looked my direction.

"It wasn't enough," I said to Grayson, remembering the way they'd so easily dismissed me. Earlier I'd wondered how it was possible to be so happy and sad at once, and I kept waiting for that feeling to go away.

But it didn't, and I was left with feeling like I was pulled in too many directions at once. Grayson kissed the back of my hand and my pendulum swung the other way. My heart was suddenly so full I could burst.

A single tear escaped and I brushed it aside.

What a great way to start a relationship.

"Why on earth are you crying?" My coach walked in the room, and all eyes swung first to her, then to me. Great. There were only a few team members hanging out in this room, but even a one-person audience was one too many. Carter pulled out his earbuds and placed them on the desk in front of him. I tried to ignore him altogether.

"You know why," I mumbled. "You were right about me getting distracted. You can tell me 'I told you so' already." If I spoke softly enough, eventually my teammates would look away and busy themselves with something else. They did, but only after Coach surveyed the room and gave them all a withering stare that would make any parent proud. Then she came and settled next to us on the ground.

I didn't bother to hide my shock. She was not a "sit on the floor" kind of person. She was a "don't you dare get my suit dirty or I will crush you into oblivion" type of person.

"I can admit when I was wrong. This is one of those times. You have no reason to cry." She crossed her legs out in front of her, like that settled the deal.

I wasn't about to unload all my hurt about Carter to my coach, so I was glad when she didn't mention it. It was better to stick to the competition for now. One thing at a time.

"You know that's not true," I said. "I interrupted a round, and those judges are going to take it out on me." There was way too much water in my eyes. I blinked furiously, trying to keep it all from spilling over.

Coach sighed. "You know I just came back from the tab room. Would I really be telling you not to worry if I hadn't seen your results?"

"You're my coach. You're supposed to say stuff to make me feel better."

Grayson still hadn't said anything, but he stayed by my side, holding my hand. That alone made me like him that much more, if it was possible.

Coach Bates shifted and took my face in her hands.

"My dear, you have *nothing* to worry about."

"You know I—" I tried to say, but Coach cut in.

"Quinn, you won."

I stopped breathing. She'd said it so softly, I could have misheard her. I could have heard the things I wanted so desperately for her to say. But the way Grayson squeezed my hand told me I wasn't dreaming right now.

"Really?" I breathed.

Coach nodded. "If anything, I think that little stunt of Carter's might have given you some leverage, because the judges knew you were the one to beat." She released my face and brushed some hair out of her eyes. "Now you have to pretend to be surprised and you can't tell anyone I told you. But enough with the waterworks already, okay?"

I threw my arms around her neck. She stiffened in surprise before lightly patting my back until I drew away.

She stood up, wiped dust off her pants that wasn't visible to the human eye, and then gave me a nod as she walked out of the room. Grayson attacked me in a hug and kissed my cheek.

I turned so he could have my lips instead.

Who cared if everyone was watching us? They'd already been eyeing the way we held hands, so they had to know something had changed between us. Besides, I wanted the whole world to know that Grayson was taken. By me.

I smiled as I kissed him, letting myself get lost in the moment. Truthfully, he could have been upset. If I got first place, that meant he didn't. But Grayson brought his hand up to play with the stray piece of hair that had fallen from my French twist, and I knew we weren't competitors anymore. We were on the same side. When I won, he won.

Someone cleared their throat and we broke off the kiss.

I looked up to find Carter standing a few feet away. His hands were in his pockets and he was very carefully looking at the wall above our heads.

"Hey, Quinn. Can I talk to you for a second?" He looked at me then. "Please?"

His expression was apologetic, but this time I didn't feel the wavering I normally did whenever Carter did his whole "ask for forgiveness later" thing he was so fond of. I was sad at the friendship we'd lost, but not sad enough to roll over and take another hit. The sadness was fleeting, slowly being replaced with anger.

Not only did he sabotage my chances at this competition, but with Grayson as well. I didn't have it in me to smile and pretend like I was okay. I didn't want to give Carter an inch because I knew he'd take a mile.

I stood up, pulling Grayson with me.

"What could you possibly have to say to me right now?" I asked, folding my arms across my chest.

Carter rubbed his face.

"Alone?" he asked. His voice sounded so small, but I shook my head. There was no way I wanted to be alone with Carter right now, and that was more for his protection than mine. I didn't need a criminal record after tonight.

Carter still looked hopeful, so I shook my head again.

"No," I said when he still didn't say anything. "I'm tired of you thinking it's okay to put your own wants above mine every time. It's not a friendship if you only think of yourself."

"I never wanted it to be only a friendship," he said, and I pursed my lips.

"When a girl tells you she doesn't want to date you, you need to respect that. Just because she's too nice to be rude to you doesn't mean you can continue to push and think that's okay." I took a deep breath. "And it *certainly* doesn't mean you sabotage her in a competition because she doesn't like you."

Carter reached out, but I took a step away. His hand hung there awkwardly until he dropped it to his side. He shook his head. "What, like revenge? I wasn't trying to get back at you, Quinn."

"Really?" I could tell my voice was rising to dangerous levels, and no one in the room bothered pretending they weren't listening, but I didn't care. "Then what was it, Carter? Because I've been racking my brain trying to think what could have possibly possessed you to do that to me, and I can't come up with a single thing that would justify you being that cruel. Something that would justify throwing away years of friendship."

"I didn't want you to go, okay?" Carter was almost yelling now too. His face was flushed and his shoulders were tense. "I knew if you got that scholarship, you'd be out of here. You already got accepted into your dream college. So forgive me for liking you enough that I wanted you to stick around for a bit longer." His breathing was fast and uneven.

I shook my head. "Maybe before you did that you should have asked me where I was going. Did you ever consider that?" I raised my chin. My nails were biting into my palms, but I couldn't unclench them even a little. "The university I was talking about was Boise State. I'm not going anywhere.

239

But thank you, for making it so obvious to me who my real friends are. And aren't."

"Quinn, don't be like that. I was . . . I was *counting* on you to forgive me. Even if it took some time. I know what I did was extreme, but you weren't listening to anything else. If I could just make you *see* how serious I was about you, I thought maybe you'd understand why I did it. We can work through this. We always do." Carter was doing that puppy-dog eye thing he was so good at, but I was already grabbing my bag from the floor so I could go somewhere else. Anywhere else.

"No, Carter. That's because I kept forgiving you when you did nothing to deserve it. But not this time. This was too big, and it's not something I'll be able to simply forget anytime soon."

I didn't like being so harsh. But I was done being the only one bending in this friendship.

"Friends are supposed to build you up. Not tear you down. They make you want to be a better person, not feel bad for having dreams that exist outside of them. I'm sorry, but I'm done."

I'd never been so bold about anything ever before in my life. I pulled Grayson along behind me and exited the room.

I was shaking, but Grayson squeezed my hand, and that little gesture was enough to make the hurt disappear. It'd been hard, but I knew it was all going to work out okay.

Maybe even better than okay.

Chapter Thirty-Two

The next night my mom rinsed her dinner plate off in the sink while I pretended to be helpful by getting the brownies out of the oven. Naomi was watching me intently, like that might make dessert come faster, while Grayson looked adorably lost without having some kind of task.

He'd brought my mom some wildflowers, keeping up with his rule of always bringing something to social gatherings. He'd also brought me some daisies that were now in my bedroom. My bouquet was bigger.

He'd finally gotten his wish to eat diner leftovers at my apartment. There'd been lasagna and salad, and I considered it a win since the leftovers actually went well together. That wasn't always the case.

I brought the brownies back to the table and sat down. Grayson took my hand under the table, so I was left trying to dish up the dessert with one hand. I didn't mind.

Naomi got tired of watching me struggle and swiped the spatula from my hand. "You two are impossible," she said, but she was smiling.

I broke a piece of brownie off and popped it in my mouth, just as my mom came back to the table. She swatted my hand, then placed a fork in it.

"Manners, Quinn. We have guests."

I rolled my eyes.

My mom sat down and placed the rest of the forks in the middle of the table for everyone else to grab one. She gave an encouraging smile to Grayson, who, as far as she was concerned, practically walked on water. At least, she acted like he could do no wrong. Whenever his face was turned, she'd give me a big thumbs-up and make kissy faces.

Her cheerleader-ways knew no bounds. She'd even put a candle in the brownies to celebrate my win at the state championship. I'd insisted that we also celebrate the fact that her Instagram had officially hit ten thousand followers, and we'd successfully booked the next four months of weekends with photography gigs. It was only a matter of time before she'd be able to quit her diner job.

She put two brownies on Grayson's plate, which he ate with gusto.

When it was time for Naomi to leave, she stole one of the wildflowers from the bouquet, took an extra brownie for Dax because she was a sap, and gave me a hug. She'd totally had my back with the whole Carter fiasco. While it wasn't like her and Carter were incredibly close before, Naomi made it clear where her loyalties were and she'd cut all ties with my former friend.

Grayson offered to help with the dishes, but my mom ushered us out the door after Naomi.

"You two go have fun. I'm sure you don't want to hang out with an old woman all night."

Grayson sputtered and adjusted his glasses, likely trying to figure out what he could say that wouldn't be against his countless etiquette rules. I just smiled, took his hand, and led him down the walkway to the lot where his car was parked.

"Where to?" I asked while buckling my seat belt. He reached over to hold my hand, intertwining our fingers over the middle console. It was such a simple thing, but it made my heart bang erratically in my rib cage. Every nerve ending from my fingers to my toes was alive at his touch, and I couldn't help but smile. He pushed the button to start the car and pulled onto the street.

"It's a surprise," he said.

I pursed my lips, but he was too busy watching the road to see it.

"What did your mom say when you told her we were . . . together?" I asked. I stumbled over the word like the awkward person I was, but Grayson didn't mention it, like the gentleman he was.

He smiled and squeezed my hand.

"Considering I laid it on her all at once—college choices, wanting to major in programing, new girlfriend, I'd say pretty well since she didn't pass out."

Girlfriend. It was the first time he'd used the word. My smile was so big it could have been seen from outer space.

"She couldn't have been happier about you, though. I've told you before. She likes you. Once you're around her more, you'll see it. Promise. Nothing to be intimidated about." Grayson looked over and caught my smile. He could have said his mother wanted to make a voodoo doll in my image so she could stab me with pins all day—nothing could bring me down right now. Of course, it helped that she actually liked me. That was a weight off my shoulders.

"Besides, how can anyone not like you once they get to know you?" he asked.

I could feel the blush overtaking my cheeks, and I didn't bother hiding it.

"I don't know," I said, tilting my head. "It took you long enough."

"Speak for yourself." He laughed and I watched the scenery go by, basking in the evening sun.

"You know, you're the reason I finally told her I wanted to go into computer science and programming," he said. "You chase your dreams, and if anything gets in the way, you find another path to make it happen. I used to think you took everything too seriously, but now I admire that about you. Even if it makes you the toughest competition."

There were so many things I liked about Grayson, I could have spent all night naming his positive traits. I liked that we were so evenly matched too. That I didn't have to pretend I wasn't competitive or do worse at speech and debate because his ego couldn't handle it. I could be myself, confidence and all, which made it feel all the more right.

"I think that describes you more than me," I said. He shook his head and laughed.

It had been so long since I'd been there that I didn't recognize our destination until Grayson took the final turn and parked the car. We were at the same city overlook that he'd taken me to for the fall fling in September. Now that it was the beginning of March, the weather was colder, but the temperature couldn't begin to touch me. Warmth spread through my stomach and chest until I could practically burst with happiness. Grayson kissed the back of my hand, released it, then said, "Wait here."

He got out of the car and ran around the front of it to open my door.

As I stepped out of the car, my lips were already tingling in anticipation of his kiss. My body reacted to Grayson whether he was twenty feet away or only one inch. It'd been too long since his hand was in mine, so I reached for it while we walked to the bench, relishing in the feeling of his skin touching mine.

We didn't sit down, though. When we reached the edge of the overlook, Grayson turned and cupped my face in his palm.

"I still can't believe this is real," he whispered. "For so long, you were this dream in my head. Words on a paper that drove me up a wall. Then you were real and in my life, and I messed it up." He kissed my forehead and I leaned into him, placing my hands on his chest. "But I'm never going to do that again," he whispered into my hair. "Forget about being my better half; you're both halves I need put together in one person. The dream and reality right here in front of me."

I looked up between my lashes to see him watching me with such tenderness it made me ache.

I reached up on my toes to kiss Grayson on the lips. They were soft and full, and fit perfectly with mine. My fingers curled into his hair as he held me close. I'd never known kissing could feel this perfect, this complete, until I was kissing the right person. The kind of person who made my pulse race, who cared about me more than himself, and who made me melt simply by looking at me.

There was still so much we didn't know. Our futures were wide open, with family, grades, jobs, expectations, and everything else still competing for space.

But if there was anything I knew about competition, it was that some things were worth fighting for. The stronger the competition, the stronger I became as a result. And Grayson? This relationship? My future?

Those things were definitely worth fighting for.

Acknowledgments

As a former speech and debater, it makes my heart happy to see this geeky book out in the world. There are so many people who made it possible, so I want to thank everyone who had a part in it.

Firstly, thanks to my publisher Swoon Reads, for making my dream a reality. It's because of you my books are on shelves, and there's no greater feeling in the world. My editor, Kat Brzozowski, is a saint for putting up with my random questions and mishaps. She made this book so much stronger than it would have been.

Eric Smith, who is the most supportive and encouraging agent I could ever hope to have in my corner. Thank you for believing in me. Thanks for loving quiet YA stories and books that feel like a hug. The world needs more people like you.

Freelance editor Holly Ingraham, thank you for helping me solidify what was and wasn't working. Production editor Taylor Pitts and production manager Raymond Colon, you both are amazing for all your work. Huge thanks to Sophie Erb, for designing the most beautiful cover a girl could ask for. My publicist, Madison Furr, for helping get this book into the right hands. This book exists because of the team behind it.

Major love goes to my family for all their support. My husband, Brad, is basically Superman. He's the reason I believe in love stories. Without him, this book would never have made it past chapter one. My son, who was super understanding whenever I was on deadline and was all too happy to get some extra iPad time. My siblings, who cheer me on and spread the word about my books whenever they get a chance. And my parents, who fostered my love of reading and writing, turning me into the Ravenclaw I am today.

Thanks go to my writer friends, including my critique partners Brookie Cowles and Kelly Lyman, plus everyone on Team Rocks and the Swoon Squad—you all keep me sane. The Utah Novel 19s—Samantha Hastings, RuthAnne Snow, Crystal Smith, Erin Stewart, Sofiya Pasternack, and Dan Haring—thank you for all the adventures we've gone on together.

I mentioned that I participated in speech and debate when I was in high school, so I'd be remiss if I didn't mention my coaches, David Gay, Lila Michael, and Anne Sullivan. They dealt with teenage me and turned me into a state champion, so they're miracle workers. Also, thanks to the team at Lone Peak High School and their coach, Natalie Johnson, for letting me crash their practices and judge their tournaments so I could brush up on my speech and debate knowledge.

Last, but not least, thank YOU, dear reader, for picking up my book and giving it a chance. You're the real MVP.

Check out more books chosen for publication by readers like you.

DID YOU KNOW...

readers like you helped to get this book published?

Join our book-obsessed community and help us discover awesome new writing talent.

1 **Write it.**
Share your original YA manuscript.

2 **Read it.**
Discover bright new bookish talent.

3 **Share it.**
Discuss, rate, and share your faves.

4 **Love it.**
Help us publish the books you love.

Share your own manuscript or dive between the pages at **swoonreads.com** or by downloading the **Swoon Reads app.**